Adventure
by Jamie Dodson

The popular Nick Grant series continues with China Clipper, a fast-moving, fun tale of adventure, living boats, spies, and the sea. I love this series.
Homer Hickam, author of Rocket Boys/October Sky

****

China Clipper is a terrific read! It's accurate, fast moving and filled with surprises; perfectly for young people interested in history and aviation.
Walter J. Boyne, multi-published author; Former Director National Air & Space Museum, and enshrined in National Aviation Hall of Fame

****

China Clipper, a Nick Grant Adventure is an engaging, action-packed escapade! Dodson ingeniously weaves fact and fiction and captures the Golden Age of flying boats, including the most romantic aircraft of all, the China Clipper. Nick Grant is a teen caught in a world struggling with the Great Depression and heading into World War II. It's a dark, violent world. The murderous spies, diabolical sabotage, and dedicated counterintelligence contrasts the bright world of adventure, fast cars, and a senior year romance. Dodson's second Nick Grant novel is fast-paced and does not flinch when confronting the prejudices and heroism of the time.
Larry Weirather, author of China Clipper, Pan American Airways And Popular Culture

CHINA CLIPPER

Advance Praise for
China Clipper, A Nick Grant Adventure
by Jamie Dodson

The popular Nick Grant series continues with China Clipper, a fast-moving, fun tale of adventure, flying boats, spies, and the sea. I love this series!
Homer Hickam, author of Rocket Boys/October Sky

****

China Clipper is a terrific read! It's accurate, fast moving and filled with surprises; perfectly for young people interested in history and aviation.
Walter J. Boyne, multi-published author, Former Director, National Air & Space Museum, and enshrined in National Aviation Hall of Fame

****

China Clipper, a Nick Grant Adventure is an engaging, action-packed escapade! Dodson ingeniously weaves fact and fiction and captures the Golden Age of flying boats, including the most romantic aircraft of all, the China Clipper. Nick Grant is a teen caught in a world struggling with the Great Depression and heading into World War II. It's a dark, violent world. The murderous spies, diabolical sabotage, and dedicated counterintelligence contrasts the bright world of adventure, fast cars, and a senior year romance. Dodson's second Nick Grant novel is fast-paced and does not flinch when confronting the prejudices and heroism of the time.
Larry Weirather, author of China Clipper, Pan American Airways And Popular Culture

Action-packed and full of intrigue, the China Clipper transports you to a fascinating time in America's biography with its loving attention to historical accuracy.
Rich Pearce and Ken Story, authors of Dorkman

****

In 1935, America is looking for heroes. Amelia Earhart, Charles Lindbergh and Howard Hughes are heroes to some. But the real heroes are the honest, hardworking people; the ordinary folks who do the extraordinary when called upon. Nick Grant is just such a hero. From the first page of China Clipper I was on a white-knuckled ride through paradise with Nick, Leilani, and the evil Japanese spy, Miyazaki. I can't wait for the movie!
C. M. Fleming, author of Finder's Magic

****

Once again, Jamie Dodson has written a book chock full of skullduggery, history, and inclusion of the human impact. The story line and plot is riveting, leaving one with the urge to jump hurriedly into the next chapter, and looking forward to the next book of the series. Jamie has a very colorful ability to write.
Rev. Evan G. Butterbrodt, author and newspaper columnist

****

China Clipper is a thrill ride. The action and perils never stop as young Nick Grant faces attacks on his life and his reputation while he helps Pan Am test its new plane. And his problems continue at school where he deals with anger and prejudice while making new friends. It's an exciting way to learn about a fascinating time in our history!
Ann Marie Martin, Huntsville Times book columnist

CHINA CLIPPER

A Nick Grant Adventure

BY
JAMIE DODSON

CHINA CLIPPER

A NICK GRANT ADVENTURE

BY
JAMIE DODSON

MARTIN M-130 *China Clipper*

Martin M-130 China Clipper

Photograph courtesy of the Pan American Historical Foundation, used with their kind permission. (www.panam.org)

China Clipper
A Nick Grant Adventure

Published by OnStage Publishing
190 Lime Quarry Road, Suite 106J
Madison, AL 35758

Visit us on the web at www.onstagepublishing.com

Visit Nick Grant and learn more about Pan American, the Flying Clippers and other nations' flying boats
at www.nickgrantadventures.com

978-0-9790857-3-4 Paperback
0-9790857-3-X
Printed in the United States of America

To the Reader:

During the Century of Flight Celebration, the Smithsonian National Air and Space Museum designated the China Clipper as one of the most influential aircraft of the twentieth century. In conjunction, they opened a flying boat exhibit featuring models and artifacts from the China Clipper. It's a must see for anyone who is a Clipper "wing nut."

In 1935, the China Clipper and her two sisters, Philippine Clipper and Hawaii Clipper, were revolutionary aircraft. They had five times the range of contemporary aircraft and they were the first plane capable of lifting more than their own weight. They were faster than most military aircraft and the Clippers had a Top Secret US Government mission. They carried Japanese signals intelligence intercepts from US outposts back to the code breakers in Hawaii. Six months after Pearl Harbor, the US scored a massive victory over Imperial Japanese forces at The Battle of Midway Island. The US had broken the Japanese RAINBOW codes and sprung a trap on superior Japanese forces. The decisive defeat forced the Empire on the defensive for the remainder of the war. Pan American radio operators, at outposts spanning the Pacific, provided crucial early intercepts that facilitated the code breaker's work.

From 1935-1941, the Clippers also carried critical resources to the Chinese Resistance. Resource-poor Japan coveted China's abundant natural resources and invaded in 1933. America tried peaceful means to stay Japan's ruthless ambitions. However, trade embargos and the like failed to persuade the Japanese. When the Chinese death toll reached genocidal levels, the US set a course of covert intervention with battle field advisors and intelligence actions. Japanese Intelligence Services suspected that Pan Am's Pacific air route was somehow involved and retaliated. They attempted to sabotage the Clippers and steal the advanced US technology. I have set the Nick Grant Adventure series in this silent but deadly cold war.

The China Clipper has always fascinated me. At ten, my parents gave me The Wonder Book of Knowledge, with a chapter devoted to the first transoceanic transport aircraft--flying boats. There was even a picture of the China Clipper. As a teen, I watched the *China Clipper* on TV. Warner Brothers released the movie in 1936, only a year after the historic US mail flight from Alameda, California to Honolulu, Hawaii. As a newly minted Army Lieutenant, my young son and I stumbled upon the China Clipper Historic Marker while stationed in Hawaii. The die was cast. I had become a Clipper "Wing Nut." I hope you enjoy China Clipper.

Jamie Dodson, Madison, Alabama

Many people helped me write China Clipper, the second in the Nick Grant Adventure Series. Some sweated through multiple iterations of the manual script, others provided invaluable technical and historical information, family and close friends provided encouragement and neck rubs.

- Members of the WYSIUR (What You See is Under Revision). Writer's Critic Group, Madison, AL. Through all the years they gave me great feedback and tough criticism. Bottom Line – they made me a better writer with tough love.
- Members of the Coffee Tree Fiction Writers Group. Their support and enthusiasm keep me writing in my darkest hours. And some great material!
- My editor Dianne Hamilton and the great people at OnStage Publications. Thanks for your patience and encouragement .
- David Allen Lambert, of The Literate Evolutions Co-Operative Unlimited. He explained Joseph Campbell's hero concepts and helped me with the final layers of Nick story.
- Louis Stannard, Former Pan American Clipper Pilot, novelist and screenwriter. Thanks for all the "Pilot Stuffs".
- Pan Am Historical Foundation for the use of many of their photos, graphics and historical files.
- Renown Aviation Artist Keith Ferris. For use of his wonderful "Clipper Arrives in Paradise" , the art work that graces the China Clipper cover.
- Roger Pugliese of Black Sheep Entertainment. Thanks for all the Hollywood instructions. We'll make a movie yet!
- Homer Hickam, Walter Boyd, Michael Dobson, Ralph Peters, Annie Laura Smith, Rev. Evan G. Butterbrodt, C. M. Fleming, and the many other authors who took time out of their busy schedules to read and comment on my work.
- Finally to my family near and far for their endless enthusiasm and tireless efforts to help prepare Nick's latest adventure.

CHINA CLIPPER

Chapter One: The Butt of the Matter

7:10 a.m., Saturday, October 19, 1935
Alameda Airport, Alameda, California

Nick's footsteps echoed in the light fog as he made his way along the deserted flight line. Ahead he could barely make out the glowing end of the night watchman's cigarette. The cold San Francisco Bay fog defused and muted its weak orange light. Nick shivered and his breath showed against the chilly grey backdrop. It did little to lighten his glum mood. His recurring nightmare had returned to haunt his dreams and rob him of his sleep.

He walked on, and the night watchman's nebulous form morphed into the familiar. The watchman jumped and then smiled. "Morning, Nick! You gave me quite a start!"

"Sorry, Mr. Jackson. Good morning. Quiet night?"

"It's been quiet ever since the murder. It's a shame that the killer's still out there somewhere."

Nick recalled the death of his mentor and friend Joe McMillan. *Had it only been six months since Mac's death?* "Someday, I'll find that murderer."

"Well, I wouldn't hold my breath! The police have no leads." He stubbed out his cigarette and gazed toward the airfield. "There's been lots of changes around here. Even Mac would have to admit things have gotten better since Pan Am arrived."

"Maybe." A fresh wave of sadness swept over Nick and he tried to push it out of his mind. "Nice talking to you, Mr. Jackson, but I've got to get to work."

"See you, Nick."

Nick waved and walked on towards the old yacht club building. A single light bulb illuminated the sign over the door: Headquarters, Pacific Operations Division, Pan American Airways. It was a grand name for a dilapidated building, but the new hangar next to it was very impressive. Inside, Nick felt the warmth of row upon row of high intensity ceiling lights. The lights glinted off the metal hull of the world's largest airliner, the *China Clipper.*

He had watched with a mixture of envy and frustration as the last survey flight lifted off for Guam on October 5th. He so wanted to be aboard. Captain Sullivan and Tilton were out over the Pacific even now, flying a heavily modified S-42, the *Pan American Clipper.* It was the same plane he'd saved from destruction in August. Tilton had asked to take Nick along "for good luck" and Colonel Young considered it for a time. Then Nick's mother found out and squashed his trip. She'd been emphatic. "No more gallivanting to God knows where! Your job is to finish high school!"

Nick smiled at the memory. His mom sure was something! His thoughts returned to the plane in front of him. The clippers were flying boats and the *China Clipper* sat high and dry on her beaching cradle. Even out of the water, she looked sleek, elegant and huge. Mechanics fussed around the giant airliner like worker bees tending their queen. Some workers were on high scaffolding in front of the four massive engines. Others stood underneath polishing her hull.

A short middle-aged man of Japanese ancestry clapped

Nick on the shoulder. "Hey, Nick, you're early. You afraid the Clipper might go without you?"

"Something like that, Mr. Nieshe." Nick was scheduled to fly on a test flight later in the day.

Nieshe looked up at Nick's six foot two frame. "Good. I can use you. Get into your coveralls, pick up a wrench set, and come join me plane-side."

In the locker room, Nick struggled into white coveralls. The wall mirror reflected his sun-streaked blond hair. Five months' work on the Pacific atolls had done that, but his deep tan had long ago faded.

The indigo blue Pan Am logo emblazoned on his coveralls was the kicker. When so many were out of work, he had landed a dream job - working on the Pan Am's flying boats! He still could not believe the way it had played out, that he got to work on and fly the most technological advanced marvel in the world.

Nieshe saw him as soon as he returned to the hangar. "Follow me and don't forget that wrench set."

They climbed caster-mounted wooden stairs that led to the forward crew hatch, some two stories above the concrete floor. Nick followed Nieshe through the hatch and aft into the first passenger lounge. The smell of the new leather permeated the air, but so did something else – gasoline.

Nieshe looked at a set of blueprints and pointed toward the deck. "Nick, pull up these access panels."

The panels revealed a compartment several feet deep and a maze of tubing.

Nieshe stabbed a finger at the plans. "We are here. Crawl forward to the next bulkhead and check for a fuel leak."

"Where the fuel lines exit the main tank?"

"Exactly."

"Why? We just installed the fuel lines last weekend. I screwed them in place."

Nieshe chuckled. "Screwed them up is more likely."

"You can't hang that on me. I followed the manual to the

letter and you certified the work."

"True, but it's great fun teasing you. Anyway, yesterday, during a power run up, the engines quit right after the engineer switched to that tank."

"An obstruction?"

"Maybe. That's what I need you to find out. In you go."

Nick lowered himself into the hold, careful not to damage the fragile fuel lines. Flashlight and wrench in hand, he got down on his belly and shimmed along on his elbows. The passage was tight and Nick bumped his head repeatedly. The closer he got to the bulkhead, the more powerful the smell of high octane gas. Nick pulled out a kerchief and tied it across his face in an attempt to cut the fumes. It was no good. The foul smell seemed to pass through the cloth untouched.

Nick called back over his shoulder. "Don't light a match! There are small pools of fuel everywhere down here." Nick rolled on his side, careful to avoid the spilled fuel. He transferred the flashlight to his mouth to free up his hands and started the inspection. Surprisingly, the fuel lines were loose to the touch and came free by hand. A small rivulet of fuel poured out of the loose end and soaked into Nick's overalls.

Great, I can't breathe and now I'm a human wick.

Nieshe yelled down the compartment. "Smelled it yesterday but couldn't locate the source. Aren't you done yet?"

Nick ignored the question and continued the inspection. He discovered that all four fuel lines were loose and leaking. He tightened the nuts, fixing the problem, and began to back out on his elbows. At the access panel, he poked his head out of the compartment and gulped in the fresh air.

Nieshe took the wrench. "Geez, Nick, you smell like a gas station."

"Thanks a lot! Hey, pass me some rags and a bucket. I need to mop up the fuel that leaked out of the tank."

A bundle of rags tucked inside his coveralls, Nick

maneuvered the bucket to the bulkhead. Half an hour later, he emerged with an armful of fuel-soaked rags and a bucket of spilled aviation gas.

Nieshe looked at the wall clock. "Come on, it's coffee break time. Besides, you need to get out of those clothes."

The Clipper lay deserted but they could hear the men in the adjoining canteen. "Dump those shop rags in the laundry and change your coveralls. Then, if you don't smell too foul, come join us in the canteen."

"You're too kind, Mr. Nieshe." Nick's sarcasm was lost on the older man.

In the deserted locker room, Nick tossed the rags into an open hamper. He noticed the window next to the hamper was open. *Strange - it's too cold for an open window.* He started to pull off his coveralls when, out of the corner of his eye, he caught a flicker of movement. A lit cigarette butt sailed in the window and landed in the open hamper. The gas-soaked rags instantly ignited and flames shot towards the ceiling.

Nick yelled, "Fire!" at the top of his lungs, and rushed to close the lid. Even closed the flames continued to lick out of the sides. One arm of his coveralls caught on fire. He hopped on one foot as he struggled out of them.

First one leg then the other...it's taking too long! Nick's frantic movement had moved him around and his back was toward the window. He thought he heard movement outside. He turned to investigate, felt intense pain sweep through his head, and he collapsed into darkness.

Chapter Two: G-Men

11:10 a.m., Saturday, October 19, 1935
Alameda Airport, Alameda, California

Nick was sprawled on his back with a crowd of men gathered around him. "Oh, my head! What happened?"

Nieshe gently lifted his head. "Here, drink this."

Nick took the cup and drank. The cooling liquid washed away the taste of the aviation fuel. Then he remembered. "The fire!"

"It's out, Nick. Don't worry. Are you hurt?"

He looked down at his body, relieved to see that the fire had not burned his clothes. But his left arm was red and angry. "My arm hurts and my head feels like it's in a vice."

"You've got first degree burns on your arm, but no blistering. You were lucky."

"I don't feel very lucky. Was there any damage?"

"Some charred window shades and a blackened wall... not much. The good news is you're okay. Hold still! I want to dress this wound." Nieshe started to wrap Nick's arm with a white gauze bandage.

"Ouch." Nick winced as Nieshe tied it off.

A burly redheaded man pushed his way through the crowd. It was Gunter Haas, the first shift leader. "Move over, Nieshe. You're coddling the boy." His ruddy face flushed as he bent down, and stopped inches from Nick's face. He sniffed. "You were smoking around fuel!"

"Mr. Haas, I don't smoke! Remember? Someone attacked me!"

He held something in front of Nick's nose. "We found this pack of cigarettes and matches on the floor next to you. You want to explain that?"

"I can't"

"Get up! We're going to see Colonel Young! The rest of you – back to work!"

Nieshe stood up. "I'm going too."

Haas shot him a look. "No you're not. I'm the union steward and I'm telling you to go back to work. We've wasted enough time this morning on account of him." Haas pointed at Nick then turned to the assembled men. "I said everybody back to work." He pointed at a workman close by. "Johnson, I want that airframe report on my desk this morning.

The men grumbled as they dispersed and soon only Haas, Nieshe and Nick were left in the locker room. Nieshe looked at Nick. "I will speak for you, if Colonel Young asks."

Nick stood up slowly feeling a little woozy and smiled at Nieshe. "Thanks, but I'm sure that Colonel Young will believe what I tell him."

Haas turned to go. "Come on Grant. Let's get this over with."

Nick walked next to Haas as they left the hangar and moved towards the Pan American Airways Administration building. He noticed that the sun had burned most of the morning fog away, but it hadn't warmed up yet. Nick wished he'd grabbed a jacket as he gently rubbed his bandaged arm. "Why don't you believe me, Mr. Haas?"

"You're such a prima donna, Grant. You see a boogieman

behind every bush and in every dark corner. And it seems like every time something goes wrong, you're there. Why is that?"

"I told you – somebody doesn't want the clippers to fly to China."

"I'm going to demand that Colonel Young remove you from my team."

"Remove me? You mean *fire* me?"

Haas stopped walking, grabbed Nick's burned arm and swung him around violently.

"Ouch! That hurts! Let me go!" Nick protested.

A wicked half-smile crossed Haas's face and he squeezed Nick's burnt arm harder. "You're through, Grant." He released Nick's arm and started walking again.

Nick caught up, his arm still stinging. "What if Colonel Young doesn't fire me? What if he believes me instead of you?"

Haas smiled. "Then I'll call a general strike and then we'll see what Pan Am does. The clippers won't fly anywhere."

Nick looked at Haas in stunned silence. *Whose side was Haas on?*

* * *

Once inside the main hallway of the admin building, Nick followed Haas into Colonel Young's outer office. Betty Smyth, Young's secretary, looked up from a big black typewriter. She peered at them over the top of her reading glasses, clearly perplexed. "Yes, Mr. Haas?"

Haas leaned over Smyth's desk. "I need to see Colonel Young immediately."

Betty was an attractive middle-aged woman who was also Young's gatekeeper. "Well, you can't. He's on the phone with the head office in New York." She looked at the date book on the desk. "Would you like to make an appointment? I have one open tomorrow at ten. Or would you care to wait on the off chance that he'll see you?"

Haas looked like he was about to explode. Red-faced, he pointed at Betty. "You go in there and tell him that we've had a fire and I have the man here that started it."

Betty looked at Nick. "He can't mean you, Nick?"

"I'm afraid that he does, Miss Smyth. But he's wrong!"

Smyth did not seem the least bit rattled. "Humph... sit down there both of you." She pointed to a leather couch. "And I will give the Colonel your message, Mr. Haas."

Haas and Nick sat on the couch while Betty opened the door to Young's office. Nick caught a glimpse of Colonel Young talking on the phone behind his desk. He looked up briefly and made eye contact before the door closed.

A minute later the door opened and Betty beckoned. Haas and Nick stood, but Betty shook her head at Nick. She ushered Haas into the office and closed the door in Nick's face. This time Young did not look up to see Nick.

Nick sat down. He felt confused. *Why won't Colonel Young see me?* He put his head in his hands and waited. His arm ached and he waited some more. *What's taking so long?*

Ten minutes later, the office door opened and Haas walked out. He looked a Nick and a sly smile appeared on his face. He slowly drew his finger across his throat and pointed at Nick — the meaning all too clear. Then he left the office.

Nick jumped up and paced the outer office. Betty appeared and returned to her desk.

"Will Colonel Young see me now?"

Betty looked up at Nick. "Not just yet. He's placed a person-to-person long distance call to Juan Trippe. They're trying to find Mr. Trippe now. As soon as the Colonel is through, he will see you."

"Miss Smyth, am I going to be fired?"

Betty looked up at Nick with something that looked like sympathy. "I can't say, Nick. Haas was very insistent and made several threats. That's what the Colonel wants to discuss with Mr. Trippe."

Betty's words did little to calm Nick's worries. "I've going to go down the hall to use the restroom. I'll be back in a few moments."

"Don't be long. I don't want you to keep the Colonel waiting."

"Okay, be right back."

Down the hallway from Colonel Young's office, Nick dropped a nickel into the pay phone and dialed. The phone rang twice and a man answered. "Oakland 2-2171."

"Hello, this is Nick Grant. Commander Boltz of Naval Intelligence told me to call this number if I ran into trouble."

"Okay, what's your situation?"

"Someone attacked me. I think someone is trying to kill me." Nick's hands shook as he thought about the incident. *What horrible way to die!*

There was a pause. "Where are you now?"

"I'm in the Pan American Administration building at Alameda Airport."

"We'll send a car. Someone will contact you."

Nick heard the click as the line went dead. *Great. Lot of help they were!* Nick returned to Young's outer office to wait. Unconsciously, he rubbed his burned arm and winced as pain shot to his brain.

A short while later, two men in suits entered the room and walked past Nick without a word. They stopped in front of Betty's desk.

The shorter one handed her a business card. "We want to see Colonel Young."

Nick noticed the surprise on her face as she stood. "Just one moment, please, Agent Cook." She disappeared through Young's door.

Colonel Young appeared in the doorway an instant later, walked towards the two men and extended his hand. "Special Agent Cook? How nice to meet you."

Cook shook Young's hand. "Likewise, I'm sure. This is Special Agent Franks. We heard you had some trouble this morning."

Young looked intrigued. "Really? What makes you think so?"

Cook jerked his thumb over his shoulder. "Grant called us and said someone tried to kill him."

Young looked at Nick quizzically. "Well then, you'd better all come in. Betty, please bring us a coffee tray and four cups."

Young's office was adorned with many pictures - most of Young as a pilot. Nick loved the one of Young receiving the Freedom Award from President Hoover. In another, Young stood with famous aviators Charles Lindbergh and Wiley Post. On a small side table were scale models of the M-130 *China Clipper* and the S-42 *Pan American Clipper*. Cook walked over to the wall and looked at a picture of a ship unloading supplies off a tropical island. "Is that the *North Haven*?"

Young walked over. "Yes, that's right. And that is Nick Grant." He pointed to a tall lanky figure. The man wore only shorts and his hair seemed almost white in the black and white print. He was standing on a barge tied to the ship and waving at the photographer.

Betty returned with the tray and set it on Young's desk. She poured a cup for Agents Franks and Cook. Nick appreciated her reassuring smile as she gave him a cup as well. Nick had learned to love the rich smell of coffee while out in the Pacific. After much ribbing, he learned to drink it black.

Cook grunted and sat in a chair facing Young's desk. He pointed for Franks to take the other. Nick continued to stand.

Young looked annoyed. "Nick, you may be seated." He gestured to the couch. "Now then, Nick, what's this all about?"

Nick blurted, "Somebody tossed a cigarette on a pile of gas soaked rags, and then whacked me on the head when I tried to put it out!" He held up his bandaged arm.

Young replied, "This morning's incident could have been tragic for both you and Pan Am. Mr. Haas thinks you started the fire with a careless cigarette or match, but I have my doubts. What makes you think someone tried to kill you?"

Nick grew frustrated. *Why can't they see that the Clipper*

was in danger? "Because somebody hit me on the head!" Nick exploded. "Colonel Young, it wouldn't be the first time. Before we go on, sir, who are these guys?" He pointed to Cook and Frank.

Cook opened his suit jacket and removed a leather bi-fold wallet. He opened it and held it up to Nick. There was a badge on one side and an ID card on the other. It read, *Special Agent Brian Cook, Federal Bureau of Investigation*. Cook pointed to his colleague. "This is Special Agent Franks."

Satisfied, Nick continued. "We know that Lieutenant Commander Miyazaki is back in the area – "

Cook interrupted. "We don't know that! You're the only one who's seen him."

"Well, he is! He tried to kill me in Honolulu! And he was here! Working here as a janitor when I returned. He'd still be here if I hadn't recognized him."

Cook looked doubtful. "What you saw was a Japanese man with a scar on his face."

"I put that scar there while he was slashing at me with a Samurai sword!"

Young intervened. "Gentlemen, please. Surely, you're not questioning the Aloha Tower attack? It's well documented."

Cook interjected. "Not the attack, Colonel Young, but with all due respect, we don't know that it was Miyazaki in Honolulu or here."

"If not Miyazaki, then who?"

"Colonel, we're not sure. The Japanese Naval Intelligence trail has gone cold. That could be this kid's imagination. Today, he could be trying to cover up a stupid mistake."

Nick leapt to his feet. "Stupid mistake? You calling me a liar? What about those loose fuel lines?"

Young said, "Sit down, Nick! Those fuel lines could just as easily been a sloppy install."

After a deep breath to calm down, Nick answered. "No, sir! Mr. Nieshe checks and double-checks every nut and bolt that I touched. The gas tank installation must have been logged with the installers and the supervisor who checked the work."

Young turned to Cook and Franks, his glance cold. "I thought the FBI was tasked to protect the Skyway to Asia. If that's not your understanding, then I need to inform Juan Trippe, the Pan American Airways President. Mr. Trippe can inquire with the senior senator from New York. "

Cook turned conciliatory. "We're here on President Roosevelt's orders, but we can't go accusing a serving Japanese Naval Officer of espionage and attempted murder on the word of a 17-year-old boy. The man's here legally, as an English student."

"Why can't you?" demanded Young. "I trust Nick implicitly. He has no reason to lie."

"Colonel Young, I'm not accusing anybody of lying. Maybe it is Miyazaki. But I've got to have more than a kid's overactive imagination."

Colonel Young stood. "Gentlemen, thank you for coming. If anything else turns up, we'll be sure to notify you. Now, good day."

The FBI agents stood, said a polite goodbye, and left. Nick started to leave too when Young called him back. "Nick, for the record, I believe you. As for Haas, he's as tough as nails. He gets the job done and on time. He's just sore at you for the work slow down. I'll have a word with him, but stay out of his way for a few days."

"Yes sir."

"But, next time speak to me first before you call the G-men."

"I was pretty scared."

"I appreciate that and it wasn't meant as a rebuke." He shook his head. "Sometimes I wonder if the FBI's on our side. Regardless, this isn't over yet. Keep your eyes open and stop by to see the flight surgeon."

"Thanks, for your support Colonel Young. I will!"

Chapter Three: Homecoming

6:00 p.m., Saturday, October 19, 1935
The Grant Home, Alameda, California

Nick's head and arm still ached as he walked into the living room. He leaned over and kissed his mother. "Hello."

Seated in her favorite reading chair, Helen Grant closed the evening paper. "Hello, love. What happened to your arm?"

Nick inspected his arm. The Doc had cleaned the burn but it was still red and the hair follicles were melted nubs. "Oh, it's nothing Mom. I got too close to a welding torch."

"Donald, look at what your son did to his arm."

His dad looked up from his trade magazine and seemed to notice Nick for the first time. "Hello Nick. Let's have a look at that arm."

"It's not too bad, Dad." He lied. *Good thing they can't see the bump on my head.* "In fact, I wasn't aware of it until Mom said something."

Donald looked up and examined the arm. "Son, if you continue to come home with injuries, no matter how minor, your mother will insist that you quit."

"Dad, I love what I'm doing! Without a Pan Am scholarship, how will I get to attend college?"

His mother looked up from the paper. "How about a scholarship from good grades? You could have used today to study your English grammar. Even engineers have to write well."

Nick couldn't argue that point. Math and science were so much easier, but English! Three times the effort got him half the return. He decided to change the subject. "Dad, can I still have the car for the dance tonight?"

"It's alright with me. Helen, do you object?"

"No, but Nick, I want you home at ten sharp."

"But Mom, that's so early!"

"It might be for you, but you're taking your sister. And, by the way, you've got mail"

Nick's heart leapt. "From Leilani?"

"Who else? It's on the mantle."

Nick grabbed the envelope and dashed upstairs. He closed his bedroom door and flopped on the bed. Before he opened the letter he closed his eyes and smelled it – frangipani! Just like Leilani was in the room.

Dear Nick,

Aloha my haole friend. I trust that you are well and haven't blown up a clipper yet. Just kidding! But sometimes I have the strangest dreams about you. They start the same, someone is chasing you but you always manage to get away. But in each one, your pursuers get closer. You aren't in any more trouble are you?

My senior year is off to a slow start and the days just seem to drag by. I'm taking chemistry, trig, English, and history of the Hawaiian Islands, so I keep busy. I have to take a Hawaiian history class and pass a Founders test to graduate from high school. It's such a bore. I could pass the test today because I helped Hanna study years ago. Sometimes I find it hard to believe that I'm related to King

Kamehameha, the first Hawaiian to unite the islands. He was a violent man prone to dreams and visions - maybe that's where I get my temper.

Speaking of Hanna, she left for the Johns Hopkins Medical School a couple of weeks before Labor Day. Sadly, her steamship docked at L.A., or she would have stopped by to meet your family. Hanna says that I'm not supposed to see you again until one of the family meets your family. Anyway, she plans to come through San Francisco on her way home for Christmas. So be warned! I don't care what she says - I can't wait for you to come back to the islands.

I must close so Daddy can take the letter down to the Matson Liner. She sails with the tide. I miss you and our special time together. Come back to Oahu and me soon!

  Leilani
  XXX

* * *

Dressed in his best suit and a jazzy blue tie, Nick pulled the family Ford into the Alameda High School parking lot. "Jude, meet me back here at 9:45 and don't be late again. Last time we were grounded!"

"Nicky, you worry too much." She adjusted the mirror to check her face. "You look goofy. It must be Leilani's letter. Did your girlfriend say she loved you or something?"

Nick yanked the mirror back. "I've told you, don't call me Nicky! And she's not my girlfriend!"

Judith Grant opened the car door and stepped out. "Okay ... Nicky." She slammed the door and sprinted toward the gym door, her long blonde hair bouncing.

Nick's friend, Tommy Burke, met him in the parking lot. "Sweet, Nick! How did you talk your old man out of the chariot?"

"Hey, my pop may seem square, but he's always been good about the car."

"That means we can take girls out for a soda after the dance."

"Then we'd better find some girls early because I've got to have my sister home by 10:00."

"Oh, man! I was looking forward to driving to Berkley, you know, up on Lookout Mountain, with some dames."

"Like any girl would park with the likes of you!"

"You never know buddy until you ask…"

"Come on, Tail Spin Tommy, while the night is still young." Nick walked toward the gym chuckling. Since they were young boys, they'd dreamed of becoming pilots. Nick started calling his friend *Tail Spin Tommy*, after the teenage character of the popular movie serial. But tonight, getting a kiss was the least of his worries as more serious thoughts pushed to the forefront of his mind. *What would Miyazaki do next and who was going to stop him?*

The gym was swinging. A band belted out a rhythm so loud that the floor vibrated. Nick felt the music thump in his chest. Green and gold ribbons and banners in the school colors streamed from the rafters and "BEAT BERKLEY!" banners adorned the walls. Tommy looked around and nodded his approval. "It looks just like a fancy downtown dance hall."

"Yeah, what do you know about that?" Nick looked around for a familiar face and saw Jude chatting with her friends in by the basketball hoop. Some couples were dancing but most of the kids lined the walls - girls on the left and boys on the right.

Tommy surveyed the hall like a bird of prey. "Look, there's Mary Jane Parker - alone! I've got to make my move! Good hunting, Nick!" He sauntered across the room and stopped directly in front of her. They exchanged a few words, then she smiled, took his arm and they moved to the dance floor.

Nick had to admit that while Tommy was fearless and pretty good with the girls, he wasn't. Usually he was tongue-tied and said something stupid. When he managed to talk, he was unable to say much beyond "hi."

Mac, Nick's mentor, had been shy around females, too. The night they had met Anne Lindbergh came to mind. Charles and Anne Lindbergh, the two most famous people in the world, had shown up at Mac's hangar. Mac had talked poor Lindbergh's ear off but could only mumble, "Nice to meet you" to Mrs. Lindbergh. That meeting had changed Nick's life forever, along with the lives of everyone he loved. For his family, the change was good...for Mac, it had proven fatal.

Nick moved toward the punch bowl. There a group of girls was engaged in a lively debate about the proper skirt length. *Boring!* A girl stood with her back between him and the punch bowl. She had jet-black hair that flowed down her back and ended below her waist. If her hair had been lighter, maybe chestnut colored and adorned with a hibiscus flower, it could have been Leilani. Now it was different with Leilani. He found conversation with her as easy as breathing.

He reached out and tapped the dark-haired girl on the shoulder. "Excuse me, please. I'd like to get to the punch."

The girl spun around fast, her hair fanning out like a dark curtain. She stopped, arm cocked ready to strike.

Startled, Nick leapt back and stumbled. To his utter embarrassment, he tipped over a small side table and landed with a crash on his butt. The damage to his pride outstripped the pain in his keister. *What a day! First the fuel leak, the fire, then the G-Men, and now this!*

The band stopped, girls giggled, everyone turned and stared. The dark-haired girl looked Japanese, but spoke like an American. She leaned over Nick. "I'm so sorry. Here, let me help you up." She grabbed Nick's burned arm and yanked him to his feet.

"Yeow! That hurt!" Nick rubbed his arm and looked in her face. He flushed, keenly aware a girl had made a fool of him in front of the entire school. *Even the freshmen were snickering!*

Nick's anger subsided as he eyed her. *Wow, what a looker!* Her clear complexion was darker than her companions', her face a perfect oval and her features flawless, eyes deep and dark. "You're beautiful . . . I mean strong. How did you lift me? I must be twice your weight?"

"It's all in your center of gravity and balance. See, you spread your feet shoulder width apart, like so." She hiked up her skirt a few inches above the knee and squatted. "This is a good horse stance, and it is very powerful."

Nick tried not to look at the girl's exposed thighs, but was mesmerized none-the-less. He looked away only to notice every boy in the gym staring at her. Her companions stood in shock, hands covering their open mouths.

A man yelled, "Nancy Tanaka!" It was Mr. Brown, the assistant principal – and he was headed their way.

Brown pushed through the crowd and strode up to Nancy. "Drop you skirt and cover up this instant!"

Nancy looked confused. "What?"

"You cannot behave like a hussy in this school, young lady!"

"Hussy?"

Nick was shocked. "She's not a hussy, Mr. Brown."

Nancy whirled. "Nick Grant, you keep out of this!"

"How did you know my name?"

"Everybody knows your name, *Clipper Boy*," a boy by the wall said.

Brown cut in. "We don't tolerate such behavior here, Miss Tanaka. Leave immediately and I will see in my office Monday morning at 7:30 sharp."

Nancy looked shocked. "Leave? But why? I didn't do anything wrong, Mr. Brown. Please! Girls in swimsuits show a lot more leg than I did. I had to lift my skirt up to demonstrate the horse stance." She hiked her skirt again but not as high.

Catcalls erupted from a group of football players who had moved in for a closer look. One guy called. "Hey, Nip hussy, show us some more of the Jap thigh!"

Brown swung around and pointed. "That will be enough out of you, Mr. Bennett."

The gym erupted with whistles and obscene yells as the

mood suddenly turned ugly. Mr. Brown, a short man with a shorter fuse, climbed up on a chair and yelled. "Attention, attention everybody! This dance is over! Pack up the band, grab your wraps, and go home. NOW!"

Silence fell over the gym as the shocked students headed for the doors. One reached up and tore a green streamer down. Nick found himself walking along side Nancy. One of the girls from her earlier group pushed past roughly. "Nice going, Nancy!"

Nick felt bad for her and a little guilty. "Look, I'm sorry. It was my fault, too. If I hadn't tripped, you wouldn't have done that horse thing. What was that anyway?"

She did not meet Nick's eyes. "It's an elementary *Kendo* fighting position. My uncle taught it to me at his *Dojo*."

"I don't mean to seem stupid, but I have no idea what you're talking about."

She spun to face him. "It's a Japanese Martial art!"

"You mean like Karate or Kung Fu?"

"How is it you're such a smart round eye?"

"Round eye?" They stopped next to the Grant's Ford.

Another voice explained "It's a Jap term for us whites." It was Bennett, surrounded by a group of football players.

Chapter Four: Rumble!

8:48 p.m., Saturday, October 19, 1935
Alameda High School parking lot, Alameda, California

Nick towered over Bennett, but Bennett easily outweighed him by 100 pounds. "I wasn't talking to you, Bennett!"

Bennett took a step closer. "I was talking to *you*, Jap lover! Now step aside while we teach this Jap bitch a thing or two."

Nick scanned the football players. He wouldn't stand a chance. He gulped down his fear and said calmly as he could, "Not on your life." He grabbed Nancy's hand, pulled her behind him, and opened the car door. "Get in the car!"

She snatched her hand back and stood next to him. "Stop that! I can take care of myself."

Catcalls erupted from the players. Bennett taunted, "Yeah, baby, I'll bet you can. Come over here. I've got something you can take care of!"

Nick had enough. "Shut up, Bennett!"

"Yeah, who's going make me? You?"

A new voice spoke from the shadows. "If necessary, I will. That will be your choice."

Everybody turned as the newcomer walked out of the shadows. He was a young Japanese man, maybe eighteen. As he walked past the towering football players, he asked, "Who among you has insulted my sister and our family?"

Nancy called, "No, Roger, forget it! Let's just go home!"

Bennett mocked Nancy. "No Roger, don't hurt the poor little football players." Then he looked at Roger. "What if I said it was me, Roger?"

"Then I would say that it is too bad for you."

Nancy pleaded. "Roger, let it go. Just take me home! Please don't hurt anyone."

Bennett chuckled then lunged for Roger. But Roger wasn't there. He had sidestepped Bennett and then punched him in the kidneys as he passed.

Bennett howled and turned. "I'm going to smash you!" He rushed Roger again. The next series of events happened very fast and Nick wasn't entirely sure what occurred. Roger seemed to leap into the air and kick Bennett in the face at the same instant. Bennett toppled over backward and Roger landed on him feet first. Nick heard a couple of cracks in Bennett's chest.

Roger leapt off Bennett as two other players rushed him. He planted two snap kicks in quick succession. They went down, screaming, gripping their crotches. The four remaining players surrounded Roger. Then they rushed him. Nick rushed forward to assist and grabbed the player closest to him. The player turned and punched Nick's ear. His ear hurt, but the blow had also jarred his earlier head injury. As they fell, he felt dizzy.

Nick regained his feet as the player stood up and pushed him hard. Nick landed on the Ford's hood and left a huge dent. Nick shook his head and reentered the fray.

Roger had felled two more football players, and then used a closed fist to drop the third. The last one standing attacked Roger from behind. Nick swung as hard as he could and caught him on the ear. The player seemed dazed and stopped momentarily. Then he turned on Nick. Roger leapt between them and delivered a roundhouse kick to the player's chest. The football player crumbled to the pavement in agony.

Roger and Nick stood back to back and surveyed the parking lot. Moaning, prostrate members of the high school football team surrounded them. Nancy had stood her ground in a fighting stance. She did look like she could take care of herself.

Nick heard running feet approach from the school. It was Mr. Brown followed by two other teachers and his sister. Brown pulled up short. "Oh, my God! What did you do to the football team? We've got the Homecoming Game next week! Who's left to play?"

Jude ran up and hugged Nick. "Are you alright, Nick?"

"Fine, Sis." The gravity of his situation hit Nick and he faced the Assistant Principal. "They started it, Mr. Brown! We were just trying to go home!"

Brown was shaking with anger. "Where are the others?"

Nick was puzzled. "What others?"

Brown spat out. "The ones who helped you attack the team?"

Roger replied in a calm voice. "There is no one else. The players are not seriously hurt, Mr. Brown, which is more than they deserve."

"All of you, up to my office – NOW! We'll get to the bottom of this. Call your parents."

Nick dug into his pocket and pulled out a nickel. He tossed it to his sister. "Jude, call home!"

* * *

Brown slammed his fist down on the table. "What are we going to do with you?"

Roger, Nancy, and Nick sat on the bench outside the Principal's office. The siblings sat stoically, heads erect, eyes to the front, hands folder in their laps, faces emotionless masks.

Nick's head and ear hurt but he was still fuming. "You heard what those oafs called Nancy in the Gym. We left peaceably." He stood and jabbed his finger at Bennett. "But you jumped us in the parking lot!"

Bennett sat on the bench across from them attended by the school nurse. He looked up, his head bandaged. "Mr. Brown, we were going home when Nick confronted us. He was spoiling for a fight and then Mr. Jujitsu jumped us from behind. It was a trap!"

"That's a lie!" Angry, Nick started to rise.

Brown stood up. "Grant, sit down and shut up!"

Nick sat down. He glared at Bennett with all the hatred he could muster. And he mustered quite a lot. Then to Nick's utter amazement, Mr. Nieshe walked in. "Mr. Nieshe, what are you doing here?"

Nancy leapt to her feet. "Uncle Yoshe!" She lost her composure and fell into his arms.

"Calm yourself, Niece. Do not let these *banjin* see your emotions. Remember your training."

Nancy seemed to regain her composure. "Yes, Uncle." She took a couple of deep breaths and sat down.

Brown looked at Nieshe. "So I take it you're these children's uncle. Where are their parents?"

"They are away on business. I am Yoshiro Nieshe." He bowed slightly. "I am their uncle. How may I be of service?"

"These hooligans attacked a group of students, injuring several."

Nieshe looked at Roger, Nancy and Nick. "They seem fine. What happened to the hooligans?"

Brown looked flustered. "No, Mr. Nieshe. Don't you understand English?" He pointed his finger at Nick's chest. "They are the attackers! They started a rumble, injured the football team, and I won't have it!"

Nick's anger got the best of him. "That's not true, Mr. Brown!"

Brown looked coldly at Nick. "I've had enough of you.

Apologize instantly!"

Nick had had enough, too. "For what - demanding the truth?"

"That's it, Mr. Grant. One week suspension for brawling."

Nieshe spoke up. "And what are you going to do to the perpetrators of this rumble?"

Brown gestured to Roger and Nancy. "Oh, they get a week's suspension as well. That will be all. Take them home."

Nieshe bowed and then lead them out of the office.

In the hall, Roger seethed. "That is what I mean, Uncle. The *banjin* are bigots. We never even had a chance to tell our side. Brown had already decided we were at fault!"

"And what of Nick? He's *banjin*."

"So what? He was just playing up to Nancy." He turned to Nick. "You stay away from her, *banjin*!"

Nick, still reeling from his suspension, was annoyed. "Would someone please tell me what's a banjin?"

Nieshe replied, "It has several meanings. The best is 'non Japanese' and the worst is 'barbarian'."

"So which is it in my case?"

"Nick, we mean non-Japanese." He looked at Roger. "Right, Nephew?"

"As you say, Honorable Uncle."

The disgusted look on Roger's face told Nick another story. Roger wanted nothing to do with him.

Nick looked at Nieshe. "My parents are going to kill me! What am I going to do?"

"I will speak to your parents, Nick. I am in your debt for coming to the aid of my niece."

"How could you know that, Mr. Nieshe?"

"I know you and I know my niece. You're sometimes a hot head, but in the end you would only do what you thought right." He turned to Roger. "How bad did you hurt them?"

"Not as bad as they deserved, Uncle. A few bruises, some cracked ribs, but no broken bones."

"So what punishment do you think you deserve?"

"Whatever you decide. My actions were unworthy of your teachings."

Nick was getting confused. "Wait a minute, Mr. Nieshe. They attacked us."

"While that may be true, Roger should have chosen to escort his sister away." He turned to Roger. "Your punishment will be to teach Nick in the art of *Kendo* and *Jujitsu*."

"W-What?" Roger stammered. "This *banjin* is not worthy."

"Let me be the judge of that. I will speak to Nick's parents. I will request Nick work part-time at the hangar, and start at the *Dojo* this week. After work you will bring him to the *Dojo* and train him."

Chapter Five: Bushido and Starvation

3:45 p.m., Monday, October 21, 1935
Corner of Pacific and Alameda Streets, Alameda, California

Nick stood on the corner for fifteen minutes. *Where was he?* Nieshe had dropped him off in a strange section of town and told him to wait.

An unexpected voice whispered in his ear. "I see you're still here, white boy. Or would you prefer *banjin*?"

Nick jumped. He hadn't heard Roger approach. Nick turned and extended his hand. "That was some fight Saturday night."

Roger did not take the offered hand. "Look, white boy... you may be favored by my uncle, but I don't like you."

Nick dropped his hand and felt a little foolish. "Why?"

"Isn't it obvious?"

"No."

"We're different, buddy boy. I'm Nip and a member of the dreaded 'Yellow Peril'. You're *banjin*, a white boy, a round eye, and we hate each other."

"I don't hate you. I don't know you!" Nick was growing tired of this discussion. "You going to show me the way to your uncle's *Dojo*, or do I have to find it myself?"

"Follow me, *banjin*, if you can." Roger took off running.

Nick sprinted to catch up, but Roger always stayed tantalizingly out of reach. They ran down alleys, crossed busy streets and hopped fences as they cut through yards. Nick's lungs felt on fire, but he was determined not to give up.

Finally, twenty minutes later, Nick rounded a corner and almost ran into Roger. He had stopped in front of a storefront in the Japanese section of the city.

Nick bent over, his hands on his knees. He felt like he was about to barf. He hadn't been this winded since swim team workouts freshman year.

"So, white boy, you still want to learn *Jujitsu*?"

Nick straightened up gasping for breath. "Why-Why not?"

"Tomorrow I will run faster."

Nick replied through clenched teeth, "Bring it on!" He followed Roger into the *Dojo*.

The smell of cotton mats, sweat and disinfectant greeted him. He stopped in front of a class of Japanese girls of varying ages. Two girls stood apart from each other wearing full-face masks, each armed with large padded sticks. One wore a yellow facemask, the other wore green. Mr. Nieshe stood in front of the two combatants and yelled, *"Kaishi!"*

The girls bowed to each other, yelled and attacked. Green lunged and yellow repelled. Yellow struck and green blocked. On and on it went, until yellow feinted at her opponent's head. When green raised her guard, yellow swung her stick at knee height. Green thudded to the floor. Yellow moved in for the killing stoke, stopping her stick an inch from green's throat.

Nieshe yelled, *"Shuushi!"*

Yellow reached down and offered her hand to green. Once on their feet, the girls removed their masks and bowed to each other, and then to Mr. Nieshe. Nick recognized the winner. "Hello, Nancy."

She bowed slightly. "Hello Nick. Welcome to my uncle's

Dojo."

Roger stepped between them. "This way, Grant." He led them to the changing room. Roger opened a cabinet. He took out two neatly rolled cotton bundles and tossed one at Nick. "Change into this."

Nick unrolled the bundle to discover a thick pair of white cotton trousers and coat. "How do you keep the jacket closed?"

"With this." He tossed Nick a thick, white cotton belt. "You tie it thus." He demonstrated with his black belt.

Nick changed and hung his clothes in an empty locker. "Now what?"

"Follow me to the mat."

Each day that week , the pattern remained the same. Nick tried to catch Roger and each day Nick got a little closer. For his part, Roger ensured that Nick had fresh bruises, scrapes and sore muscles everyday after their time at the *Dojo.*

Nick's parents did not hide their disappointment. He would have to pay for the Ford repairs and work extra chores. After he finished, he stayed up long hours into the night to keep up with his schoolwork. It was a long, tough week but worth it. He had flown twice on the Clipper and toughened up at the *Dojo.* He wasn't sure that he ever wanted to go back to high school.

* * *

7:30 a.m., Saturday, October 26, 1935
Alameda Airport, Alameda, California

Nieshe looked up from his tea. "Good morning, Nick. How's that shoulder? That was quite a whack Roger gave you yesterday."

Nick rotated his arm around his shoulder socket. "It's pretty sore but I can work."

"You learn fast. You surprised Roger with that ridge-hand counter blow. I'd say the match was a draw."

"Does Roger know?"

"He knows. Why?"

"Great. Now he'll really beat on me!"

Nieshe smiled ruefully. "True, but if he chopped off your arm you'd still show up for a Clipper flight. Nothing would keep you away."

Nick could hardly contain his excitement. "Is she checked out and ready?"

"So far yes, but there's still much to be done. Let's get to it." Nieshe handed Nick a pair of metal snips. Nick followed him up the scaffolding to the main wing spar and then carefully out onto the wing.

Nieshe pointed at number one engine cowling. "The Flight Engineer reported that the engine cowlings were sticking. You check number one engine and I will check number two."

"Right, Mr. Nieshe." The engines were numbered from left to right as the pilots sat in the cockpit. Carefully they moved out onto the port wing avoiding the "**NO STEP**" marked areas. They worked side by side for half an hour in silence. Nick's mind worked overtime.

Nieshe pulled a rag out of his pocket wiped his brow. The high intensity lights were close overhead and hot. "Nick, thanks for coming to the *Dojo*. It means a great deal to me."

"I should be thanking you. It's a great opportunity. Not sure that's true for Roger, though. He seems to have taken a real dislike to me."

"Your tuition under Roger serves two purposes. You learn our ancient art of hand-to-hand combat – the skills you need to protect yourself. Roger learns that not all *banjin* are our enemies."

Nick massaged his arm where Roger had landed a particularly vicious knife kick. "I'm not too sure he's making much progress."

"Give it time."

Nick pulled back his shirtsleeve to show the mottled black and blue of his bruises. "I hope my body holds up!"

Nieshe chuckled. "It's tough for Roger, too. He's torn between two worlds, yours and that of our ancestors."

"But you don't seem torn. Why is it so tough for him?"

"My situation is different. Roger's father, Mr. Tanaka, is samurai class. But he fell in love with a commoner, my sister - a woman of much lower social class. My brother-in-law had to choose between my sister and his family."

Nieshe picked up his metal file and started to shave the cowling carefully. Nieshe handed Nick a large box wrench and continued. "It's a matter of class, honor and *Bushido*."

"*Bushido?*"

"It means 'Way of the Warrior.' It's a Japanese code of conduct and a way of life, similar in some ways to the European concept of chivalry. The Tanaka family traces their lineage back to the Emperor's family. The Nieshe family is from the burakumin although they are now mostly merchants."

"I'm finished here, Mr. Nieshe. And you're killing me with all this Japanese. What's *burakumin*?"

They moved back to the fuselage and climbed the ladder that led to the tail entry hatch. "You must learn Japanese if you are to master karate and kendo, so pay attention. The Buddhist and Shinto tradition condemned people who worked as butchers, executioners, and tanners as unclean. They are called *burakumin*."

"So, after your sister married Mr. Tanaka, he became *burakumin*?"

Nieshe shook his head. "No, he became *Rohin*, or a masterless samurai."

"So what? If Mr. Tanaka loved your sister, then that is a small price to pay."

"Perhaps in the West but not so in Japan. Many say *Bushido* dictates *Seppuku* for *Rohin*."

"*Seppuku?*"

"It's what westerners incorrectly call *hari-kari* which is but one form of *Seppuku*. *Seppuku* is a ritual suicide normally committed with a special knife and with a second Seppuku is also expected for those vanguished in battle."

"Remind me never to lose again at the *Dojo!*"

Nieshe laughed. "My family does not interpret *Bushido* in that manner. We accepted the disgrace of defeat as a fair trade for continued life. It is a very un-Japanese concept. No, there was nothing for me in Japan and so I decided to emigrate to America. Here, at least, I have a chance, even if most whites are not welcoming."

"Mr. Tanaka and your sister left Japan because he was *Rohin*?"

"Yes."

"She must be very beautiful."

Nieshe and looked at Nick. "You are correct. But most whites would not see her beauty. They see only a flat face and slanted eyes. But I digress – back to your question. My sister told me it was an all consuming passion that changed their lives forever."

"A love story like Romeo and Juliet, huh? So they moved here for the same reasons?"

"Quite so. Tell me, do you think my niece is attractive?"

Nick felt his face get hot and looked away. "I'd rather not say. Roger will kill me if he finds out I have an opinion."

Nieshe gave a hearty laugh. "Yes, I believe he would. He is very protective of his sister."

"What does Mr. Tanaka do? He's always away on business."

"He has a successful import/export business. His firm handles trade between America and Japan. He has done very well for my sister and her children."

The crew hatch opened a few feet below them and Gunter Haas's baritone voice boomed. "Hey you two, a little less talking and a lot more work. We've got a clipper to fly this afternoon!"

* * *

3:32 p.m., Saturday, October 26, 1935
9,000 ft above the California coast

The smell of vomit was overpowering in the main cabin. Nick asked, "Are you okay, Mr. Nieshe?"

"Not really. I hate flying. It always makes me sick." The *Chipper* lurched unexpectedly and Nieshe grabbed another airsick bag and retched again.

Nick looked around in awe. "The size of this plane still amazes me. The Martin 130 is 10 tons heavier than the *Pan American Clipper* and almost 50 knots faster. Still, it doesn't seem as stable as the old Sikorsky 42."

The Clipper dropped a good fifty feet and Nick felt his stomach lurch. Nieshe looked a lighter shade of green as he folded the top of the barf bag and placed on the floor next to the others. "Has Captain Tilton let you pilot the M-130 yet?"

"Not yet, but he says I'm almost ready. Says I could use more time at the flight engineer position and managing the fuel flow."

The cockpit door opened and Vic Wright, Flight Engineer, appeared in the doorway. "Nick, Skipper said to come forward."

Nick leapt out of his seat. "See you later, Mr. Nieshe. Hope you feel better."

Nieshe called after him. "You keep it steady or you'll clean up my puke!" The four engines drowned out whatever else he said. At 830-horse power each, the Pratt and Whitney engines produced more power than a steam locomotive.

* * *

On the flight deck, Nick struggled for two hours as the Clipper flew a racetrack course out over the Pacific. The big plane used cables and pulleys to activate the flight control surfaces, which, even in trim, was heavy work. He had one hand on the throttles and the other on the wheel as he tried to slow the plane to just above a stall. *Easy, easy...* Suddenly the *Clipper* dropped like a stone. Nick dropped the nose and pushed the throttle forward to recover airspeed. He used the opportunity to wipe the sweat from his forehead. It was strange to be sweating in the cold cockpit.

Nick heard Tilton's voice through the headphones. "Damn it, Nick, you stalled it again! One more time and I'm taking her back!"

He keyed his mike. "It snuck up on me, Mr. Tilton!"

First Officer Jack Tilton sat in the jump seat behind the two pilot positions. "Nick, the M-130 is fickle. You need a much lighter touch on the controls than the Sikorsky. You've got to anticipate the stall before it hits you. Listen to what the M-130 tells you. She announces she is at the edge with a light shake of the control wheel."

"I'm trying Mr. Tilton, but it's not as easy as I thought."

At 9,000 feet altitude, there was ample time to recover before they slammed into the ocean. However, the mechanics in the back would not be happy. They would be convinced they were falling out of the sky. If Nick didn't master the M-130's stall threshold soon, it would be a while before they would let him fly again.

Tilton yawned and stretched his arms up against the cockpit ceiling. "Nick, let's change places. It's time to take her back to the barn."

Nick unbuckled his seat belt and moved past Tilton, disappointed. "When can I try again?"

Tilton answered. "After my stomach gets back in place. Vic, the auxiliary fuel tank is reading near empty. Switch to the main tank."

"Roger, Skipper." Flight Engineer Vic Wright sat in the co-pilot seat getting some pilot hours along with Nick. He reached up and moved the valves from AUX to MAIN. Almost at once, engine one quit.

"What the heck?" Nick searched the instruments for some explanation. The main tank read full, more than 800 gallons. Then engine two quit. The Clipper started to lose altitude and turn to port as the wind-milling propellers created a lot of drag on the port wing. She was going into a spin.

Tilton and Wright heaved with all their might to keep it level. Tilton called into the intercom. "Flight Engineer Position"

The crackly voice came back through the intercom. "Jackson, here."

"What have you done to my engines?"

Jackson's voice came back. "Nothing, Skipper. I was doing paperwork."

Nick thought he knew. "Skipper, I think it's the fuel line. The bay was choppy and our take-off was pretty rough. Maybe they came loose again. I'm going to check!"

Wright reached up and switched back to AUX. "Hurry Nick! We've only got a few minutes of fuel left in the auxiliary tanks. Then we'll have to ditch into the ocean. The waves are running eight to ten feet and the Clipper won't last long in those seas!"

Nick raced back to the lounge in time to see Nieshe removing the last inspection hatch. He still looked sick, but had a flashlight and a wrench in his hands. "Seems we are of a similar mind, Nick."

Nick nodded, grabbed the tools, and crawled into the hull. On his stomach, he elbow-walked back to the main tank and shined his light around. Nothing. He sniffed No smell of fuel. He yelled back over the engines' roar. "No sign of a leak, Mr. Nieshe."

Nieshe yelled back. "Must be a blockage. Back off the number one fuel line and see if you get any leakage."

Nick expected a fuel shower, but when he removed the fitting, it was bone dry. "I don't get it Mr. Nieshe. I've got number one off and there's not a drop of fuel."

"Shine your flashlight inside the hole leading into the tank. What do you see?"

"It looks like the end of a cork."

"Okay, use your finger to push the cork back into the tank. You have to replace the fuel coupling fast!"

"Right." Nick used his pinky and received a face full of

aviation fuel. "Yuck!" He screwed the coupling on as fast as he could but still managed to get soaked.

"What's happening?"

"I got number one clear. Tell Mr. Jackson."

Suddenly the engines quit. The few minutes had expired and the silence became graveyard quiet. Nick heard Nieshe's footsteps overhead as he moved forward. Then he heard number one engine roar to life. *Great! Now for number two!*

Chapter Six: RECCE

4:24 p.m., Saturday, October 26, 1935
Benton Field, Alameda, California

Lieutenant Commander Miyazaki lowered his oversized naval binoculars and rubbed his facial scar. "Idiot! You said it would work!"

"I do not understand. It should have worked, Most Honored One."

"Are you certain that our man placed the corks?"

"Absolutely! I spoke with him right after the Clipper lifted off. But the bay was very choppy. Perhaps they were dislodged?"

Miyazaki slammed his fist down on the windowsill. "Fool! If it was done as I instructed, that Clipper should have crashed into the sea! Without fuel, the wind-milling propellers would cause impossible drag and rob the wings of lift. It should have fallen like a stone. Did the mechanics re-install the propeller brakes yet?"

"No."

"Then find out what went wrong and report back to me

tonight! Do not fail me again."

"Yes, Commander."

"If you want to be a samurai, you must learn that failure is not an option. Now get out of my sight!"

Once alone, Miyazaki sat at the table and gazed out the window. The clouds were moving in from the west and it smelled like rain. He pondered his next move. He had to sabotage the Clipper in such a way as to make it look like an accident. *But how?* Since that Grant boy had exposed him at the Clipper base, he had to rely on sympathizers, or paid agents, and they were always such fools. His report was due in Tokyo soon and he needed to show some progress. His superiors were getting impatient, and he couldn't keep ahead of American Counter Intelligence indefinitely.

His thoughts wandered to what they had tried. The disruption of the Wake Island radio direction finder had failed, as had the bomb at Honolulu Harbor, and the fire. Now he could add this latest failure. It was time to take direct action. *But what would be the best way to go?* He did not mind sacrificing his own miserable life in the bargain but he must not tip his country's hand. *Not yet anyway.*

* * *

5:23 p.m., Saturday, October 26, 1935
Alameda Airport, Alameda, California

Colonel Young met the Clipper at the dock. Tilton stepped through the forward hatch and walked over. "First Officer Tilton, great job bringing the Clipper home safe. I want a written report on my desk before you leave today."

"Yes, Colonel Young. But if the mechanics weren't aboard, we'd be swimming with the sharks! Nieshe and Nick got the fuel lines clear in time, but had we been any lower, I'm not sure what would have happened."

The mechanics filed by looking pale and tired. Young called out. "Mr. Nieshe, you look like you had a rough time of it."

Nieshe stopped and made an almost imperceptible bow. "Yes, Colonel Young, it was far from a pleasant journey."

"First Officer Tilton tells me that your efforts ensured a safe return. Thank you."

Nieshe pulled Nick forward. "Nick figured out the problem, too. And he's the one who crawled into the hull to fix it."

Nick protested. "Mr. Nieshe taught me everything I know about the Martin 130. This is similar to the fuel problem a few weeks ago. This goes beyond incompetence! How could anybody be so careless?"

Young asked, "What do you mean?"

"Someone installed a new main tank, but neglected to remove the fuel line corks? I don't think so!"

"What's the purpose of the corks?"

"They keep dirt and dust particles out during painting, or while in storage or transit. The Martin Company checklist specifies removal before installation. Martin then calls for a double-check to insure they are removed before connecting the fuel lines."

"Are you suggesting that it was deliberate?"

Nieshe interjected, "Colonel Young, we'll know soon enough. First I'm going to check the maintenance logs."

"The FBI agents have them, there in the Ground Crew Foreman's office." Young pointed.

* * *

6:04 p.m., Saturday, October 26, 1935
Alameda Airport, Alameda, California

Agents Franks and Cook were waiting inside the hangar when the crew walked in. "Nieshe and Grant, over here!" Cook ordered.

It had been a tough day and Nick was in no mood for more of Cook's verbal abuse. "Well, if it isn't the G-Men. You guys are sure doing a bang-up job protecting the Clipper!"

Cook gestured to a chair outside the foreman's office. "Grant, sit down and shut up!" Two uniformed police officers stood on either side of the door. Franks opened the door, motioned Nieshe inside, and then shut the door.

Nick could hear the agents' raised voices through the door, but couldn't quite make out the words. Still the tone told a great deal. Haas walked by and sneered at Nick. "What's the matter, you little Jap lover? Your friend get caught?"

"Mr. Haas, normally you're a fool. But today you seem intent on besting your previous efforts. Mr. Nieshe *saved* the Clipper. Maybe you should find out who was the last person to handle the fuel tank. Unless I'm mistaken, you're the one who signed off on the air worthiness certificate."

"Shows what you know, Grant. Nieshe was the last to handle that tank and he signed off on the certificate."

Shocked, Nick tried to mask his emotions.

Haas grinned. "What's the matter, Grant? Cat got your sarcastic tongue?"

"Mr. Nieshe would never sabotage the Clipper. Think, man. He was on board!"

"You watch your tone with me! It just so happens that Nieshe asked to be relieved from the flight."

"What? I don't believe you."

"Said he always get sick and hates to fly. Lousy excuse, if you ask me."

"Just for the record, Mr. Haas, I didn't ask." Nick glared at Haas with an intensity he hadn't felt since last he'd seen Miyazaki. "Just leave me alone."

"Sure, kid, but after Nieshe is gone, you're next! This time even Young can't save you." Haas whistled as he walked away.

Agent Cook opened the office door and Nieshe walked out. Cook barked, "Sit down and don't move. Grant, inside." Nieshe looked serene, almost calm and composed, unlike the G-Men. They looked a bit frazzled. Nieshe winked as he passed, causing Nick to smile.

Chapter Seven: Where There's Smoke...

6:24 p.m., Saturday, October 26, 1935
Alameda Airport, Alameda, California

Cook and Franks questioned Nick for another hour. They were brusque, demanding, and accused him of complicity. They kept asking the same questions, repeatedly.

"How did you know where to look?" Cook asked.

"I'm a mechanic, it's what I do."

"You were just trying to beef up your earlier claim. Everyone believes that you were smoking and careless."

"Yeah, then how come I haven't been fired?" Nick kept thinking about Nieshe's wink.

"Who are you working for?"

"I work for Pan Am. You've got my personnel file in front of you."

In the end, the agents gave up. "We're going to let you go for now, but don't leave town."

"Just where would I go? I've got school on Monday."

Outside the office, Nieshe sat waiting patiently. When he saw Nick, he asked, "I think the agents are through with us for the time being. Can I give you a lift home?"

"That would be great, Mr. Nieshe. Thanks."

"Don't mention it."

Nick hopped into the passenger seat and Nieshe started the engine. The car was old but the engine sounded smooth as silk. "Did you rebuild the engine, Mr. Nieshe?"

"Several times."

"I can tell. Sure sounds sweet and there's no plumes of black smoke from the tail pipe."

Just then the engine back-fired with a loud bang. Nieshe looked embarrassed. "However, the timing still needs some work." He shifted into gear, engaged the clutch, and drove away.

The more Nick thought about their treatment the angrier he got. "My God! You'd think those clods would realize that we saved the Clipper, not sabotaged it!"

Nieshe shifted the car into third gear. "The maintenance log clearly shows that I was the last one to handle the tank."

"What? When?"

"The day we worked on the engine cowlings."

Nick pondered the new information. "So that's why they kept asking me if I was with you all day."

"It appears that you are my alibi. And your word is golden, at least with Colonel Young. Rumor has it that you have saved the Clipper before."

Nick tried to change the subject. How Nieshe knew about that was beyond him. *Wasn't it supposed to be a secret?* "You know, I was thinking. Haas was inside the Clipper that morning. Remember he chewed us out for too much talking and too little work?"

"Indeed, I do. He was also closest to the main tank access. It might not have been a coincidence."

"But Haas is a bigot! He hates the Japanese. Why do anything to aid the Imperial Japanese Government?"

"His anti-Japanese words may be an effective way to cast off suspicion. What better way to throw off the diligent

G-Men?"

Nick chuckled. "I don't know, Mr. Nieshe, that's awfully subtle for those two knuckle heads!"

"Nick, had you considered the agents' prejudicial manner belies what they were really thinking?"

"Well, I've got to tell you, they sure fooled me! What about the log entry for our cowling work? That should have cleared you."

"Sadly, it has gone missing."

"How? Is that possible?"

Nieshe shrugged. "Haas might have pulled the original record, replaced it with one containing my signature, then hidden the real work record."

"That's possible. So what are we going to do?"

"We're going to compare that signature."

Nick slumped. "How? The agents have it."

Nieshe stopped the car at Nick's house "We must go to Colonel Young. He is our only hope."

"It will have to wait until Monday, I'm afraid. He left the building earlier this afternoon."

"Nick, can you meet me at the airport after school on Monday? I'm going to need help searching the records."

"Sure Mr. Nieshe, I'd be glad to help."

* * *

4:43 p.m., Monday, October 28, 1935
Alameda Airport, Alameda, California

Betty Smyth had bad news. "He's gone to New York on business and won't be back for a week."

Nick felt defeated but decided he would still help Nieshe search through the mountain of maintenance records. He found Nieshe inside the hangar cafeteria. It had long since closed but the smell of fried chicken lingered in the air. Nieshe sat at one of the long tables surrounded by open boxes and piles of records.

He looked up as Nick entered. "Thanks for coming, Nick." He looked exhausted.

"Did you find anything?"

He shook his head. "No. I've gone through them twice. I searched all the Martin logs, then all the Sikorsky records. Colonel Young left word to allow free access to all records, but Agent Cook insisted on being present." Nieshe pointed to a dark corner.

Surprised Nick looked and saw Cook silently watching. "Well, maybe a fresh set of eyes will help." He sat down, rolled up his sleeves and picked up the closest pile.

Two hours later, Nick threw the last record down in disgust. "Nothing! Someone has covered his tracks very carefully."

Cook stood and walked over. "So? You done?"

Nieshe stood and stretched. "No, but there is nothing more we can do here. I didn't place the corks, Agent Cook. If you knew I did it, you'd have already arrested me."

"Give me a little more time, Nieshe, and I'll nail you."

"You are wasting your time, Agent Cook. However, that is your affair, not mine."

Nick was annoyed. They had searched through piles of dusty records for nothing. "Mr. Nieshe, I've got to get home. I have midterms tomorrow, and I need to review."

"Of course, Nick. I have to drop off some things at the *Dojo*. Then I'll run you home."

It was too late for his workout with Roger, but he didn't mind. His shoulder was finally beginning to heal. The ride to the *Dojo* was short and uneventful, but that changed as they got closer. Nick noticed a flickering light in the sky before he noticed the acrid smell of a burning building.

"Oh, my God, Mr. Nieshe! You don't think it's on your block, do you?"

Nick's worst fears were confirmed as they turned the corner. Three fire trucks, a chief's car, and many firemen blocked the street in front of the *Dojo*. The firemen were valiantly trying to douse the roaring flames but without much success. The flames shot out of the roof and climbed hundreds of feet into the evening sky. The building housing the *Dojo* was a total loss.

Nieshe slammed on the brakes and jumped out of the car. He ran to the opposite side of the street where his students had gathered. Nick leapt out and followed him. He saw Nieshe say something to Nancy then cross the street to speak with the Fire Chief. Something loud exploded and a fireball arched into the sky. Burning debris fell across the street but luckily it missed the gathering crowd of on-lookers

Nick reached Nancy and noticed she was crying. "Is everyone okay?" The heat was intense and hurt his exposed face, even from this distance. Steam rose as the firemen sprayed the flames. It added a sooty taste to air he breathed.

"Yes, but I'm so afraid."

Nick touched her arm. "Are you hurt, Nancy? Was anybody hurt?"

She answered as if from a great distance. "No, I don't think so, but Roger left."

"Left? Where'd he go?"

"He said he knew who did it and he was going for retribution."

"What do you mean? Is this arson?"

"The Fire Chief seemed to think so. He asked if anybody held a grudge."

A bad feeling descended over Nick. *Roger would kill them!* "When did he leave?"

"He left about five minutes ago. He took my parents' car. Find him Nick! Find him before he does something dumb!"

"Where did he go?"

"He said something about Alameda Stadium."

Nick looked around for Mr. Nieshe. "Find your uncle and tell him that I borrowed his car. Is there someplace I can call you?"

She pointed to a Japanese Grocery store behind her. "Call Mr. Sanyo's store." She gave him the number. "Can you remember that?"

"Yes, I think so." He ran back to the car and looked inside the window. *Yes, the keys are there!* He slid behind the wheel, started the engine, and depressed the clutch. He dropped it into first gear, popped the clutch, and sped away into the dark night.

Chapter Eight: A Friend in Need

7:45 p.m., Monday, October 28, 1935
Alameda High School, Alameda, California

Nick slowly drove through the stadium parking lot. At first, it seemed deserted, and then he noticed car lights leave from the far end. It didn't look like the Tanaka car but it looked familiar. As he sped closer, he realized that it had been Bennett's car. At least he didn't see any of the other football players.

Nick found Roger's car parked at the end of the stadium, tucked behind the end of the building. The engine was running and the driver's door was open. Nick turned off the engine, shut the door, and looked around. The weight room lights were on and the door ajar.

The stadium was a huge affair. Recently built by the Works Progress Administration, it was grand as only a federal government building could be. The slanted stadium seats formed the roofs of two large concrete buildings. They housed equipment rooms, team locker rooms, the coaches' offices, and the weight room. Nick was familiar with the weight room from a sophomore class and the swim team workouts.

Nick cautiously walked to the opening and peeked inside. *Whew! And I thought the Dojo smelled bad!* It reeked of old sweat and dirty cloths. However, the smell of disinfectant was noticeably absent. *How on earth could the players stand it?* Ruefully, he wondered if that was what made football players so angry all the time.

The weight room consisted of three separate areas. The first was vandalized. Benches stood upended and dumbbells lay among the shards of smashed mirrors. He stopped and listened but heard nothing. Slowly he advanced into the second room. It, too, was ransacked and then he thought he heard a moan.

"Roger? Are you there?"

Nothing.

Nick moved toward the third room. A single light bulb cast eerie shadows as it swung back and forth from the ruined ceiling mount. He heard the faint moan again. It seemed to come from outside, beyond the door to the stadium.

"Roger! Come on, Nancy's worried. Answer me!"

"Ohhh…"

Nick stepped through the door and stood in the small circle of light the open door provided. Beyond the circle, the stadium lay in darkness. He cocked his head to listen to another moan, this time much closer. His eyes quickly adjusted and he saw a crumbled figure lying face down on the grass about 30 yards onto the field. He ran over and knelt. It was Roger.

"Roger, are you okay? What happened?"

No answer.

Nick felt Roger's neck, located the carotid artery and located a strong heartbeat. *Good!* Roger's breathing seemed okay so Nick gently felt around the skull. His fingers touched something wet and sticky. He smelled them. The scent was strong, coppery, and familiar - blood!

Trying to recall what he had learned from the *North Haven's* surgeon, Nick gently felt around Roger's body. He found another laceration. He used his shirt as a compress, and applied direct pressure to the wound. The bleeding slowed dramatically. *At least it wasn't arterial bleeding or I'd need a tourniquet.* Then he continued to check for other injuries. Roger's right wrist was broken and Nick thought he might have a couple of busted ribs. Nick ran back inside, picked up the phone, called the police and asked for an ambulance.

*   *   *

8:22 p.m., Monday, October 28, 1935
Alameda Hospital, Alameda, California

Mr. Nieshe and Nancy arrived at the hospital by cab about twenty minutes after Nick.

Nancy ran up to Nick. "Where's Roger?" Her eyes were red and swollen.

"He's in surgery."

Nieshe asked, "What happened?"

"Someone whacked him over the head and knocked him out."

Nancy looked horrified. "You're covered in blood!"

Nick looked down at his ruined work shirt and pants. "It's Roger's. It was only a scalp wound. But it bled profusely."

Nancy collapsed into a chair. "Oh, my poor Roger!" Tears welled up her eyes again.

Nieshe spoke firmly but kindly. "Niece, control your emotions. They will not help Roger. I need you to be strong."

She dabbed her eyes with a handkerchief. "Yes, Uncle."

Nieshe turned to Nick. "Did the medics say anything about his condition?"

"Not much, but I've seen this type of injury before. Unless there's uncontrolled bleeding behind that hematoma, he's probably going to be fine."

Nancy blurted out, "Oh, no!"

"Nancy, he probably has a concussion, but hematoma is

just a medical term for a bruise." Nick paused. "How many times has Roger been bruised?"

"Lots of times."

"See, he's going to be fine. Lucky for him he took the hit on his head – it's his hardest part." Nick's poor attempt at levity fell flat.

The Operating Room doors opened and the surgeon walked out. He stopped in front of Nieshe. "You the boy's father?"

"No, I am the uncle. His parents are away on business."

Nancy rose out of her chair. "Doctor, how is my brother?"

"He's doing very well. However, he's going to have one heck of a headache."

Nick asked. "Doctor, any evidence of bone splinters under the hematoma?"

The surgeon turned and stared at Nick. "Are you a medical student?"

"No, but I worked for the surgeon on a ship last summer. We saw a lot of different injuries."

The surgeon lifted an eyebrow quizzically. "We've controlled the bleeding and the X-ray confirms that there are no bone splinters in his brain. Now, if you'll excuse me, I have other patients." He turned and briskly walked away.

Nieshe guided Nancy to a waiting room chair. Nick followed and sat facing them.

Nieshe looked over at him. "You might as well go home. I've put in a call to my sister's hotel. They should call the hospital soon and then return. It seems that I am again in your debt. You continue to come to the aid of my family."

"No way, Mr. Nieshe. You don't owe me anything. I do have a question though."

"What is it Nick?"

"Who could have done this to Roger?"

"Excellent question, my honored student."

Nick stood and so did Nancy. She threw her arms around him causing Nick's heart to leap and his blood to race.

She pushed herself back and looked into Nick's eyes. "Thank you for finding Roger." Then she lightly kissed him on the cheek and sat down again.

Nick gave the car keys to Nancy, said goodbye, and walked out the door. His mind kept drifting back to Nancy.

The dark streets helped to hide his rumpled and blood stained clothes during the long walk home. Try as he might, he couldn't get images of Nancy out of his mind. She was a very attractive girl, and he knew that she wasn't dating anyone. Roger was laid up…but what about Leilani? Deep in thought, he was surprised when he found himself at his front door. His parents were sitting in the front room when he walked in.

His mother looked up and a shocked look crossed her face. "Nick, what in the world?"

His parents stood up and rushed over. His dad asked, "Are you hurt, son?"

"No Dad, I'm fine just a little tired that's all."

His mother looked him up and down. "Come in the kitchen. I've left your supper out and you can tell us all about it."

Wearily, Nick followed his parents. "There was a fire at the *Dojo*, that's all. I helped some people until the ambulances got there." He looked down at his cloths. "Do you think the stains will come out?"

Nick's mother handed him a plate of food and studied his clothes. "I doubt it. Now, sit and eat. Then tell us all about it."

Nick complied and, as he ate, concocted a story that was close to the truth. If he left out the events at the stadium, the morning newspaper would confirm most of his story. His mother listened with a skeptical expression, but they seemed to accept Nick version. He felt terrible about omitting the key facts. But what could he do? If he told them everything, he wouldn't be able to train anymore. And he really was starting to like the training a great deal.

His father took a sip form his glass on water. "Nick, where will the students practice since the *Dojo* is damaged?"

Nick wiped his mouth with his napkin. "The Shinto Temple has offered up their basement until Mr. Nieshe can get another place."

His parents seemed satisfied. His mother stood and picked up Nick's plate. "There's a letter from Leilani on the mantle."

Nick's mind raced as he struggled to cage his raging thoughts. He tried to sort his conflicting emotions of elation and guilt. "Ah, thanks, Mom. I'm pretty tired and I've still got to study for a midterm tomorrow. If you'll excuse me, I need to get upstairs."

His mother nodded and he left. He grabbed the letter, and walked upstairs to his room. He closed the door and inhaled the sweat fragrance of Leilani's envelope. He tore it open.

Aloha, Nick!

I'm sorry it's been so long since I've written. I have been very busy with the Hula Dance Troop and school. I still have two midterms, but I felt I had to drop you a line.

I miss you, Nick! I've re-read your last letter so many times that the edges are frayed. Momma has threatened to take it away if she sees it one more time. I was so worried after the locker room fire. Thank goodness your injuries were minor. I hope you have since healed. The fight at the dance was awful and your punishment so unfair. I was tempted to write to Mr. Brown, but Daddy said it would only make matters worse. I still might.

So tell me about that girl you protected. Is Nancy prettier than I am? Does she dance as well as I do? How old is she? I'm dying to know all about her. Is there something you're not telling me, Nick? Remember, you promised, no more lies.

As I look out over the Pacific, I can see the Matson Liner coming into Honolulu Harbor. I must close this letter to make sure it's aboard before she departs for California tomorrow. I desperately hope that she carries a letter from you. I couldn't bear to wait another week.

Thinking of You Always,
Aloha, Leilani
P.S. Hanna writes to say hi and wonders if you have
heard from John Borger?

Oops! Nick had not written to her in a week. He sat down to compose a reply. Maybe she'd get it in a week – if he were lucky.

Chapter Nine: Seagulls, Rats and Bats

2:31 a.m., Tuesday, October 29, 1935
Alameda Hospital, Alameda, California

Roger Tanaka slowly opened his eyes. *Where am I?* He surveyed his surroundings illuminated only by faint light from the door. He was lying in a hospital bed in a darkened room.

"At last, you are awake."

A chill stabbed at Roger's heart. *It was him!* "Most Honored One, why are you here?"

Miyazaki, dressed in *ninja* black, was deep in the shadows near an open window. "I came to ensure they were taking proper care of you."

"Your words earlier this evening... I thought you were through with me."

"Like you, Roger, I was incensed not only with the actions of the football players, but of my prize student. I acted in anger and attacked you. Now I regret my deeds."

"No, it is I who regret my words and actions. I would have killed those who burned my uncle's *Dojo*. I am most humbly in your debt." Roger tried to rise up but his injuries restrained him.

"Easy, Master Tanaka. You will need weeks to heal. I did what was necessary but it was unfortunate. Had you harmed those football players, an investigation would have followed. That is attention we do not need."

Down the hall they heard voices and then footsteps headed in their direction. Roger cocked his head. "Commander, that sounds like my worthless parents. Perhaps you should depart."

The drapes moved gently in the open window, but Miyazaki had already gone.

* * *

8:30 a.m., Saturday, November 16, 1935
Pan American Hangars, Alameda, California

Nick waited with a group of mechanics and ground support crewmen under the *China Clipper's* wing. Colonel Young, Captain Ed Musick, and Captain R.O.D. Tilton were deep in conversation.

Finally, Young nodded. "Ed, you're the captain and it's your call. What's it going to be?"

Nick stood close to Musick and could see deep lines and dark shadows of fatigue around his eyes. Musick stared at the floor, deep in thought. Finally, Musick looked at Colonel Young. "I believe that we're ready."

The ground crew let out a deafening roar of approval. Colonel Young raised his hands. "Quiet, lads. We've all worked hard but none harder than the ground crew. Men, your efforts have made this a reality."

Someone in the crowd wisecracked. "Yeah, that's because we don't get no crew rest!"

Musick and Tilton laughed dutifully. They held up their hands and shook their heads as if to say, we don't make the rules. It was all in fun and Nick laughed along with the older men.

Colonel Young continued. "Tuesday, November 22, 1935. It's a date that will go down in the annals of history. The first scheduled air mail flight over the Pacific."

The men let out another wild cheer. What an accomplishment, thought Nick. Many had worked every waking hour poring over the Clipper to make sure she was ready. While they labored, the aircrews were far out over the Pacific. The long haul flights tested their navigation skills. Musick was a stickler for details and repetition was his mantra.

Young raised his voice. "We've still got lots to do, so let's get back to it."

Nieshe put a hand on Nick's shoulder. "Come on Nick."

Together they walked back to the hangar and stopped in front of a work stand. It supported a partially disassembled Pratt & Whitney radial engine. Pound for pound, it was the most powerful engine in the world and years ahead of all competition.

Nick picked up a monkey wrench and turned to Nieshe. "I don't get it. This engine has less than 100 hours on it. Tell me again, why we're doing a maintenance tear-down?"

Nieshe picked up a wrench. "It's the fuel starvation problem. Musick wants to make sure we've covered every possibility. An engine failure or, God forbid, two, would mean disaster."

Nick pondered a few moments. "Wait a minute... All those incidents stopped the day Roger wound up in the hospital. What a strange coincidence."

Nieshe did not meet Nick's eyes. "Yes, isn't it?"

Afraid he'd insulted Nieshe, he changed the subject. "I can't believe it's been three weeks since the *Dojo* burned. How's Roger doing?"

"He is recovering very nicely, thank you. I saw him last night and he's almost healed. He will be at the *Dojo* Monday waiting to resume your instruction."

"Great! The day of my green belt test! Have you noticed how much better I do when he's not around?"

"It has not escaped me. Roger will not sit on your green belt board." He looked at Nick. "He will go easier on you once you no longer wear a white belt."

"No offense, Mr. Nieshe, but I doubt it."

"None taken."

Nick persisted. "I'm doing so well without him. Why does he have to be my instructor again?"

"Your instruction in our ancient martial art is only one part. Roger must also learn from you, Nick."

"Oh, like not to hate round eyes?"

Nieshe chuckled, and then tried to look stern. "I have told you that is not a polite term for members of the white race."

Nick grinned. "I figure I'm a round eye so I can use it."

Nieshe thought for a moment. "Yes, I suppose that is correct. However, I would not use it on other round eyes." He smiled ruefully and they both laughed.

* * *

7:00 p.m., Monday, November 21, 1935
Pan American Hangar, Alameda Airfield, Alameda, California

Nick wiped his hands on a rag, attempting to remove the accumulated grease, oil, and dirt. "That should do it, Mr. Nieshe. She's as snug as a bug in a rug." He admired the newly mounted engine.

"Indeed it is, Nick. We can quit at a decent hour tonight."

"Good. I've got homework and I'm sore."

"Your performance was good, Nick. You honored your instructors when you earned your green belt."

They paused before descending the ladder and looked across the bay. The lights of San Francisco twinkled in the distance. The new moon spun a river of silver across the dark water. As he watched, Nick noticed something cross the reflected moonlight. "Did you see that, Mr. Nieshe?"

"Yes, it was probably a boat."

"Without running lights? Good way to get run over by a ferry boat."

Nieshe raised his finger to his lips and whispered, "Shush!"

They listened in the early evening quiet. Nick heard the faint throb of a small boat engine coming closer. "Sounds like a fishing boat."

Nieshe looked out at the bay. "No one has fished this side of the bay in years." Then he shrugged. "Come on, let us replace our tools and then I will give you a ride home."

They climbed down from the scaffold, put their tools away, and then washed up in the locker room. They changed out of their overalls and walked out towards Nieshe's truck. It was parked beside the launching ramp. The ramp was close to the line of old destroyers the navy had sunk a few years earlier to form a breakwater.

Nick looked out over the half submerged shapes. "Funny, isn't it?"

Nieshe fished in his pocket for the keys. "What?"

"The Navy sinking all those perfectly good war ships."

Nieshe nodded. "They make an excellent breakwater for the Alameda Seaplane Harbor."

"No, that's not what I mean. Now the Navy needs more ships to counter the Germans and Japanese. Only there's no money on account of the Depression. Yet, only a couple of years ago the United States was scrapping ships left and right."

Nieshe looked at Nick for a long time before answering. "Nick, you never cease to surprise me. Do you know about the 1928 Naval Treaty?"

"Yes, I pay attention in history class."

"Ah, just so. I remember it well." Nieshe sighed. "Everybody was sick of war. England, France and the US, flush with victory in the Great War, forced the losers to reduce their naval fleets. Then the three powers decided they no longer needed a large expensive Navy. And so the democracies of the world voluntarily disarmed."

"But that was so stupid! Look where we are now."

"Many things look stupid in retrospect, Nick."

"It's ironic." Nick paused and pointed. "What's that?"

Nieshe looked. A large shadow was lying on the bay side of the breakwater. "It is that fishing boat. But why is it there?"

"Maybe they're in trouble! Come on, let's go have a look." Nick ran to the transom of the first dilapidated warship and clambered aboard.

Nieshe followed. "Wait, Nick! It is too dangerous!"

But Nick was already racing toward the next ship. Nieshe climbed up over the transom and followed. He caught up with Nick at the bow. They stood in the faint shadow of the forecastle. Two ships further out, the fishing boat was illuminated in the weak moonlight.

Nick squinted. "I think I see movement on the breakwater and on the fishing boat."

Nieshe looked but shook his head. "My eyes and ears are too old. What can you hear?"

"They're moving something heavy from the boat to the breakwater."

Nieshe's interest was obviously piqued. "Let's get a closer look."

They crossed over to the next ship and continued forward. This ship was smaller and its deck was awash with cold bay water. They had to climb up ladders to reach the upper deck and stay dry. When they rounded the ship's bridge, an explosion of squawking seagulls erupted from the foredeck. Nick jumped back in fright and slipped on the copious amounts of bird droppings. He landed with a wallop that reverberated like a steel drum.

"Shush!" Nieshe admonished. But it was too late. A voice boomed out from the fishing boat now only fifty feet away. "Who is dare? Vhat do you vant?"

Nick got to his feet as Nieshe called. "Ahoy, there! It's Pan American. Do you need any assistance?"

They heard something heavy slam onto the metal deck of the ship ahead. Then men rushed around and voices spoke in an un-recognizable foreign language. The first voice spoke again. "No, thank you. A little engine trouble - dat's all. We have fixed it."

Then they heard an engine roar to life. Nick dimly saw movement and the boat made a hasty escape into the darkness of the bay and off towards San Francisco.

"Funny," said Nick as he tried to brush the bird poop off his pants. "They're still not running any navigation lights."

Nick moved forward carefully as not to slip on the bird droppings again. "Come on, Mr. Nieshe. Let's see what they were doing."

This hulk was the largest so far. Its main deck was several feet above the water and the superstructure was huge. They searched in the moonlight as best they could but found nothing. They checked below decks only to find their way blocked. Most of the hatches were welded shut. Others led down but soon terminated in cold bay water. Everywhere rats scurried out of their path.

At the bottom of one blocked stair case, Nick saw a dark opening suggesting a doorway. "Let's check out that compartment." He walked in and quickly beat a hasty retreat. Hundreds of bats followed. The disturbed bat colony streamed past him and out an open porthole.

Nieshe had had enough. "Nick, we're unlikely to find anything. Let's return to the base and report this incident."

Nick, who had gotten quite a start from the madly flapping bats, was ready to call it quits. "Okay, I guess you're right. Besides we need flashlights to do a proper search."

Chapter Ten: Nancy's Question

7:45 p.m., Monday, November 21, 1935
Pan American Administration Building,
Alameda Airfield, Alameda, California

They entered the darkened building. Nick looked around. "Did everybody already leave?"

Nieshe pointed to a light escaping from Colonel Young's secretary's office. "I do not think so."

They moved down the hall and entered Colonel Young's office suite. Young's office door was ajar. The heard two men talking - Colonel Young and a voice Nick did not recognize. Nick burst into Young's office with Nieshe in tow. To his great surprise, he saw that Colonel Young was speaking with Juan Trippe, the President of Pan American Airways."

Without hesitation Nick blurted, "Colonel Young, there's something strange going on out on the breakwater!"

Young seemed startled by Nick's sudden appearance but quickly regained his composure. "Where?... What did you say, Nick?"

Mr. Nieshe stepped from behind Nick's towering frame.

"Forgive the uninvited intrusion, Colonel Young, but we wanted to advise you immediately."

Young looked at Nick in horror. "What is that white stuff all over you?"

Nick looked down. "Bird poop."

Young shook his head. "Sit down and tell me what happened."

They moved toward the couch.

Young held up his hand. "Not you, Nick." He pointed to a wooden chair. "Bird poop stains."

Nieshe and Nick relayed their encounter with the errant fishing boat and the crew's strange behavior. After they finished, Young looked thoughtful, then turned to Trippe. "Mr. Trippe, as you have no doubt ascertained, this is Yoshiro Nieshe, our top mechanic." He gestured to Nick. "And this is Nick Grant, our infamous underage roustabout and mechanic trainee."

Trippe was dressed in a rumpled three-piece suit. His Mackintosh and Fedora lay across the back of a chair. At 35 years old, Trippe was an imposing figure, trim and athletic, with only the hint of a middle-aged paunch.

Trippe stared at them for a few seconds. He moved over to Nieshe, hand extended. "Mr. Nieshe, Colonel Young speaks highly of you. Frankly, I doubt the *China Clipper* would be ready to fly tomorrow without your efforts."

Nieshe stood and bowed. "You are most kind.

Trippe turned to Nick. "So, you're Nick Grant." He extended his hand.

"Yes, sir." Nick stood and took it and felt a firm shake in return.

Trippe cocked an eyebrow. "Have you been swimming with the sharks lately?"

"N-n-no sir!" He wasn't sure if Trippe was ribbing him. "But other things have been happening around here."

"So I've heard." He glanced over at Nieshe. "You two did some very nice work repairing that fuel line in-flight. Most impressive." He glanced back to Nick. "Seems you are making a habit of saving my Clippers, Mr. Grant. How is that?"

"I don't know, sir. I just seem to be in the wrong place at the right time, I guess. Something strange happened on the breakwater tonight. That's why we're here."

Trippe cocked an eyebrow. "Indeed."

Nick explained about the fishing boat and his suspicion that something was not right.

Trippe turned to Young. "Clarence, I don't like the sound of this one bit. The State Department warned me that the Japanese government might be up to something and I tend to agree. We've had many instances of unexplained accidents that could be sabotage. We can't ignore this. What do you propose, Clarence?"

Young took a drag from his cigarette and slowly exhaled. "We call the FBI. Have them coordinate security until the Clipper is safely away tomorrow."

Trippe brooded. Nick wondered what was so tough about this decision. It was a no brainer. *What was he waiting for?*

A minute later Trippe pointed at Colonel Young. "Clarence, call the FBI, but for God's sake tell them to keep it quiet. Not a word of this must reach the press!"

Young reached for his phone. "Yes, Mr. Trippe."

* * *

9:56 a.m., Tuesday, November 22, 1935
Alameda High School, Alameda, California

Nancy Tanaka called, "Nick! Wait up."

Nick continued walking as fast as he could. The school was huge and he had to make it to the other side in less than four minutes. "I can't. If I'm late again to drafting, I'll get detention!"

A burst of energy brought Nancy alongside. "Nick, I have to ask you something."

Nick continued to pound the hallway. "Ask." He dodged

left around two slow-moving girls. Nancy dodged right and managed to keep up.

"You did well on your green belt test. Only Roger did it in less time."

"Can't this wait until we're at the *Dojo*? This is not the time!" Nick glanced at his watch.

"No, this is important!" She reached out grabbed Nick's arm and swung him around with surprising force. They came to an abrupt halt as other students streamed around them like river water around a boulder.

"Ouch!" Nick winced at her touch and tugged his arm away, annoyed. He was going to be late. "What is it?"

"I'm worried about Roger." She held his stare.

He showed the underside of his arms to Nancy. They were black and blue and covered with small abrasions. "And I'm tired of all the cuts and bruises he seems to enjoy inflicting on me."

Her dark eyes stared up at him and her beauty struck him once again. Nick sighed. He couldn't stay angry at her ... even if he was late to class. Resigned, he began walking again, but slower, and motioned Nancy along. "Oh for Pete's sake! Your uncle said that Roger was healing well."

She reached out and placed her hand on his arm, but much more gently. "It's not that. He's so edgy that anything sets off his temper. He's also become very morose."

"I'd welcome the change from sadistic."

"Not to you. I mean to Mom and Dad, to me and even Uncle Yoshe." She bit her bottom lip.

Nick slogged on. "Nancy, I'm confused. I'm not sure what you think I can do." He looked at his watch again. *It's going to be close!*

"If you thought Roger was involved in something illegal, what would you do?"

"Nancy, that's absurd. Some football players got the best of him and got away with it. His big fat ego can't take it. He should just get over it."

"Nick, I need to know what you'd do."

"Why, Nancy? I don't see what this has to do with me."

"What if he was plotting to do something, say against the Clipper?"

"The Clipper? Nancy, why would you think that? He's never been near the airfield. At least not to my knowledge. Is there something that you want to tell me?"

They turned the last corner. Mr. Carol was standing in the classroom door glaring at Nick.

Nancy stopped. "No. It's just a feeling, really."

"Then I think that I'd have to turn him in."

Nancy looked squarely at him. "Promise me you'll speak to me first."

"Look, Nancy. Can't this wait? Let's talk about it after school. Say at practice?" The bell rang and Nick shot past Mr. Carol just as he closed the door. Nick looked back and saw Nancy staring through the glass pane of the door. He wasn't sure, but he thought he saw a tear on her cheek. Then he turned away and moved towards his drafting table.

Chapter Eleven: Manila Calling!

12:10 p.m., Tuesday, November 22, 1935
Alameda High School Auditorium, Alameda, California

Nick walked into the noisy auditorium searching for a familiar face. He noticed Nancy, but luckily she was talking to the girl next to her. He beat a hasty retreat. He walked down the left aisle of the packed hall. Few seats remained open.

Tommy waved. "Over here, Nick. I saved a seat."

"Wow, what a turn-out."

"What did you expect? It's mandatory. You working this afternoon?"

"Yeah, I'll be there. What about you?"

"You bet! I wouldn't miss it for the world! Shush, Mr. Brown's walking out on the stage." Tommy turned his attention to the podium.

Assistant Principal Brown raised his hands for quiet and gradually the packed auditorium quieted. "Students, as you know our Principal, Dr. Rogers, has been ill of late. He's asked me to extend a special welcome to a true captain of industry, the President of Pan American Airways who has a very exciting announcement to make. Please join me in extending a warm Alameda High welcome to Mr. Juan Trippe!" Brown stepped back from the podium and began to clap. Teachers on the stage and the students gave Mr. Trippe a standing ovation.

Trippe walked out on the stage to the applause. Tommy stood, clapping madly and hollering at the top of his lungs. Embarrassed, Nick grabbed Tommy and yanked him down. But it was too late. All around him the students stared at them both. Some faces showed interest; some showed amusement; but others showed disdain.

Nick sank back into his seat. A boy seated behind him leaned forward and poked Nick. "Nice going, Clipper boy! Like I really want to sit here and listen to this stuffed shirt. Boring! Did you set this up?"

Nick rubbed his shoulder as he turned to face his antagonist. "No, I had nothing to do with it." Then he turned back to the stage.

The boy shoved Nick forward in his chair. "Ya? Well I don't believe you."

Nick seethed and swung around. "You calling me a liar?"

"Want to do something about it?"

Tommy put a hand on Nick's shoulder and yanked him back. "Will you be quiet? Mr. Carol is the aisle monitor and he is headed this way. You want detention or another suspension, Nick?"

Nick wavered. "No... but..."

Tommy pulled harder. "No buts! Turn around and be quiet. Trippe's about to begin."

Trippe raised his hands. "Thanks! Thanks, awfully! Mr. Brown, faculty members, and students, I have come here today to invite you to a historic event...the launch of the first scheduled Trans-Pacific airmail flight. Today at 3:00 pm, the mightiest airliner that the world has ever known will lift off from San Francisco Bay. The maiden voyage will fly to Manila with stops at Honolulu, Midway, Wake, and Guam. But best of all, she will depart from your very own Alameda Airport, at the seaplane harbor.

"The network radio stations will broadcast the event live. National magazines like *Time, Newsweek, Life, Saturday Evening Post*, and *Look* are there now. Newspapers and movie newsreel reporters will also cover the event. We expect a number of Hollywood celebrities to respond to the 'Manila Calling' radio link from across the Pacific. Pan American will provide refreshments, so do come out and help America celebrate this fantastic achievement."

Trippe nodded to Mr. Brown who stood up and moved next to Trippe. Brown began, "Due to the historic nature of this event, school will end today at 12:30."

The students let out a cheer and Brown looked annoyed. "Settle down, settle down."

The students brimmed with surprise and excitement, and their chatter slowly subsided.

Brown finally continued. "Go to your classes. When you hear the next bell, then school is dismissed. I expect you all to attend the inaugural lift off of the *China Clipper*. Aisle monitors take charge and see to getting the students out in an orderly fashion. Dismissed."

Pandemonium erupted as all the students got to their feet in unison and charged for the doors. The aisle monitors didn't stand a chance and were swept along with the rising student tide. Brown rushed down from the stage to try and regain order. Nick watched gleefully as a wave of students plastered Brown against the wall. Nick smiled. It was gratifying to see the man who had unjustly suspended him pushed aside like sea foam in the path of a flying boat.

Tommy struggled to maintain his feet as the student mass carried him along towards the door. Nick was being tugged in another direction

Tommy yelled, "Nick, where should we meet?"

Nick yelled his answer. "At the hangar. Tell the cop at the door to come get me." Carried along by an irresistible force of high school students released early, they exited through separate doors.

* * *

1:10 p,m., Tuesday, November 22, 1935
Alameda Airport, Alameda, California

Nick threaded his way through the crowds towards the Pan American Hangar. The crowd noise was deafening. *God! There must be thousands of people here.* As he walked on, he heard the call of the hawkers. No matter what the event, they always seemed to show up with something to sell to the masses. Today it was American flags and Pan Am pendants. His stomach rumbled as the enticing smell of hot dogs and cotton candy wafted under his nose. He looked around and saw the newsreel cameras and the press photographers, but couldn't see Tommy. Disappointed, he continued towards the hangar.

Two uniformed policemen blocked the way at the open door. Dressed in brown knee-high boots and matching Sam Brown belts, Nick recognized them as California State Motorcycle Police.

The one with corporal chevrons on his sleeve stopped Nick. "What do you want, kid?"

Nick was unaccustomed to being challenged. "I want to go to work." Anticipating the cop's next question, he dug into his wallet, pulled out his Pan Am ID card, and handed it over.

The corporal looked at the card. "You got any other ID… Grant?"

Agent Cook walked out of the hangar. "It's okay, Corporal. He works here."

The corporal handed Nick's ID back and stood aside. Nick hurried by, but Agent Cook grabbed Nick's arm. "We need to talk about last night."

Nick blew out an exasperated breath. "Let me guess. You think I made up the whole thing."

Cook scowled. "Nieshe's already provided his sworn statement and I need yours. You got a problem with that?"

Nick glared at him but didn't answer.

Cook shrugged. "We've also got to clarify a few things."

"Yeah? What things?"

"You'll see." Cook led Nick to a vacant engineering office. He pointed to a drafting table. "Sit there."

Nick spent the next forty minutes writing a detailed account of the previous night's events. He checked it once, then handed it to Cook, who immediately sat and started reading. Nick got to his feet and started for the door.

Cook didn't look up. "Sit down."

Nick returned to the table and wondered if he'd ever get to work.

A few minutes later, Cook finished reading. "Stand over here and raise your right hand."

Nick stood in front of the now standing agent, who had raised his right hand. "Nick Grant, do you swear that the statement provided is true to the best of your knowledge?"

"I do."

"Sign here." Cook handed Nick the pen. "You're free to go."

Relieved, Nick hurried to the locker room, donned his PAA coveralls, and raced outside to join in the festivities. Everyone was down at the launching ramp where Pan Am had erected a pavilion. The national flags of the United States, the Philippines, and China, along with the California state flag and the Hawaiian Territorial flag flapped in the stiff bay breeze. Nick recognized the Governor, a senator, a couple of congressmen, and the mayor standing to the left of Juan Trippe. Naval admirals and Army generals stood to Trippe's right. Their medals glinted when the sun poked out from behind the scattered clouds. The *China Clipper* was on her beaching cradle at the top of the launching ramp.

Trippe's voice boomed in the public address system. "Ladies and Gentlemen! Pan American Airways welcomes you to the inaugural flight of the world's first scheduled trans-Pacific airmail flight!"

The crowd of more than thirty thousand people roared their approval.

Trippe continued. "My fellow Americans, this achievement is surely a turning point in the economic downturn that some now call the Great Depression. It shows what America is capable of when we all work together as a team."

Nick was only half listening as Trippe went on and on. *God! That man had the gift of gab!* The crowd provided polite applause at the appropriate pauses as Trippe introduced his distinguished guests. "And now ladies and gentlemen, I give you the man who made this possible, Postmaster Farley!"

Farley waved to the cheering crowd and held a leather saddlebag marked US MAIL over the side of the pavilion. Nick heard the clatter of horses' hooves and turned to see a Pony Express rider gallop towards the stand. Without stopping, the rider grabbed the mail pouch and continued around the pavilion at a gallop. He rounded the other side and drew up alongside a Wells Fargo stagecoach pulled by a team of trotting white horses. The express rider tossed the pouch to a man riding shotgun. Whooping and hollering, the stage driver drove the stage only to stop alongside the Clipper's sea wing.

Postmaster Farley had moved from the pavilion and now stood on the sea wing. The man riding shotgun stood on the stage roof and handed the pouch to Farley. Trippe had narrated the action over the PA for those unable to see.

Farley handed the pouch to Captain Ed Musick, also standing in the sea wing. They posed for the press, each holding a side of the pouch. Then Musick handed the pouch to Captain R.O.D. Sullivan who stood in the open Clipper hatch. Tilton held the pouch up and presented it to the crowd. Then he handed it to Flight Engineer Vic Wright, who took it inside and closed the hatch.

Farley, Musick and Sullivan descended from the Clipper. Farley returned to the pavilion, Sullivan stood at the front of the assembled flight crew, while Musick took up a position at a microphone in front of the pavilion.

Trippe looked down at Musick. "Captain Musick, is all in readiness?"

Musick, Nick knew, hated Trippe's insistence on pomp and ceremony. But he played his part and stepped up to the microphone. "This is Alameda calling. Are all stations ready to receive the *China Clipper*?" The hiss of static rose in the PA system. Then, through the long distance phone lines, Nick heard the first station report. "Alameda, this is Hawaii. All ready!"

Musick waited as Midway and Wake Island bases reported ready. In the background, Nick saw the tractor launching the big airliner and ground crewmen securing her to the wharf. As soon as Guam reported ready, Musick stepped back to the microphone. "This is Alameda calling. Are the Philippines prepared to receive the *China Clipper*?"

"This is Manila calling. We are ready to receive the *China Clipper*! Standby...more to follow." There was a slight pause. "Please be advised that the President of the Republic of the Philippines has decreed a national holiday to mark the arrival of the first trans-Pacific airmail. Expect a crowd of half a million people to greet the Clipper!"

The California crowd roared its approval and now Trippe took over. "This is Alameda calling. Captain Musick, go forth and execute your orders forthwith."

Musick tossed a casual salute in Trippe's general direction and moved to the front of his crew. The twelve men marched in single file out on the wharf as wild applause and cheers rose from the crowd. Nick remembered proudly marching in that line in August after the *Pan American Clipper* had returned from her Wake Island survey flight. Silently, he renewed his vow to march with a Pan Am crew once again.

Chapter Twelve: The Trap

3:21 p.m., Tuesday, November 22, 1935
Seaplane Harbor, Alameda Airport, Alameda, California

Someone clapped Nick on the shoulder, startling him. He spun arpund and saw Nancy. "Nick, where you been? I've been looking for you everywhere!" she asked.

"The FBI held me up again. I swear those guys think I'm the one trying to sabotage the Clipper."

Nancy looked stunned. "Sabotage the Clipper? What are you talking about?"

Nick realized his mistake. "Look, Nancy, you've got to promise me you won't say anything about this. I'm in enough trouble already and I'm not supposed to discuss it."

Nancy's surprised expression changed to one of concern. "I was going to ask you if you've seen Roger, but now —"

What about Roger? Did he come with you?"

"Yes, I rode with him. But when I asked him for a ride, he seemed annoyed and tried to talk me out of coming."

"Maybe he thought you'd be bored."

"No, he said I might get hurt. And you just said something

about sabotage. I'm worried."

"Where is he now?" Nick wondered aloud.

She folded her arms across her chest. "I don't know. When we arrived, he ditched me."

Nick rubbed his chin. "That is strange. Which way was he headed?"

She pointed. "Toward the breakwater. What's going on?"

A sinking feeling filled him with dread. *Is Roger involved?* Feeling guilty about breaking his word, Nick gazed across the small harbor. "Someone is trying to sabotage the *China Clipper*."

"Who? When?"

HE looked into her face and wondered. *Can I trust her?* However, he needed Nancy's help and he'd have to take the chance. "It started last month when a mysterious hangar fire and they tried to frame me. Later, somebody stole aboard the Clipper and blocked fuel lines before we took off. Whoever it was, they knew what they were doing. We started to spiral into the ocean as one engine after another quit.

Nancy injected, "But the Clipper made it back."

"Your uncle and I were able to make a quick repair before we had to ditch in the ocean. We were 200 miles out to sea and lucky."

"Oh, my God! Uncle Yoshie never told me."

Nick nodded. "He couldn't. The FBI swore us to secrecy."

She looked suspicious. "But now you're telling me. Why? Do you suspect Roger?"

Nick said nothing but looked over her shoulder at the huge crowds of people that ringed the lagoon eager to witness history unfolding. *What is it? What is the enemy planning?*

Nancy continued. "It's not Roger! Maybe he's trying to stop the next attempt. Maybe Roger thinks if he saves the Clipper, he'll be a hero. He's had so many disappointments lately because we're Japanese."

How could Roger suspect something? And why didn't I tell the authorities about my suspicions?

Feeling guilty about breaking his word, Nick gazed across the small harbor. Huge crowds of people ringed the small body of water, eager to witness history unfold. He turned his attention to the row of sunken ships that formed the breakwater and wondered again about the strange events the previous evening.

"So...what are thinking about?" Nancy stared at Nick.

"I don't have time to explain it to you. I'm not sure but I think it's something to do with the breakwater."

Nancy followed Nick's gaze. "Why the breakwater?"

"If something does happen, it won't be blatant. It will look like an accident. Something that makes Pan American look incompetent or worse, negligent." A wave of fatigue swept over Nick. *God, I'm tired.* He just wanted the Clipper to get off safely so he could go home and flop into his bed. Nick hurriedly chased the thought away. He had a big chemistry exam at the end of the week, and he hadn't studied enough. In fact, he hadn't studied at all.

Nick pointed toward the end of the line half-submerged ships that formed the breakwater. "Nancy, look at the narrow gap between the half-submerged ships. The Clipper captains have a tough time getting through the gap. If they scrape the fragile wing, they must return to base for repair. They won't meet their schedule and they could lose FAM14."

Nancy looked back at Nick. "FAM14?"

"Foreign Air Mail Contact fourteen. It's how Pan Am gets paid to operate Clippers. The government is most unforgiving about disruptions in the mail service. No contract – no clipper service.

Nancy nodded. "So captains hug the shore line on the other side of the harbor?"

"Exactly, even though the water's much shallower over there, it's deep enough for Clippers."

"I'll say it's shallow. Look, you can see the water breaking on the shoals."

Nick's head jerked up. "What shoals?" Nick looked to

where Nancy pointed. "O, my God! That's it! That's what they were doing last night. Why didn't I think of it before?"

Nancy looked befuddled. "You mean there aren't any shoals?"

"No. I think someone added a few last night. Look, I've got to get out there and take a closer look." He dug into his pocket and fished out a small notebook and pencil. Hurriedly he scribbled a note, tore off the piece of paper, and handed it to Nancy. "I need you to find you uncle." Ask him to give this note to Juan Trippe."

She looked at the sea of people and shook her head. "I'll never be able to find him in this crowd."

Nick grabbed Nancy's shoulders. "I don't know how, but you've got to try. The Clipper's in danger! You've got to give them a warning!"

Nancy looked shocked. "Why don't you. You run faster than me, anyway."

"Can't. I've got to get out there in case you can't get the note to Trippe in time."

"To do what?"

Nick released Nancy and started running for the breakwater. He called out over his shoulder, "I don't know yet!" As he ran, he heard the unmistakable sound of the Clipper's engine come to life. *That's one – three more to go. I hope Nancy and Mr. Nieshe can warn the Clipper in time!*

* * *

3:51 p.m., Tuesday, November 22, 1935
Seaplane Harbor, Alameda Airport, Alameda, California

By the time Nick reached the breakwater, he heard the second engine catch. A uniformed policeman stood at the end of the breakwater. He scowled. "What do you want, kid?"

"Officer, how long you been here?"

"Since daybreak. Now, you going to tell me what you're doing here?"

This guy would probably laugh in my face if I told him that I thought the waterway was sabotaged. "I'm with Pan Am's ground crew and need to go out on the breakwater in case the Clipper gets into trouble."

The cop crossed his huge arms. "My orders are clear. Nobody goes out there. Beat it."

Nick looked back at the Clipper as ground crewman started untying mooring lines. Nick shook his head. He moved to go around the policeman.

The cop barred Nick's path. "Nope. Nobody goes out there without permission."

"It's a change in plans." Nick dug out his Pan Am ID and showed it to the cop. As the cop reached out, Nick dropped it. Instinctively, the cop bent down for the ID. Nick saw his chance. He bolted to the breakwater. He clambered over the first ship's transom, and he yelled, "Keep the ID until I return."

The cop straightened up. "Hey, you! Get back down here, pronto!"

"Sorry, officer, I don't have time to argue." He trotted along the slippery deck just as the third engine came to life. *Come on Mr. Nieshe. Get the lead out!*

As Nick made his way along the breakwater, the final engine fired up. The Clipper would be moving out towards the harbor mouth at any moment. He stopped and looked back towards the grandstand.

No sign of Nancy, Mr. Nieshe, or Trippe. It looked like it was up to him, but what could he do?

As he made his way along the rusty hulks, he thought about the latest attempted sabotage. An obstruction below the surface was clever. The clipper would rip her hull open and sink before reaching the shore. Sabotage would be hard to prove. It would take months to repair or get a replacement. The next Martin airliners wouldn't be ready for months. That would be catastrophic to American prestige but there was a more sinister reason.

Last August, when Nick returned to Hawaii from Wake,

CHINA CLIPPER

Commander Boltz had summoned Nick to the *USS Arizona*. She was moored at the Pearl Harbor Naval Base. Deep in the bowels of the mighty battleship, Boltz swore Nick to secrecy and he told an amazing story. The Clippers were part of a clandestine U.S. operation. America was supporting the Chinese National Government against Japanese invaders.

The Clippers took three weeks off the usual time of the fastest ship. With the Japanese Navy blockading China's sea ports, the Clippers were the last lifeline. Combined with the Chinese National Airline Corporation, or CNAC, the Clippers would help the Chinese resistance immensely. Without Pan Am, and its subsidiary CNAC, China would be cut off from critical US money and supplies.

Most Americans supported helping China, but few people knew the real motivation. War loomed between the US and Japan and the Clippers would be vital to survival.

Chapter Thirteen: Traitor's Gate

4:06 p.m., Tuesday, November 22, 1935
Seaplane Harbor, Alameda Airport, Alameda, California

At last Nick reached the ship he and Nieshe had searched that night before. From the rail, he took a closer look at the shallows. The water was a murky brown, but he could see something below the waves. He wondered if Captains Musick and Tilton would be able to see it, too. Nick heard the deep rumble of a diesel engine at the harbor mouth. Then the small launch, *Pan Air*, came through the gap and moved slowly down the breakwater. Nick recognized the coxswain. It was Gunter Haas. Nick started waving and shouting, "Over here. I'm over here!"

The launch stopped below Nick. Haas cupped his hands and yelled. ""What are you doing up there? That's off limits!"

Nick yelled back. "Mr. Haas, I think there's something under the water on the shallow side." He pointed. "Do you see it?"

Haas didn't bother to look. "We've already checked. It's clear. Now get off the breakwater!"

One of the other crewmen was looking where Nick pointed. "Mr. Haas, I see something, too."

Haas spun around and pointed a finger at the man's chest. "And I said we checked it and it's clear."

"But we didn't check that area. How can you be sure?"

Haas was turning red. Nick saw him stab his meaty finger into the man's chest. "I said we checked. I'm in charge here! You got a problem with that?"

Clearly shaken the man shrank back. Haas turned back to Nick and yelled up to the deck some twelve feet up the corroded hull. "Grant, get your butt back on shore and wait in my office. I want a word with you."

Nick didn't answer. Haas's behavior was strange to say the least. He turned away with the clear understanding that they weren't going to help. He heard the flying boat engines accelerate and turned to see the Clipper shove off and move towards the harbor mouth. Resigned, he sat down and leaned back against the railing, pondering his options.

I guess it's up to me.

* * *

4:06 p.m., Tuesday, November 22, 1935
Seaplane Harbor Breakwater, Alameda Airport,
Alameda, California

Commander Miyazaki had watched Nick climb out over the ships and steadily move towards his position. Roger Tanaka had also seen Nick approach. "Master, do you think that Grant suspects the trap?"

Miyazaki responded in his native tongue at a whisper. "Fool! Keep your voice down. Of course he does."

He whispered into Roger's ear. "He would be dead now, had your meddlesome uncle not been along."

They were hiding in an old gun turret. It was out of sight but offered a clear view of the breakwater's approaches and the harbor. He had chosen the position last night while the fishing boat crew had unloaded and hidden the maulers.

"Why didn't you subdue my uncle while I took care of Grant?"

"Will you never learn to think strategically? Too risky. Had we taken them, they would have been missed. The resulting search may have found our little welcoming gift."

Roger bowed his head. "Of course, Master, but I welcomed the chance to dispatch Grant."

Miyazaki thought about the maulers. They were elegant and yet simple devices fashioned after ancient Japanese river obstacles. However, these were much improved. Made by an unsuspecting local workshop out of hardened American steel, they consisted of four-foot arms wedded vertically to an "X." The X was in turn welded to eight-foot steel poles set into concrete blocks. The vertical spikes would rip through the thin duralumin hull of the Clipper like a knife through tofu.

Miyazaki had directed Haas to place himself aboard the launch, clearing the route of floating obstacles. Haas would ensure the maulers remained unseen before the Clipper arrived. By then it would be too late. All was going well until that Grant boy started nosing around. Grant would have to be eliminated. He turned to his eager assistant. "Roger, has Grant gone by yet?"

Roger slowly peered over the top of the turret housing, looked around, then slid back down beside Miyazaki. "I do not see him, master. Should I go and check?"

"Yes, and if you see him, eliminate him. But it must look like an accident."

"What did you have in mind?"

"Perhaps a drowning?"

Roger smiled and bowed slightly. "This is a task I have longed for, master."

"If you handle yourself well, without any slip-ups, I will reward you with admittance to the Imperial Japanese Naval Academy. You will enter the Intelligence Track if you are worthy."

Roger stood, bowed, and silently and then moved in search of his quarry.

* * *

4:12 p.m., Tuesday, November 22, 1935
Seaplane Harbor Breakwater, Alameda Airport,
Alameda, California

Nick stood and took off his coveralls. He could see Haas and the Pan Air launch out in the bay patrolling the *China Clipper's* watery runway. They were looking for flotsam and jetsam from passing ships or other debris that could hole the Clipper on takeoff. *What was the point? The* Clipper *would never get that far.*

He looked back toward shore and saw the Clipper moving closer to the harbor mouth. He yelled and waved his coveralls over his head but it was no use. He doubted the pilots could see him anyway. The windshield wasn't all that big. He looked down at the dirty water. It was going to be cold. The breeze was building out of the southwest as Nick removed his pants, shirt, and t-shirt. He was already chilled to the bone.

He stood in his underwear and wondered how deep the water was next to the ship. He looked for some way to lower himself down. He didn't want to take the chance jumping. Anything could be in the dark water and he didn't want to land on it after a ten-foot jump. Then, to his great surprise, he heard Roger's voice from behind him.

"Nick, Nick, Nick. You can't leave well enough alone, can you?"

Nick swung around and was shocked to see Roger walking calmly towards him. "Roger, what on earth are you doing out here?"

Roger continued walking. He stretched his arms out, fingers interlocked, and cracked his knuckles. "You know, buddy boy, I was just about to ask you the same thing."

"Nancy said you might be planning something for the

Clipper." Nick glanced over Roger's shoulder at the Clipper, now less than 100 yards from the seaplane harbor opening.

"I have come about something else. It is a problem that has long plagued me."

"Problem? Roger what are you talking about?"

"You. I'm here to kill you before you can interfere again."

Realization dawned on Nick. "You're working with Miyazaki!"

Roger smiled and leapt. He planted a kick at the center of Nick's chest.

Nick flew backwards and landed hard on the deck. He rolled away as Roger's foot landed where his head had been a moment before. Nick swept his legs around in a wide arch and knocking Roger's feet out from under him. He crashed to the deck.

Nick hopped to his feet and tried to reach the rail. Roger flipped to his feet and moved to block Nick's path.

Nick took up a fighting stance and faced Roger. "Why are you working with Miyazaki? He's only using you." Nick dodged a kick and blocked a ridge hand strike to his head.

"He is my *ninja* Master. He'll get me into the Japanese Naval Academy."

Nick let fly a left snap kick then threw a roundhouse punch that connected with Roger's side. Roger stepped back and Nick followed. It was a mistake. Roger attacked in a fury of combination kicks and punches. It was all Nick could do to block Roger's onslaught. He was trading space for safety and there wasn't much space left. Roger was fast but Nick had the reach. It was an uneven match that favored Roger.

Roger leapt up and delivered a double snap kick barely missing Nick's head. Nick dived for the deck and rolled away. He came up with a rusty piece of metal about two feet long. He welded it like a sword feeling a little foolish.

Roger laughed. "That isn't going to save you! You're getting desperate, Nick."

"Perhaps...catch!" Nick drew back and threw it with all his

might.

Roger easily dodged the missile as it passed harmlessly to the side and clattered to the deck. Nick seized his chance and broke for the rail. He threw his earlier caution to the wind and dove over the side praying he wouldn't hit something submerged in the dark bay water.

Chapter Fourteen: Nick's Stand

4:13 p.m., Tuesday, November 22, 1935
Seaplane Harbor, Alameda Airport, Alameda, California

Roger ran to the rail in time to see Nick splash into the water. Nick surfaced ten feet out and started swimming like mad for the opposite shore.

Miyazaki stepped out from a passageway. "Fool! After him!"

"But Master, I do not swim!"

"What? Why didn't you tell me?"

"I am ashamed. It is a deep fear for me."

Clearly enraged Miyazaki slapped Roger hard across the face, then drew a dagger from his boot and laid it against Roger's shirt. He stopped. "After him now, or I'll gut you where you stand." Miyazaki shoved the knife until it pricked Roger's flesh. Roger looked down and saw a small stain of blood appear on his shirt. Roger backed away and toppled over, head first, into the bay.

* * *

Nick surfaced. *How could water be this cold?* Then he

concentrated on the task at hand. He knew it would be a race. *Can I reach the obstruction before the Clipper?* He put his head down and began his best Australian crawl. All those years of swim team just might pay off after all.

After a few minutes, he reached the obstruction, or rather the obstructions. There appeared to be two of them about eight feet apart. Nick treaded water as he turned around. The *China Clipper* was about 100 feet away and bearing down on him. He felt around underwater trying to discern the outline and composition of the obstacle. It was something like a giant's comb with the teeth up. It was attached to a pole that held it just below the surface. It was directly in the path the Clipper always took. The pilots would never see him in time to turn if he stayed in the water. He had to be more visible. *Can I stand on this thing?*

* * *

Roger felt the impact of the water on his upper back and neck. It slammed his head into his chest and knocked the wind out of him as he sunk below the surface. Panicked and struggling, he tried to claw his way back to the surface. *But which way was it?* He opened his eyes but saw only a defused dark green blur. He had to figure which way was up!

* * *

Nick felt the tip of one of the teeth. It was rounded, not sharp. He put his foot on the cross bar and stood. He was about two feet out of the water. He could hear the roar of the *Clipper. It must be so close!*

He struggled and turned around to face the aircraft. He waved frantically.

They've got to see me!

The Clipper was close and Nick could feel the suction from the mighty engines. Nick could clearly see Musick and Sullivan's faces and they looked back in disbelief. Musick reached up to the engine throttles. Engines three and four on the starboard wing immediately slowed and the *China*

Clipper yawed hard to starboard. The port sea wing cleared the obstacle by mere feet. Elated, Nick splashed back into the water to avoid the port wing spar.

As the Clipper turned, he saw Vic Wright at the crew door waving at him. Then he put both hands together and shook them over his head making the sign of a champion. He was grinning from ear to ear.

* * *

Roger broke the surface like a breaching humpback whale. He grasped for air and struggled to stay on top of the water. He thrashed with all his might but slowly slid back below the surface. He got one last gulp of air and a mouth full of water that found its way into his lungs. He gasped, involuntarily inhaling water, then gagged and retched as he tried to again fight his way back to the surface.

* * *

It was close, and Nick thought the starboard wing was going to strike the breakwater. Somehow Musick or Sullivan or both, were able to maneuver the giant flying boat past the obstacle. The churning water subsided after the Clipper passed. It moved through the harbor mouth and out into the bay.

Nick had more pressing matters to attend to. He had never felt so cold... so numb. He shivered so badly that his teeth hurt from their constant chattering. He had to get out of this water!

He started swimming for the beach a few hundred yards away. It would be a hard swim, but he knew it would warm him. He was about to put his head back into the water and begin the crawl when he saw something large break the surface across the harbor mouth. Fear shot through him as he remembered the sharks of Pearl Harbor. Then he realized that it was no shark. It was someone in the process of drowning.

Roger?

* * *

Roger bitterly thought with bitterness about his worthless life. It was hopeless, he was drowning. He came to the realization that he deserved to die, he had failed his master. He was especially bitter about failing his ancestral home. It was his destiny to die here and now. He thought about *Bushido* and hoped that in his next reincarnation he would be more worthy. He stopped struggling and gave up to the inevitable. He let himself drift motionless down into the dark depths and the bottom. A few bubbles escaped his mouth and moved towards the surface. He briefly considered trying to follow them, but decided he was too tired. He closed his eyes and thought about sleep.

* * *

When Nick reached the last place he'd seen Roger, there was no sign of him. He swam in a circle slowly searching for some clue. After his second circuit he thought he was too late. Then a stream of bubbles surfaced about two feet in front of him. He took two big breaths and did a surface dive. Bending at the waist he lifted his feet up in the air. The weight of his legs shot him straight down.

God, it's dark down here!

He felt his ears begin to hurt and equalized them until they popped. His hands sank into the bottom ooze before he saw it. He stirred up some muck and couldn't see much beyond a few feet. After about twenty seconds of searching, he headed to the surface exhaling all the way. He surfaced, grabbed a couple of deep breaths and returned to the bottom. *Where was Roger?*

It was hopeless. Nick couldn't see anything but the bottom muck. Nick decided to continue his search until his air ran out and then give it up. Then he saw something. He kicked hard only to come upon an old tire. *But wait a minute. There's a shoe and it's connected to pants. Yes! It's him!*

The body seemed inert. He reached out gingerly and

touched the leg. It moved, scaring him half to death. He'd heard the lifeguard stories about bodies coming back to life. Sometimes the victims would struggle and drag the lifesaver to the bottom where they would both drown. Afraid but determined, Nick grabbed Roger under the armpits and pushed off the bottom. The silt squished between his toes, but finally gave some resistance.

Once free, he kicked with all his might as he pulled Roger upward. His lungs burned and Roger was much heavier than he'd imagined. He wondered if they'd ever reach the air. Finally, after what seemed an eternity, they broke the surface. Nick rolled the still inert Roger on his back and kicked for the closest safety - one of the half-sunken ships of the breakwater. He hoped that it held no more surprises for him this afternoon.

Chapter Fifteen: Roger's Lament

4:58 p.m., Tuesday, November 22, 1935
Seaplane Harbor, Alameda Airport, Alameda, California

Nick swam for a beached ship that formed part of the breakwater. When he reached the partially submerged deck, he dragged Roger's heavy and unresponsive form out of the water. Nick's adrenaline rush had peaked and fatigue began to take its toll.

Wearily, he pulled Roger to a dry spot, rolled him over, and checked his carotid artery for a pulse. It was weak, but worse, Roger had stopped breathing. Nick opened Roger's mouth, reached in, and cleared the airway. Then Nick rolled Roger on to his stomach to begin artificial respiration.

With elbows locked, Nick pushed down hard on Roger's back. Water flowed from Roger's mouth, but still he did not breathe. Nick repeated the procedure again and again until at last Roger coughed. Then he wretched as more water, mucus, and vomit gushed from his mouth. Roger jerked awake and tried to get up.

"Easy Roger, just try to breathe. I think you swallowed

most of the bay." Nick thumped Roger's back, trying to ease the passage of air in and water out. It was up to Roger now.

Roger gagged and vomited again. Finally, his ragged breathing eased and became less labored.

"Okay, Roger, let's try sitting up."

Roger pushed up and rolled over onto his side. He rested for a minute, turned the rest of the way and then sat up.

Roger's face was ashen. "Why did you save me?"

Nick sat down on the deck next to Roger. "I don't know. Until this moment, I didn't give it much thought. I guess because you were drowning and it seemed the thing to do."

"I told you I was going to kill you."

The cold clawed at Nick and he started to shiver. "Yeah, I remember. You still want to do that?"

"No." Roger looked at the deck. "It would've been better if I had drowned. I have shamed my parents."

"What made you join with Miyazaki?"

Roger's head jerked up. "How do you know his name?"

"We've met before. He tried to kill me then, too. That's when I gave him that scar on his face."

Roger stared at him aghast. "But he said the wound was from his China service."

"Sorry, buddy boy, it was me. I slashed him with a broken bottle while he chopped at me with a sword. But that was in Hawaii, not China. What other lies has he told you? And why did you throw in with him?"

Roger's gaze returned to the deck. "He is an honorable man. Someone who cared for me. He was always there for me...unlike my father."

"Your father loves you. He was really proud when you won that karate match last month."

Roger's face flushed with anger as he once again met Nick's eyes. "That was the first time I'd seen him in months. He's always too busy with his business for me... or Nancy for that matter."

"Times are tough and your Dad's just trying to give you

and Nancy a good life."

They heard shouting from somewhere back on the breakwater. Nick called out, "Over here!"

They heard the footsteps approach and saw several uniformed policemen moving towards them.

Roger asked, "So what will you tell them?"

"The truth. That I pulled you out of the water and nearly drowned in the process."

"Why?"

Nick shook violently with the cold and he forced his response between clenched teeth. "Because your sister asked me to!"

They heard someone yell, "There they are! Bring some blankets and coffee."

Someone threw a scratchy woolen blanket over Nick's shoulders as they hoisted him to his feet. He wrapped it tightly around himself and watched another man help Roger to his feet.

The first policeman asked Nick, "What happened here?"

Nick pointed at Roger. "Why don't you ask him?"

Then Nick remembered. "What happened to the *China Clipper*? Did she get away?"

The policeman smiled. "I'll say. Captain Musick flew her right under the Bay bridge and out towards the Pacific. What a sight! Everybody cheered. Didn't you see it?"

"No, I was a little busy at the time."

* * *

The California State Police escorted Roger and Nick back to Colonel Young's office. Betty, Colonel Young's secretary, brought them brandy-laced coffee and a mechanic had provided two sets of dry overalls. The coffee burned as Nick swallowed, but it also spread wonderful warmth through him. Then a deep fatigue spread through him. He wanted to lay down on the couch and sleep, but he shook it off. He needed to be on his toes with the FBI.

Gradually, Nick stopped shaking and regained feeling in his extremities. Colonel Young sent for the Pan American flight surgeon who quickly pronounced Roger and Nick cold, tired, but otherwise okay. All the while two uniformed police officers kept a careful watch.

Nick considered his options and wondered what to tell Agent Cook, who would surely question them soon. The door opened, but to Nick's surprise, First Officer Tilton walked in. Tilton showed a piece of yellow paper to one of the cops, who nodded.

Tilton approached Nick. He eyed Roger. "Is this the guy you fished out of the harbor?"

"Yes."

"Way to go Nick!" Tilton clapped him on the back. "This radiogram is for you." He handed the yellow paper to Nick.

FROM: CHINA CLIPPER, MUSICK STOP
TO: ALAMEDA BASE, NICK GRANT STOP
THANKS NICK! STOP
MESSAGE ENDS

Nick looked up at Tilton, puzzled. "When they changed course, I was pretty sure they were cursing at me. Why would Captain Musick thank me?"

Tilton smiled. "Ed Musick knows what you did. You saved the Clipper and the crew. Trippe knows, too. Thought you might be a bit nervous in here waiting for the FBI. I thought that I'd give you some good news."

"Gee, thanks Mr. Tilton!"

Tilton smiled and left. After a few minutes, Agents Cook and Franks walked in accompanied by Colonel Young. Young walked over, hand extended. "Well done!"

Nick wearily got to his feet and shook Young's hand.

Agent Cook stood next to them. "Okay, Grant, good job." He nodded at Roger. "What's his story?"

"You'd better ask him."

Cook looked at Roger who refused to meet his eyes. "Tanaka, you're under arrest for trespassing and unauthorized entry into a restricted area. Those are the local charges. We're working Federal charges like sabotage. But I need to ask you a question."

Roger continued to stare at the floor. "What?"

"Are you a citizen?"

Roger nodded.

"Good, then we'll add treason to the charge of aiding and abetting a foreign agent. We're going to lock you up and throw away the key. You got anything to say for yourself?"

Roger didn't respond, his gaze remained fixed on the floor. Frustrated, Cook turned to Nick. "Grant, you'd better tell me what you know, pronto!"

Nick looked at Cook then at Roger. *There's got to be a better way!* Strangely, he felt compelled to help Roger though he couldn't figure out why. Maybe it was Nancy? However much he wanted to help Roger, he didn't want to lie to a federal agent. He came upon an idea. "Could I have a few minutes alone with Roger?"

Cook looked startled, then annoyed. "What, so you two can concoct a cover story? No way!"

Colonel Young stepped forward. "Agent Cook, on several occasions Nick's taken enormous personal risks to protect the Clippers. He's not going to do anything to jeopardize operations now. You're getting nowhere with Tanaka. I think we should give Nick a few minutes."

Cook, normally decisive, looked nervous. "I'm not sure that's such a good idea, Colonel Young. It's against procedures…"

Young picked up his desk phone. "Hello, Betty. Please book me a long distance person-to-person call to Washington, DC. Yes, that's right… to J. Edgar Hoover at FBI headquarters… Yes, I'll be here, ring back when you have the Director on the line. Thank you."

Cook and Franks eyed each other.

Young replaced the receiver and looked up at the two FBI agents. "Did I mention that Edgar and I know each other?"

Franks poked Cook in the ribs and nodded. Cook looked defeated. "Okay, okay! Five minutes, but no more, Grant. I'm holding you responsible if he doesn't cooperate."

Cook pointed a finger at Roger. "I've got two men armed with shotguns outside the office window. They've got orders to drop you if you make a break. I've also got police officers right outside the door. Grant, yell if he tries anything." Cook turned and walked out of the room followed by Franks.

A sly smile crossed Colonel Young's face. "This better be good, Nick. I've never met Hoover, and I'm sure our intrepid agents will figure that out in about five minutes." He winked, turned on his heel and left, closing the door.

Alone with Roger, Nick began. The brandy had loosened his inhibitions and his anger and suppressed emotions exploded. "What were you thinking? Working for Commander Miyazaki? He's a cold-blooded killer and almost got you killed tonight!"

Roger showed no emotion as he stared back at Nick.

Nick leaned over right in Roger's face. "I asked you a question. Why did you help that murderer? He kills innocent people without regard to who they are! How could you?"

Roger answered in a whisper. "Miyazaki kills his enemies only when he has no other choice. He is an honorable Japanese officer."

"Honorable? He beat Mac to death after he tortured him for hours!"

"Who's Mac?"

"My old boss, Mac McMillan. Miyazaki was trying to get to me, but Mac didn't give me up, so he died."

Roger's expression softened as he appeared to take in Nick's words. "I know nothing about that, but lately I've begun to question some things my sensei has told me."

"Roger, he was just using you! Tell me, how did you wind up in the harbor? Even I knew that you don't swim."

Anger flared in Roger's eyes. "How could you know that?"

"Nancy told me. I asked if you were afraid of anything, and she told me you fear deep water."

Roger seemed to deflate before Nick's eyes. "Miyazaki offered me a choice. Jump in or feel his blade. I wasn't afraid. I was ashamed that I had failed him and decided I'd rather die trying to finish my task."

"Don't you see that he's just using you?"

"He offered something I wanted – entrance into the Japanese Naval Academy. The exchange was honorable."

"*He's* not honorable! He may wrap himself in all that ancient homeland crap, but it's just a way to get to you. Face it, Roger, whether you like it or not, you're American."

Roger stiffened. "White boy, you don't know what it's like to live as a second class citizen in your own hometown. I tried out for the football team, and the coach told me, 'No Japs.' It was the same with everything except academics. There, at least, I was judged as an equal."

Nick softened his approach. "I know a little about that. Walking down the street with Nancy, people come up to me and say, 'What's the matter, a white girl's not good enough for you?' Sometimes we get cat calls from passing cars. They'd call out, 'Stick to your own kind!' or some such thing."

"They're right. Stick to your own kind and away from my sister."

"Roger, Nancy is just a friend, nothing more."

"You are a fool. She's in love with you, *Banjin*!"

"What?" Nick was startled. He's never given Nancy any reason to think he was interested. *Had he?* He shook off those thoughts and returned to more pressing matters. "Roger, in a few minutes, the FBI is coming back through that door to take you off to jail for a long, long time, maybe the rest of your life."

Roger looked resigned. "You think that I don't know that?"

"Come clean, Roger. Maybe they'll make a deal if you tell them everything. Regardless, I'm sure they'd go easier on you."

"What can I offer them?"

"Information. Things that they don't know about. Like Haas for one thing."

Roger looked at the floor. "Haas is a thug, nothing more. He's in it for the money but he hides that behind his professed love of the *Fuhrer*."

Nick was startled. "You mean Adolph Hitler?"

"Yes."

"My guess is that information would be very important to the FBI. What do you say?"

"I don't know. We'll see."

"Don't be a bigger fool than you've already been. The choice is yours." Nick stood, walked to the door, and opened it. Two huge policemen blocked his path. "Tell Agent Cook that I'm finished here. There's nothing more I can do. The rest is up to Mr. Tanaka."

As Nick walked away, he decided not to mention Roger's attempt on his life. He hoped he was doing the right thing. A cop blocked the door. "Excuse me, I'd like to go home now."

The cop crossed his arms across his chest. "Sorry kid, not until the G-men give the okay."

"Why am I being held?"

"Look, I don't know, but they said *nobody* leaves until they say so.

Chapter Sixteen: Worry Ward

7:42 p.m., Tuesday, November 22, 1935
Pan Am Administration Building,
Alameda Airport, Alameda, California

An hour and a half later, Nick awoke to a prodding foot. He swung his feet off the couch and sat up, scratching his head. "Did you catch Haas?"

Agent Franks looked down at Nick. "No, he's flown the coop."

Nick felt groggy from too little sleep or maybe too much brandy-laced coffee. Slowly the fog began to lift from his frazzled brain. "Did you check his apartment?" He yawned and stretched.

"We're not fools, Nick, of course. But he's cleared out. We put out an all points bulletin, he can't get far."

"I hope you're right, Agent Franks."

Franks nodded. "We've decided that you can't go home tonight."

"What! Why?" Nick was now awake.

"Agent Cook and I have concocted a little story to catch a

big fish. And you're part of it."

"Just how does it involve me?"

"Tanaka told us about your little set-to on the breakwater ships. Why didn't you tell us?"

"Tell you what?"

"That Tanaka was trying to kill you before you pulled his butt out of the drink."

"Oh, that. Well, he already had so many charges against him and I thought it wouldn't matter."

"Look, Grant, you tell us everything, and I mean *everything*. Miyazaki wants you dead, and next time he might attack at your home. How'd you like him sneaking around your house with that knife of his? Might run into your mother, your dad, or even your sister."

A sickening feeling settled in Nick's stomach. "My God, I hadn't thought about that. I made a promise to Roger's sister, that's all." Nick sat up straight. "Okay, Agent Franks. What do you need me to do?"

"The plan is simple. You and Roger are bait to lure Miyazaki into a trap. The cover story is that you were injured saving Roger and both of you required hospitalization. The Pan Am press agent will take pictures of you two in the hospital and get the story to the Bay papers in time for the late edition. Cook hopes that Miyazaki reads it, or hears it on the radio, and comes calling. We'll be waiting with the police next door."

Franks handed Nick the phone. "Call home. But keep it simple, I'll be listening on the extension."

Nick dialed the number. The phone rang twice before he heard his father's voice. "Hello, Grant residence."

"Hello, Dad, it's Nick."

"Nick, where have you been? Your mother's made a fine supper and she's hopping mad that you missed it... again."

"I'm sorry, Dad. There's been a bit of trouble at work and the FBI is holding all the ground crew members until they can figure it out."

"What? Was there another sabotage attempt?"

Nick looked to Franks who shook his head no. "Look Dad, I can't talk about it, but they say I might be here all night."

"That's outrageous! I'm coming down to give them a piece of my mind!"

"No Dad, please don't. It'll just make matters worse. There are cops everywhere and they're turning back people all the time. You can call the Pan Am switchboard about midnight to check on me, if you like. But I've got to go now."

Franks mimed for Nick to end his conversation and hang up.

"I'll hold off until midnight, but then if you're not home, I'm coming to get you. This is a school night, Nick. You know that I've had just about enough of that airline. Who do they think they are?"

"Dad, can we talk about this later? I've got to go. Bye." With a huge pang of guilt, he hung up the phone and looked at Agent Franks. "I'm going to be in so much trouble. You promise to square it with my parents?"

Franks smiled as he hung up the extension. "Sure, Nick. We'll set it right."

"Okay then, off to the hospital."

* * *

The ride to the hospital was thankfully short, sirens blazing, red lights flashing, and windshield wipers slapping back and forth. The rain had come suddenly and in sheets. It made the streets darker and more dangerous. Nick felt like he was a character in some spy thriller movie with a lousy plot. Cook and Franks were confident that they could take Miyazaki alive. Nick wasn't so sure. He'd seen Miyazaki fight and he feared for the agents.

Franks, seeing Nick's look, opened his coat to reveal a snub-nosed .38 caliber revolver on his belt. "Don't worry. If he gives us any trouble, we're armed." He closed his coat and patted his side. "The state police will be in the adjacent room, so he'll be out-numbered and out-gunned."

Nick smiled but remained silent. *Perhaps I do worry too much. But I don't like being the bait on the hook!*

* * *

Agent Cook strode into the hospital room and took off his sopping wet raincoat. He shook it and water cascaded off and fell on the floor. He gazed around the room. "This will have to do." He pointed to the door that led to the adjoining room. "Nick, Franks and I will be in that room. There'll be two uniformed police officers next door. You got any questions?"

Nick looked from his bed over to Roger, who was in the other bed, then back to Cook. "Just come quick if you hear me yell, or when I push the button."

He griped the black button in his hand. It was connected to a black phone line that ran behind his bed, across the floor, and into the heating vent. Cook had said that it was connected to a light in the next room. Nick still wasn't convinced about the wisdom of the plan. "Miyazaki is quiet and fast. I wish you'd just stay in the room."

Cook shrugged. "We've been through that. If he sees anything out of the ordinary, he won't bite. You just lie back and push the button when you see him, and we'll handle Miyazaki."

Nick shook his head in disbelief. "I hope you're right."

Cook walked to the door and turned off the room lights. Nick lay back on the pillow, his arms folded under his head. He stared at the ceiling and watched as car lights reflected from the rain slick streets raced across the ceiling. The corner stoplights flickered there as well. With each change, the stopped cars and trucks would start moving, often sending a cacophony of backfires and sounds of over-worn mufflers. *How was anybody supposed to sleep with that racket?* Nick listened to too many traffic cycles to count until he finally dropped off.

* * *

CHINA CLIPPER

3:30 a.m., November 23, 1935
St. Jude's Hospital, Alameda, California

Nick walked on a warm tropical beach hand-in-hand with Leilani, enjoying the easy sound of the surf. Her red *mu'u mu'u* fluttered in the trade wind and contrasted with the dark greens of the tropical forest. It reminded Nick of Christmas. She turned and tickled him, and then she sprinted away just out of reach. Her waist length dark hair bounced enticingly under the flower head lei. *But the smell was wrong!*

Leilani turned to face to him as she ran. "You're such a slow poke, Nick. I'll bet you can't catch me."

Nick awoke sweating. He had wrestled the sheets off in his sleep. It had only been a dream but it had seemed so real. The dream state lingered in his foggy mind like scattered fragments of an alternate consciousness. Slowly he brushed the cobwebs from his mind. Sleep, so far, had been fitful. He had awakened with every noise, real or imagined, and he wondered if this was yet another false alarm. He opened his eyes and scanned the room, careful not to move or make a sound.

Nothing but the gentle sound of the waves lapping on the beach. *What?*

He was about to roll over when a deep sense of dread passed through him. The window was open. *It had been closed when I last looked.* He felt the presence of someone, other than Roger, in the room with them. His heart racing, he slowly reached for the panic button. *Where was it?*

A shadow moved across the open window and stopped. A human apparition held something and gently swung it back and forth. "Looking for this, *Grant-san*?"

Ohmigod! It's Miyazaki! His mouth was dry. He tried to cry out. "Help!" The croaking sound was barely a whisper.

Miyazaki chuckled. "Don't bother. I've dispatched the police officers. They can no longer help you."

The police? But what about the G-men?

116

In a swift motion, Miyazaki was at his side and Nick felt cold steel against his throat. "Not a sound, Grant, or I'll cut you, ear to ear."

Fear gripped Nick. *Why didn't Roger act? Had he truly repented or would he still serve his former sensei?* Nick had to do something and quick. But what?

Nick thought quickly. Miyazaki would kill him regardless. He might as well die fighting. He looked up at Miyazaki and then at the door to the adjoining room. *Look, at the door, for God's sake, please!* Nick looked again.

Miyazaki's eyes darted towards the door. It was the break Nick needed. He pushed hard on the knife hand and lifted his legs towards Miyazaki's head. His right hand found a pillow and he tossed it at Miyazaki's knife. As Nick's legs wrapped around Miyazaki's head he pushed harder on Miyazaki's knife hand. The knife slashed the pillow open, and a cloud of feathers exploded between them. Nick released his leg headlock. He bounced off the opposite side of the bed milliseconds ahead of the slashing blade.

Nick rolled away across the bedside table and knocked the lamp over. It smashed on the tile floor. Nick did his best crabwalk backing away from the bed as fast as his hands and feet would carry him. He kicked over the table for good measure.

The cacophony of noise brought both Cook and Franks in from the adjoining room. As the light flooded the room, Nick saw that they had both drawn their revolvers. Then Nick caught the flash of a fighting star as it zipped across the room and imbedded in Frank's right arm. Franks screamed and dropped his revolver. It discharged as it hit the floor. The bullet harmlessly buried itself in the ceiling and the gun skidded across the tile out of sight. Franks collapsed against the wall clutching his arm as blood spurted from the wound.

Everything and everyone was in motion in the hospital room except Roger. Nick raised his head and tried to see what was happening.

Cook yelled. "FBI! Freeze!"

Miyazaki dove for the floor and Cook snapped off a couple of shots. The muzzle flashes and resulting booms stunned everyone. The bullets missed Miyazaki, but smashed into the wall clock, spreading shards of metal and glass everywhere.

Nick crawled across the broken glass, looking for Frank's pistol, heedless of the cuts on his elbows, hands and knees. He pawed under the bed. *Where is it?* The hallway door opened and the ceiling light suddenly snapped on. A voice said, "There he is, men. Get him!"

Then Nick heard a scream and more breaking glass. The room plunged back into darkness once again. Off to his left he heard glass crunch under fast moving feet and then two bodies collide.

Someone said, "Uuff!" and a body hit the floor followed by muffled scream and a gurgling sound. A chair flew through the other window and the glass seemed to explode outward. A dark figure leapt through the jagged opening and disappeared down the fire escape.

The hallway door opened and several uniformed men stormed in, flashlights in hands, weapons drawn. A cop came over to Nick just as he stood up with Frank's pistol in his hand. The cop growled, "Drop it, son!" Nick looked over his shoulder and saw the cop had a gun leveled at his midsection.

Nick slowly raised his hands and let the pistol hang from his index figure. "If I drop it, it might go off. It's already happened once."

The cop looked wary. "Okay, slowly hand it to me butt first."

Nick handed it over just as two cops leaning out the window started blasting away. One of them said, "Damn, he got away. Murray, get on the horn and put out an all points bulletin. We got to get this guy! He's a cop killer!"

Cop killer? Who got killed? Then Nick saw Franks face up on the floor, his unseeing eyes staring at the ceiling. "Not another murder! But where's Roger?"

Roger pushed his way out from under Frank's inert body, covered in blood. "I'm here."

Nick was puzzled. "Are you alright?"

"Yes. Agent Franks stood between me and Miyazaki. He took the blade meant for me."

Nick looked at Roger's blood-soaked shirt. "Are you sure?"

"It's not my blood."

"Where were you during the fight? I didn't see you once."

"Miyazaki asked me to leave with him. I was trying to decide, go or stay and fight him. Then you woke up and all hell broke loose."

"So, what did you decide?"

Roger looked hard at Nick. "I'm here, aren't I?"

Nick shrugged not completely convinced. He turned to the cop. "Can I put my hands down now? They hurt and so do my feet." They were bloody from the broken glass covering the floor.

The cops shrugged. "Sure kid, why not." He called over his shoulder. "Hey Mac, get somebody to look at this kid's hands and feet. They're a mess."

Cook was kneeling at Frank's side. He reached out and tenderly closed his colleague's eyes. "I'll get him, buddy. I swear that I'll get him." Cook's eyes were red and tears streaked his cheeks.

Nick limped over toward them. He found a section of the floor not covered in glass and seated himself next to Frank's body. He sat in silence for a few minutes, picking a couple of glass and metal shards out of his hands and feet. *Ouch!* After a while, he looked at Cook.

"Agent Cook, I heard what you said about Miyazaki."

Cook looked over, anger on his face. "Yeah, so what?"

"So," Nick continued, picking at a piece of glass in his knee. "We've got something in common."

"What could you and I possibly have in common?"

"We both want to get Miyazaki." Then he turned to Roger. "But what about you?"

Roger looked back at Nick. "I, too, have a debt to settle with Commander Miyazaki."

The medics rushed in and attended to the dead and wounded. Some guy poured what seemed like a pint of iodine into Nick's cuts. *Ouch!* The medic who patched him up said, "Your cuts are superficial. You're lucky."

Nick looked the hapless orderly in the face. "Funny, I don't feel very lucky."

The man shrugged and moved on to treat the others. The smell of cordite and blood abated as orderlies mopped the floor. The mop heads ran red with blood as the orderlies squeezed them dry.

Afterwards, Cook drove Nick to his house.

Nick asked. "Will you come in and square it with my parents? Agent Franks said he would and now…"

Pain and sadness etched Cook's face. "Sure kid, but nothing about the spies."

"So what you going to tell them?"

"The organized crime cover story."

"Agent Cook, my parents aren't stupid. Why don't you level with them?"

"Can't. Orders."

"Good luck. You got a cover story for these?" Nick held up his bandaged hands.

Cook opened his door. "I'll think of something. I always do."

"It better be good!"

"It will be."

Nick opened the door and walked in. He parents were sitting up waiting for him. His mother looked old with worry. He father looked angry.

"Mom, Dad, this is Agent Cook, FBI."

Cook removed his hat and stepped into the front room. "Hello, Mr. and Mrs. Grant." He held up his ID badge and began. "There was some trouble with organized labor tonight at the airport. They threw some bricks and Nick got cut with flying class. I thought I'd better bring him home after his visit to the hospital. Pan Am will pay all medical expenses, not to worry."

Nick turned to look at Cook. *Oh, my God! That was supposed to be a good cover story?*

Mr. Grant extended a hand. "Thank you, Agent Cook. There's been a lot of labor unrest this year. Frankly I'm not surprised."

Mrs. Grant walked over and hugged her son. "Are you cut bad Nick?"

"No Mom, just a few cuts on my hands." He didn't dare tell them about his feet! *I think they're buying it.*

Cook replaced his hat. "If you'll pardon me, I really must get back to the office. I've got so much paperwork to finish."

Mr. Grant shook his head. "I fully understand, Agent Cook. Thanks you for bringing my son home."

Cook tipped his hat to Mrs. Grant and turned to go.

Nick caught up. "Thanks again, Agent Cook. Let me walk you to your car."

Cook looked suspicious, but only nodded. Once outside Nick asked. "How did you know that my parents would buy that cockamamie story?"

"I didn't."

Chapter Seventeen: A Promise

Saturday, November 30th, 1935
Alameda Airport, Alameda, California

Agent Franks' death was national news. He was buried in his home town of Erie, Pennsylvania, and J. Edgar Hoover attended the ceremony and gave a short speech. FBI agents and uniformed police formed an honor guard, and they escorted the flag-covered coffin to its final resting place. Hoover presented the flag to his widow. Mrs. Franks stood in the snow with their four children and cried.

Nick heard it live on the radio and saw it a few days later in a Movie Tone Newsreel that also featured the inaugural *China Clipper* flight. It irked him that the media had not connected the two events. During Hoover's eulogy, he had gone on and on about the evils of organized crime and how the FBI would bring the murderers to justice. Hoover never mentioned that Franks had died trying to protect the Clipper from foreign agents. Cook stood in the front row with the assembled dignitaries. He had looked miserable.

When Cook got back from the funeral, the FBI put him in

charge of Clipper base security. Nick was so agitated after viewing the newsreel, he decided to confront Cook. "Why all the subterfuge? Why don't we just level with the American people? They have a right to know the truth."

Cook looked disgusted. "I don't agree with the organized crime cover story either, Nick. However, that decision was made at a higher level. I'm just following orders."

"That's a load of bunk and you know it!"

Cook took a more consolatory tone. "You know the score. We can't let the American people get riled up. Can you imagine the public outcry if they knew that a foreign agent had killed an FBI man? They'd want his head on a pike."

"And you don't?"

Cook's eyes flashed with anger. "Of course I do! You know better than to ask me that! Franks was my partner for years. Our wives are close friends and our kids play together. My wife is devastated by his death and wants me to quit. She's terrified and couldn't console Mrs. Franks. Thank God she's with family now. Perhaps they can console her. We sure couldn't."

"I didn't mean any disrespect. It's just so frustrating!"

Cook's anger faded. "None taken. It's been hard, that's all."

"Why didn't you believe me when I first called you?"

"Who said we didn't? Franks believed you immediately."

"And you?"

"No... not at first."

"And now that you do, Franks is dead. Why does everything have to take so long? I've known Miyazaki killed Mac for months and he's still at large. He'll kill again if someone doesn't stop him. The more people that know, the better chance that we get him."

"I know that. Look Nick, the gag order comes from the very top. So drop it."

"Oh, you mean, J. Edgar Hoover?"

"No, his boss."

Realization dawned on Nick. "President Roosevelt?"

"I said drop it, Nick."

"Okay. Okay!"

* * *

Tuesday, December 3, 1935
Study Hall, Alameda High School, Alameda, California

Nick had just finished a long letter to Leilani. He should have been studying Calculus, but he was having trouble focusing on schoolwork. He'd written to her about the dream of walking hand-in-hand down a tropical beach. He wrote about viewing the *China Clipper* ceremony, but he'd left out any mention of his part in that day's activities. Finally, he's told her about his recent karate test and winning a brown belt. And about his concern with the upcoming Pan Am Flight Engineer exam on the 21st.

He wrote Leilani's address on the envelope and let his thoughts roam. Roger was out on bail. Charged with interfering with a U.S. Mail carrier and vandalism, he seemed to have turned over a new leaf. He wasn't condescending and sarcastic to Nick. Instead, he had actually helped Nick prepare for his karate advancement.

Nancy was amazed, too. "Who was it you pulled from the bay? It can't have been Roger. This guy's way too nice! It's got to be an imposter!"

They had laughed until Mr. Nieshe had admonished them, and even Roger had smiled. That prompted Nick to ask Roger. "I'd be glad to teach you how to swim, Roger. What do you say?"

"Perhaps, but not until the water is a lot warmer! And after my trial."

Nick remembered the bone-chilling bay water. "Okay, you're on." Then on a more somber note he asked. "Do you have a date for your trial?"

Roger looked at the floor. "Yes, it's set for January. Will you come and be a character witness?"

Nick looked at Roger. He lifted his face to look at Nick. Nick thought a moment. "If you're through with Miyazaki, I will."

"I'm through. I made a deal with the FBI. I spill the beans on Miyazaki and they drop the attempted murder and espionage charges."

"I'll speak for you, Roger. I would be honored."

Roger stood and extended his hand. "I made a big mistake, Nick. I still hate the way that *Banjin* treat people of Japanese descent, but I'm committed to my country now. Someday, I'll be able to pay the U.S. back for my treachery."

Nick shook the offered hand. "I know you will, Roger."

* * *

11:10 a.m., Tuesday, December 11th, 1935
Pan Am Administration Building, Alameda Airport
Alameda, California

Fall had flown by. First it was Thanksgiving and then the *China Clipper* returned without incident, but Nick was consumed by studying, not only for semester finals, but also for the upcoming Pan Am Flight Engineer Exam.

Nick continued to work when he could, but Colonel Young put a stop to that. "You'll never be an airline pilot, let alone a college-trained engineer, if you don't do well in high school."

"But Colonel Young, I want to work! It helps me keep my mind off of Agent Franks' death and – "

"I won't hear of it. I don't want to see your smiling face around here again – not until you finish your finals."

Nick looked out of Colonel Young's window. "Why does Agent Cook allow all these people on the airfield for each Clipper launch and recovery operation?"

"Because, my inquisitive young friend, that's his orders. Besides, it's good for the country *and* Pan Am."

"But, Colonel Young, that's when the Clippers are most vulnerable!"

"I am aware of that Nick, but it's a risk that President

Roosevelt has asked Pan Am to take."

"I don't get it. Didn't the President put the kibosh on releasing the truth about the *Pan American Clipper* sabotage incident in August?"

Young stubbed out a cigarette. "Yes, Nick, but the Clippers offer excitement as well as hope for millions of Americans affected by the depression. Juan Trippe and President Roosevelt actually agree on this minor point."

"*Minor* point? We have no idea where Miyazaki is or what he'll try next."

"Be calm, my young friend. You need to concentrate on finals and the Flight Engineer Exam. Are you ready?"

Nick shook his head in disbelief. "I am, but I'm more worried about the Clippers, sir!"

"Admirable, but the police and Agent Cook have it well in hand. We'll see you when you've finished your school finals. Off you go."

"Yes, sir, but —"

"No buts. You need only worry about correctly interpreting the '*How Goes It*' curve and you'd also better be quick at your calculus."

"Yes, sir." Nick walked away shaking his head. *I'll never understand adults!* He watched the ground crew working to get the *China Clipper* ready for her next hop to the Orient. Pan American had borrowed a fortune to build the Pacific Skyway to Asia. They needed regular twice-a-week flights as early as possible to repay the exorbitant cost. The bank loans had to be repaid.

Post Master Farley had been generous with the Air Mail contract. It only required one flight a month. However, Juan Trippe wanted the next flight as soon as possible, and had scheduled it for December 22.

The engineers grumbled. But Young asked, "Can you do it safely?"

They answered, "Probably," and that was the end of all further discussions about the matter.

Chapter Eighteen: The Exam

Saturday, December 16th, 1935
Pan Am Administration Building, Alameda Airport
Alameda, California

The proctor looked up from his desk and scanned the classroom. "Five minutes, gentlemen." Then he returned his attention to the paperwork on his desk.

Nick returned his attention to his exam. *Think!* He was almost done with the last problem and it was a tough nut:

Scenario: You are the Flight Engineer on a Martin M-130 Flying Boat. The crew has been flying for 12 hours on a 2,401 statue mile hop from San Francisco to Honolulu. The navigator tells you that the aircraft is 1,100 nautical miles out of Honolulu and that the barometric pressure is 29.13 inches and rising. The takeoff weight was 52,196 lbs. with all fuel tank, oil and hydraulic reservoirs filled to capacity. The captain asks you to determine:
    a. Total remaining fuel.
    b. Given that current meteorological conditions

> *remain constant, maximum range remaining.*
> *c. Most efficient engine settings.*
> *d. Has the flying boat passed <u>the point of no return</u>?*

The point of no return? That's not fair! The navigator is supposed to determine that! Nick snapped his pencil. The sharp crack echoed around the silent room. Several heads turned and a few men chuckled. He felt foolish. *Get a grip, Nick!* He felt the glare of the proctor as he put down the broken end down on the desk.

Nick had used the provided "*How goes it*" graph, or curve, to quickly determine the remaining fuel and most efficient engine settings. Then the projected maximum range fell into place. But how the devil was he supposed to determine *the point of no return*? He didn't even have a chart of the Pacific. It was maddening!

He searched his memory. *What was it that Nieshe had said about the curve? It was an aside, and not part of his normal lesson...* Nick racked his brain but to no avail. He looked at the two lines on the graph. The black line represented the preflight projected fuel consumption and the dashed red line the actual rate. *No, the answer's not there.*

The proctor said, "One minute, gentlemen."

A groan emanated from many men. At least, he was not the only one having trouble. Then it hit Nick like a ton of bricks. It was the head wind! If they turned around, it would become a tail wind. *Could it be that simple?* He quickly did the calculations and jotted down his answer with the corresponding "proof".

The proctor picked up a small wooden mallet and struck the bell on his desk. "That's the time bell, gentlemen. Place your pencils on the desk and stand up, please."

Several men kept writing.

The proctor said, "I shall not tell you again, gentlemen. Stand away from your tests or forfeit your exam - NOW!"

The men still writing reluctantly slapped their pencils

down and joined those standing. Twenty men had tested today for two open positions. Nick's chances weren't good. He was the youngest by far, and many had said they were college graduates.

The proctor gazed around the room satisfied. "That's better. The test results will be posted outside on the bulletin board Monday noon. Good day and have a very Merry Christmas!"

Dejected, Nick followed some of the crowd to the canteen. Nick took a tray and walked through the food line in a daze. He paid for his ham sandwich and lemonade, then joined Nieshe who was sitting with Tilton.

Nick sat down and noticed something about Tilton's uniform. His jacket had four gold rings around the sleeves. *Omigod! Jack Tilton had made it!* Nick smiled and reached his hand across the table. "Congratulations on your promotion, Captain Tilton."

Tilton grasped Nick's hand. "Thanks Nick. It was official today."

Nick picked up his sandwich, unsure if he had an appetite or not. "When did you find out?"

"I was pretty sure last week but there was a snafu with the correspondence school."

"How's that?" Nick took a tentative bite.

"The school lost my celestial navigation test. Until they found it, I was still a first officer. But enough about me, how did your test go?"

Nick swallowed. "I'm not sure. The last question was unfair and I wasn't prepared. I'd like to meet the guy who came up with that question. I'd sure like to give him a piece of my mind."

Nieshe put down his coffee. "You are very lucky, Nick. Captain Tilton wrote that question."

Nick felt a blush explode over his face. "Gee, Captain Tilton, I didn't mean any disrespect..."

Tilton laughed good-naturedly. "Tell me Nick, what was so

unfair?"

Nick gulped. "Well, if you must know, it was determining the point of no return. That's a navigator's job."

Tilton leaned in. "Yes, and?"

"Why test engineers about navigator's duties?"

Tilton leaned back. "Suppose that the navigator got sick or injured. Everybody else on the crew would have to pick up his duties. That's one reason the captains have to be proficient in navigation as well as flying and engineering. If the navigator were sick from food poisoning, more members of the crew could also become sick."

Nick was starting to get the idea. "So, why not have the pilot determine the *point of no return*?"

"We might be pretty busy up there on the flight deck. You've flown the M-130. She's a beast even in the best of weather."

"So, if it's all about team work, why not tell the students ahead of time? It would have been nice to have been prepared."

Nieshe had been drinking his coffee and listening intently, until now. "Another aspect of that question, Nick, is to ensure that you have the presence of mind and the inner calm required to deal with unexpected contingencies."

Tilton added, "I'll tell you something else, Nick. No one passes the test without answering all four parts of the last question correctly."

Nick was shaken. Up until this moment, he still had a fleeting hope that he just might have passed. Those hopes seemed to recede before his eyes. "So, what was the answer to the *point of no return* question?"

Tilton smiled. "The Clipper had not reached the point of no return."

Relieved, Nick put his head in his hands. "Oh, God."

Nieshe put a hand on Nick's shoulder. "Not to worry, the test will be given again in a few months."

"Mr. Nieshe, I got that one right. Now I'm worried about

the rest of the test." He picked up his tray with the half-eaten sandwich. "If you'll excuse me, I'm going back to work and try not to think about the results."

Tilton smiled at Nick. "Don't worry. If you didn't pass this time, I know you will eventually."

"Gee, Captain Tilton, thanks."

"Sure, Nick and you can be on my crew anytime."

Nick was speechless. He nodded his thanks and walked away, elated. It was going to be a long couple of days.

Chapter Nineteen: A Phone Call

11:50 a.m., Monday, December 18th, 1935
Pan Am Administration Building, Alameda Airport
Alameda, California

School was finally out for Christmas break but Nick could only think about the Flight Engineer Exam. *I hope I passed!* The hours had dragged by, each seemingly longer than the last. Nick found himself repeatedly staring at the wall clock, willing it to move faster. But that only seemed to slow it down even further.

Finally, he jumped into Mac's old pickup truck and drove to Alameda Airport. The cop at the gate, the one who'd found Nick on the breakwater, smiled and waved him through. Nick waved back barely able to contain himself. *What would I do if I failed the test? Maybe Commander Boltz would still take me in the Navy's flying boat corps.*

He parked and walked to the Administration Building. A small group of men were crowded around the bulletin board. Nick gulped back his fear and weaved his way to the front. He tried to look as unconcerned as possible, although he felt that his world was about to be torn asunder.

One by one, the men turned and left. Nick could tell from their demeanor that none had succeeded. He stood in front of the bulletin board and now it was his turn. He started from the bottom and worked up. No one had passed by the time he reached his name. Then he saw his score–he had passed!

Relief flooded through him and he felt a little giddy. *I've done it! I'm the youngest Pan Am Flight Engineer!* He leapt for joy and let out a loud, "Wahoo!" Then seeing the dejected faces of his fellow test takers, he calmed himself and quietly left the building. However, he couldn't resist clicking his heels as he walked back to Mac's truck. *Time to call Tommy!*

* * *

7:30 a.m., Tuesday, December 19th, 1935
The Grant Home, Alameda, California

Nick took a sip of coffee, and then placed his cup on the kitchen table. "What are you doing today, Mom?"

Helen Grant sat across the table from her son, reading the morning paper. "Oh, the usual, cooking, cleaning and such." A girlish smile crossed her face. "Of course, I have my bridge club this afternoon."

Nick smiled back. "As I recall, you made some big money last week."

"Deary me, Nick, seventy-five cents is not *Big Money*!"

"I don't know about that, Mom. Seventy-five cents will buy you a great lunch at the Blue Plate Café. It sure beats losing."

"When have I ever lost more than a nickel?"

"Okay, Mom, regardless of win or lose, I'm glad you enjoy your card games."

The kitchen door opened and Tommy strolled in. "Hello, Mrs. Grant! Hey, Nick. You ready to go?"

"Almost. I forgot my logbook. I'll be right back down." Nick raced upstairs to his bedroom just as the phone rang. He heard his mother answer. "Hello, Grant residence... yes, please hold the line."

His mother called up the stairs. "Nick, it's for you. It's Alameda!"

Nick grabbed his logbook from his dresser and returned to the kitchen. His mother handed him the receiver. "Hello, Nick Grant here."

A familiar voice sounded in the phone. "Nick, it's Captain Tilton. I need you to fly with me on a training mission. It'll be for a few days. Are your folks agreeable?"

Nick couldn't believe his ears. "I hope so. Let me ask." He put the phone down. "Mom, Pan Am needs me to go on a training mission as an FE. I'll be gone a few days. Is that alright?"

Mrs. Grant looked up from her paper. "What is an FE? Where are you off to and for how long?"

Nick picked up the phone. "Captain Tilton, where to and for how long?"

Tilton replied. "For at least a week, maybe more but you'll get *per diem*."

"What's *per diem*?"

"It's living expenses for hotels and meals."

Nick answered his mother's questions. "FE is short for Flight Engineer, you know the test I just passed. It's for a week, Mom, but Pan Am pays all expenses."

"What? And be gone for Christmas! And if I know you, Nick Grant, you'll find an excuse not to attend church on our Savior's birthday."

"Mom, please! This is such a big break for me. If I don't go, another new FE will take my place!"

Mrs. Grant sat back and crossed her arms. Nick knew this look. She was thinking it over. *There's still a chance, she hasn't said no yet!*

Nick gave it his best shot. "I promise to attend service on a holy day of obligation."

Mrs. Grant raised an eye brow. "Not good enough. I want you to go on both Christmas Eve and Christmas Day. That is, should you not be back in time to attend with the family."

"Yippee!" Nick took a breath and tried to sound a bit more restrained. "Captain Tilton, I can go. What time is the pre-flight?"

"It's already begun. We lift off at 3:30. Get your butt down here pronto." Tilton sounded almost relieved.

"Okay, Skipper." Then it hit Nick and he couldn't imagine why it had taken so long. "So what tail number are we flying?"

"NC 14715, but mum's the word. I need you to keep this on the QT. You'll get the scoop when you arrive. I can't say more on the phone. Understand, Nick?"

"Yes, sir, I understand. I'll see you in about thirty minutes." He hung up the phone.

His mother wasn't fooled. "What is it, Nick? I thought you'd be delighted."

Nick grasped for words. He had to say something... but no more lies. "I just realized this might be my first Christmas away from home. It sort of hit me like a ton of bricks."

Helen Grant reached across the table and took her son's hands. She looked into his eyes for a moment. Nick could see the tears starting to well up. "My little boy is all grown up. You've long been a man physically, but I see the change in your heart. I'm proud of you, son, and I love you."

Something deep inside tugged at Nick and he wondered if he'd see his family again. "Thanks. I love you too, Mom."

Then his mother straightened up. "You'd better get along and pack your bag. You don't want to miss your plane."

Nick stood up. "Tommy, can you give me a ride to the airport?"

Tommy, who was looking more than a little embarrassed, said too loudly, "Sure, Nick, I'll be outside in Mac's truck."

Chapter Twenty: Westward with the Night

10:22 a.m., Tuesday, December 19, 1935
Pan American Operations Building, Alameda Airport
Alameda, California

Agent Cook handed Nick a package and a letter. "This came for you by Naval Courier this morning. You're to open the letter and read it in my presence."

Nick looked at the package. It was about twelve inches by ten by four and wrapped in brown paper. He ripped open the envelope and began to read.

CONFIDENTIAL EYES ONLY
OFFICIAL US NAVY
TO: Nicholas D. Grant, Pan American Airlines
FROM: LCDR STEVEN BOLTZ, US Navy Counter Intelligence, Pacific Fleet, Pearl Harbor, Oahu, Hawaiian Territories
Aloha, Nick!

(C) I have requested that Pan Am carry you to Oahu on the next available Clipper. We have just learned damaging details about the Japanese Intelligence Service activities in the Hawaiian Territories. Those details are in the package. You must deliver it to me, unopened, immediately.

(C) I have entrusted you with this extremely sensitive mission for one simple reason. We have reason to believe that our radio codes have been compromised. We have indications that a Japanese secret society, the *Black Dragons*, are involved with Imperial Naval Intelligence. They are extremely dangerous *Ninjas*. Deliver this package to Chief Ellis or me and no one else. Trust no one and be careful. There may be traitors among us. Sorry that I can't tell you more, but I don't know much more myself.

(C) On a personal note, I owe you for your help earlier. Now we have a chance to take down Miyazaki's entire mission here in Hawaii and, possibly, California. Last August, when we met aboard the *USS Arizona*, you asked me if there was any way to get Miyazaki. This is your chance. I'm counting on you, shipmate. With your help we may yet bring Mac's murderer to justice.

(U) IMPORTANT: Do not discuss the contents of this message or show it to anyone. Wait for Ellis or me at the Pan Am Pearl City pier.

> Signed
> Steven Boltz
> > LTCDR, US Navy
> > Counter Intelligence Service
> > OFFICIAL US NAVY
> > CONFIDENTIAL EYES ONLY

Nick looked up in amazement. "Have you seen this, Agent Cook?"

Cook looked at Nick a long time before answering. "No, the envelope was marked "EYES ONLY.""

"What does that mean?"

"It's short for FOR YOUR EYES ONLY. In other words, I don't have a need to know."

"Why? I thought you were running the show here?" The idea that Cook didn't have a need to know surprised Nick. Since Frank's death, Cook had changed dramatically. He had dropped much of his condescending tone, and was less accusatory. Nick had lost his disdain for the FBI agent.

Cook looked pensive. "I don't know, but I have to tell you that I'm worried. The Navy has asked you to do something and I'm betting it's something dangerous."

Nick was taken aback. "Worried? Why are you worried about me? I thought you detested everything about me!"

Cook took off his Fedora, sat heavily in a chair, and mopped his brow with a handkerchief. "Nick, I've got a son a few years younger than you. At first, I thought you were just a publicity hound, or worse, an adrenaline junkie. But now I know better. You're far from perfect, but a good kid at heart. I'm afraid that you're going to get hurt or worse."

Nick didn't care. "This is my chance to get even with Miyazaki and, by God, I'm going to take it!"

"Think a minute, Nick. Would Mac want you to risk your neck to avenge him? How about Agent Franks? His death will be in vain if you die, too."

"I thought your job was to protect the Clippers, not me. Why the sudden change of heart?"

"Frank's death has made me think about a lot of things. The dad in me is overriding the agent. It's too dangerous for a –"

"For a what?"

"For a boy! You're only a teen. Franks was a seasoned agent and he's dead. You keep going and you're next!"

"I appreciate your concern, but I'm not going to miss my chance. This may be the only shot I get. I swore I'd get Mac's killer and I will!" Nick could feel his emotions rise as he thought about Mac's death.

"If you won't think about yourself, then what about your parents? I don't want to be the one to tell them that their hard-headed son wouldn't listen to reason!"

"So what should I do, Agent Cook?"

"Decline. You're a civilian. You can just say no!"

"Fine! If you're so worried…" Nick sat down at the desk and started writing furiously on a steno tablet. He finished, tore off the top sheet, and handed it to Cook. "There you go! Read it. That should ease your conscience."

Cook looked down at the note Nick wrote:

> *In the event of my injury or death, I request that the U.S. Navy make all arrangements and handle notification.*
> *Nicolas D. Grant*

Cook looked defeated. "I guess this means you're going."

"I guess it does."

* * *

10:30 a.m., Tuesday, December 19th, 1935
Pan American Hangar, Alameda Airport, Alameda, California

Captain Tilton read from his clipboard. "I have you down as third engineer. Did you bring your logbook?"

Nick took it from his battered traveling bag. "Right here." He handed it over.

Tilton studied the logbook. "I see you still need a few more hours on the flight engineer station. However, we've got a twenty hour flight, so I'll invite you forward to the flight deck for some pilot hours, too."

"That would be great, Skipper." Nick should have been elated, but his thoughts drifted back to his discussion with Cook. *What was Cook so afraid of?*

"Nick, go down to the quartermaster and draw a uniform. Sorry, there's no time to get it fitted. I'm afraid that off the rack will have to do for this trip."

Nick was speechless. *A Pan Am uniform!* Wow! He had worn a uniform once before. That was when he had returned from Hawaii on the *Pan American Clipper* last year. But that had been a loaner. The crew had cobbled it together for him during the flight. Back then, Nick believed he was in disgrace, a runaway returning to face justice. He had been certain he would never wear the uniform again. Delighted, he tucked Boltz's package under his arm and headed off.

* * *

15:12 hours, Thursday, December 19, 1935
Aboard the *Philippine Clipper*, Seaplane Runway 31N
San Francisco Bay, California

The roar of the four Wright Cyclone engines was deafening. The noise easily passed though his earphones as the *Philippine Clipper* accelerated down the watery runway. He was strapped in next to Vic Wright, First Engineering Officer at the flight engineer station. The station was located at the apex of the fuselage, between the high wings, and too close to the engines for Nick's liking. Nick looked down and could see the top of the navigator's station, and further forward, the flight deck.

The *Philippine Clipper* surged forward as if some great weight had suddenly been cast off.

Wright leaned over, smiling. He shouted into Nick's ear. "She's on the step. It won't be long now!"

Nick checked his engine instruments. "Good thing! Those engines are getting hot! They've been in the red zone for almost forty seconds!"

"Don't worry! We've still got forty more to go before we have to warn the Skipper!"

Nick nodded back, too tired to shout anymore. It had been a tremendous amount of work preparing the Clipper. He was excited beyond all measure, but he also was starting to feel the effects of deep fatigue. So much had happened in so short a time. It would take twenty hours to fly the 2,400 miles to Honolulu and he might only get a few hours of sleep.

The Clipper was at her maximum take-off weight and lifted

briefly before lightly touching back down onto the bay. Wright yelled. "Come on baby, you can do it!" Then as if listening to her flight engineer, the *Philippine Clipper* lifted off from the bay and started a slow climb into the gathering twilight.

Nick smiled. *We're on our way! I'll bet Leilani will be surprised.*

Chapter Twenty One: No Show

7:58 a.m., Friday, December 20, 1935
Pan American Hawaiian Operations Building,
Pearl City, Hawaii

The headphones buzzed. "Finished with engines."

Nick pulled the engine mixture control levers back to the "cut off" position and waited for the engines to stop; then he killed the ignition switches. "Engines off" he called back into the headset microphone.

Flight Engineer Officer Vic Wright clapped Nick on the shoulder. "Way to go, Nick! That was nearly perfect."

Nick placed his headset on the small built-in table in front of the engineering panel. "What do you mean, nearly? That was perfect, Mr. Wright."

"Nick, a Civil Aeronautics Administration inspector would have passed you, but that's not good enough. Pan Am standards are higher than the CAA and you hesitated before acting a couple of times."

Nick rubbed his chin, deep in thought. "You're right. I wanted to make sure that I performed the correct action –

you know, get it right the first time."

"That's admirable when you're learning, but if there is an emergency – you won't have that luxury. You have to act instinctively. You won't have much time. Seconds count when you're losing altitude and spiraling into the ocean."

"Are you sure that I can't bum a ride to Wake? Think of all the training I could get in. Besides, I'd like to see John Borger and Bill Mulhahey again. I still got a lot of other buddies out there. Will you speak to Captain Tilton for me?"

"Sorry Nick, the Navy said Pearl Harbor and here you be. Be thankful that you don't have to take a boat back to San Francisco."

Nick frowned. "Darn! Okay, I'll hit the technical manuals and try to memorize all the take-off and landing actions before we head back." He tried a woeful look. "I should have a lot of time on my hands. Of course, I'd learn more if you took me on to the Philippines."

Wright chuckled. "Nice try, Nick, but the answer is still no. I'll tell you what. With Captain Tilton's permission, you can sit the engineering position for our Pearl take off and San Francisco Bay landing."

"Thanks, Mr. Wright. I won't let you down."

Wright tipped his leather peaked Pan Am uniform hat back and smiled. "I know that, Nick. You haven't yet."

Nick stood up and stretched. His tall frame barely fit in the cramped engineering space, and he could not wait to get off the *Philippine Clipper*. He'd gotten a grand total of three hours sleep during the night flight across the Pacific. He picked up his logbook and stuffed it in his coat pocket. Wearily, he straightened his tie, picked up his officer's cap and travel bag, and then followed the rest of the crew out the main hatch.

The trade winds tugged at his cap and he had to grab it before it lifted off his head. Then the wonderful smells of Hawaii filled his nostrils. It was as intoxicating as his first time nine months earlier. The palm trees swayed in the tropical breeze and flowering plumeria trees filled the world with a perfumed scent like no other. Pungent and sweet, but not overpowering, its fragrance was more like honeysuckle, mixed with a hint of cinnamon. He was thrilled to be back on Oahu, whatever the reason. It was paradise.

Some things had changed since he'd last been in the islands. Now, instead of docking at Ford Island, the Clippers tied up to the Pan Am pier in Pearl City. It was across the harbor from the island, and made getting to town much easier. No more riding a naval skiff or a long slow ferry ride from the island. He could either hop the sugar company's train or take the new inter-urban electric trolley. Either way, he could get to downtown Honolulu in less than an hour.

At the end of the pier, he looked around for Chief Ellis or Commander Boltz. A band played *Aloha Ole*, and Hula girls bestowed leis on the crew as they passed. Off the end of the pier, there was a large crowd of military and civilians. *Where were Ellis and Boltz?* Nick spied some naval officers and walked over to them. They wore formal dress white uniforms, and were engaged in a lively conversation about the merits of the navy's newest prototype fighter. Nick couldn't get their attention.

He waited a few moments, then finally interrupted. "Excuse me, Captain. I'm looking for Commander Boltz or Chief Ellis, have you seen them?"

The naval captain looked around. "Young man, I have no idea who you are talking about." He turned his back on Nick and resumed his discussion with the other officers.

* * *

3:38 p.m., Friday, December 20, 1935
Pan American Airways Facility, Pearl City,
Oahu, Hawaii Territories

Nick had completed his post flight paper work and turned it in to Wright hours ago. Still he waited. He waited until only

Tilton and Wright remained.

Tilton asked, "Nick, why are you still here? Jump in the car. This is the last one."

Nick smiled. "Can't. I'm waiting for someone."

Wright nudged Nick gently in the ribs. "It's not that cute Hawaiian girl you met last time, is it? What was her name again?"

Tilton chuckled. "It's Leilani, isn't it Nick?"

Nick felt the flush of embarrassment creep up his face but also his stomach twitched with excitement. *Leilani ... I must call her!* "Yes, her name is Leilani, but, no, it's someone else."

Wright seemed incredulous. "You mean it's a different girl? Nick, you're a regular Romeo!"

Nick smiled. "No, it's nothing like that. It's some guys from the Navy. I'm supposed to give them this package." He held up Boltz's package.

Tilton looked worried. "Why don't you bring it along to the Royal Hawaiian Hotel? We'll call your contact from there and have him pick it up."

Nick thought that sounded pretty good, but he remembered his instructions. *Wait for me at the Pan Am dock in Pearl City. I will meet you there.* "No, I've got to wait here." He pointed to the cabstand beside the terminal. "There's a cab there. I'll wait another half-hour, and then I'll take it to the hotel."

Tilton shook his head. "Okay, Nick, but I think you're making a mistake. Your contact probably got delayed. Do me a favor though?"

"Sure, Captain. What?"

"Call my room when you get in. I want to be sure my entire crew is bedded down for the evening."

"Will do, Skipper."

"Okay then. See you later." They hopped into the car and drove off.

Where was Boltz?

Nick was exhausted and tired of waiting. He sat down on the bench outside the Operations building. He leaned back, wondering what had happened to Boltz or Ellis. Looking around, he took in all that was wonderful about Hawaii. For a while, he watched the bees, busy at a plumeria tree. A couple of mocking birds called from somewhere. Vaguely he remembered Leilani telling him they were not an indigenous species. They came ashore with the first European settlers and rapidly destroyed many of the local bird species. He wondered what everybody was doing back home as he slumped on the bench. He closed his eyes and felt them burn as waves of fatigue swept his body.

Chapter Twenty Two: Mele Kaliki Maka!

5:46 p.m., Friday, December 20, 1935
Pan American Hawaiian Operations Building,
Pearl City, Oahu, Hawaii

Nick awoke with the abrupt sound of a car horn. The Middle Lock reflected the setting sun and blinded him. Nick rubbed his eyes and looked around. He'd fallen asleep on the bench. In a daze, he looked up and he saw a friendly face – a few feet away. The Asian eyes said Japanese rather than Hawaiian. His toothy smile revealed bright white teeth that offset his deep brown features.

"Hey, mister, you need a ride? Last trolley gone long time now. Where you go?"

Nick stood and rubbed his arm. He had fallen asleep on it and now, as the circulation returned, he felt the unmistakable barrage of pins-and-needles. He looked at his watch and realized he'd been asleep for hours.

Nick stood up stiffly. "*Konichiwa!*" He bowed slightly and continued in Japanese. "Nowhere. I'm waiting for someone."

The driver smiled and jumped from the cab. He stood

stock still, arms at his side and bowed deeply from the waist. *"Konichiwa! Watakushi-wa Hito, desu."* Then he rattled off at least two dozen words in Japanese like some fast-firing machine gun.

Nick threw up his hands. *"Yamete kudasai!"* He stumbled on in his kindergarten Japanese. "I only know a few Japanese words! You're speaking way too fast."

The cabbie smiled and continued but much slower, much as one might speak to a child. "I am honored that you know some Japanese." Then he reached for Nick's old, beat-up bag.

Nick clutched the package. "No. I said I'll wait." Nick picked up his bag too.

"Okay, Joe, you sorry. You get into cab. I take you to Waikiki Beach and Royal Hawaiian!" He gestured wildly as if to shoo Nick into the cab. Then he did a strange thing. He looked around at their surroundings before he got into the driver's seat.

Nick was immediately suspicious. "I said wait! *Genki desu.*" He moved back to the deserted building and found a phone booth. He dug into his pocket and retrieved a nickel. Keeping a wary eye on the Japanese cabbie, he opened his note book and dialed Leilani's number.

The phone rang twice before someone answered it. "Hello, Porta residence."

Nick recognized the voice. "Hello Consuela. It's Nick, Nick Grant, from the mainland."

"Oh, hello, Nick. Are you calling long distance?"

"No, I'm in the islands. Is Leilani home?"

"Oh, you're here! Leilani will be so excited. I'll go get her."

Nick heard Consuela put the phone down and then her footsteps receded. He thought he heard a shriek and then heard someone's footsteps running.

Someone picked up the phone and then Leilani asked. "Who is this?"

It was her! "Leilani, it's Nick. How are you?"

"Oh, Nick, is it really you?" Then her voice hardened. "This had better not be Kalani!"

"No, it's me. I flew in on the Clipper earlier today."

Leilani sounded excited. "On the *China Clipper*?"

"No, on the *Philippine Clipper*. The *China Clipper's* back at Alameda."

"Oh, the radio and papers never say which one. Everybody just calls them the *China Clipper*. Anyway, why didn't you let me know you were coming?"

Nick sighed. "I'm sorry. It was a last minute thing and there wasn't time for a telegram or phone call."

Leilani asked. "Where are you now?"

"I'm at the Pan Am building in Pearl City. Why?"

"Because I'm coming to get you!"

"Wait, no Leilani, I have to wait for someone!" Too late. The line was dead.

* * *

The cab was still waiting when Leilani wheeled the Ford Estate Wagon, or Woody, into the parking lot. It was called a Woody because Ford covered the sides with beautiful mahogany paneling. She was the only car on the otherwise deserted road. Leilani tooted the horn, stopped, opened the door, and charged towards him. Her long brown hair streamed out behind her as she ran to him. She wore a school uniform of a dark knee-length skirt and a close-fitting white blouse under an open blazer. She looked prettier than he remembered.

"Nick, I can't believe that you're here!" She threw herself into his arms and embraced him. Then she kissed him on the lips. Her lips felt full and soft and her scent – wow! It was way better than her letters! After a few seconds, they parted and she sized him up. "The uniform looks nice. Did you join the Navy?"

Nick chuckled. "No, the uniform is Juan Trippe's idea. He wants his pilots to look like merchant marine officers. His slogan is '*Pan American, America's Merchant Marine of the*

Air'. Tell me that you haven't heard it."

"Umm, can't say I have. Never mind, let's get your things and take you home."

"What?"

"Silly, Momma has invited you to stay with us. You know Momma. She won't take no for an answer."

He was tired and fed up with waiting, but felt compelled to say. "No, I've got my orders. I'm to wait here for my contacts. Besides, the rest of the crew is waiting for me at the Royal Hawaiian."

"Nick, is this more of that secret agent stuff?"

"Leilani, I'm just delivering a package for the Navy."

"Oh, well then, I'll drive you to the base to drop off the package and then take you home. You can call the hotel from there. No arguments, Mr. Grant, or would you prefer I called you by your earlier cover name – Grandmore?"

"Leilani! You're impossible!"

"You're darn tooting, Nick. But just remember, I'm worth it." She winked at him.

Nick looked into her green eyes, framed by her gorgeous hair. He wanted to touch the auburn highlights. *Later*. He sighed. "Yes, Leilani, you certainly are." He tossed his bag in back next to a pile of packages. "What are all these?"

"Christmas presents, silly. I had to hide them somewhere. How long will you be staying?"

"For about ten days. Depends on how it goes for the rest of the Clipper's trip."

"You mean you're staying through Christmas?"

"Yeah, why?"

"Mele Kaliki Maka!"

"What?"

"Merry Christmas in Hawaiian!"

Nick grinned, opened the car, and put his cap on the back seat.

Chapter Twenty Three: Alley Oops

6:16 p.m., Friday, December 20, 1935
Kamehameha Highway, Outside Pearl City,
Oahu, Hawaii Territories

Leilani pulled the Ford Estate Wagon out onto the Kamehameha Highway. She shifted the gears flawlessly as the Ford picked up speed. Nick waved at the cabbie as they left but the cabby only looked angry.

Nick sat in silence for a few seconds, but he couldn't stop thinking about the cabbie. There was something odd about his actions. "Geez, what a grump."

"Who?" Leilani depressed the clutch and downshifted as they started up a small hill.

"That cabbie. I feel sorry for him. I told him I didn't need a ride, but he insisted on waiting."

Leilani looked in the rearview mirror. "He's following us."

"Really?" Nick swung around and peered out the rear window. "Wow, he looks really angry and he's catching up!"

"We'll see about that." She punched the accelerator and the Woody surged forward.

Nick continued to look out the rear window. "He's still gaining. Can't you go any faster?"

Leilani checked her outside mirror. "No, I've got the pedal to the floor. I told Dad he should have gotten the V-8!"

All of a sudden the cab surged up on them and smashed into the rear bumper. Leilani let out a gasp as she struggled to control the Ford. Then the cab pulled out from behind and raced up alongside. His passenger side window was down and the cabbie looked at them. With a lighting quick flick of his wrist, the cabbie tossed a tire iron out the open window and at their windshield. The Woody's windshield shattered but the laminated safety glass held it together. Leilani gripped the wheel as the cracks spread. Soon it was like trying to drive while looking through a dew-covered spider's web.

They passed through the outskirts of Chinatown, but nobody was on the street. Nick looked past Leilani, out the driver's side window, just as the cabbie cut the wheel hard towards them. The cab crashed into the paneled side of the Woody. They heard breaking wood, screeching metal, and the crunch of breaking safety glass. The side window seemed to crystallize and then fell inward.

Nick opened the glove box and rummaged around.

Leilani fought to keep the Woody on the road. "What are you doing?"

"I'm looking for something to throw, like a flashlight!"

"It's under your seat!"

They entered a small town. Buildings and streets whirled by. The larger and heavier cab crashed into them again. Slowly, the cab maneuvered them toward the side of the road.

Nick reached under the seat and withdrew a huge black flashlight. It was heavy and more like a night stick. He rolled into the back seat landing next to Christmas presents.

Leilani cut the wheel back at the cab, causing it to momentarily swerve away. "Watch out for the presents."

"Okay, okay! You just drive!" Nick leaned out the window and tossed the flashlight at the cab. It hit the passenger window which shattered just as the cab slammed back into them.

He looked through the shattered windshield. They were fast approaching an alleyway.

Leilani yelled, "Hang on to something!"

She cut the wheel hard and the Woody swerved into the narrow alley impossibly fast. Nick slammed into the door as they slid into the side wall leaving a cascade of sparks. Leilani corrected and floored the gas. Nick looked ahead just in time to see a huge pile of garbage blocking the alley. Leilani was already braking, but they couldn't stop in time.

The Woody punched through the pile, scattering trash everywhere. Nick looked back to see the cab's windshield covered with discarded yellow palm leafs and old newspapers. The cabbie swerved, unable to see, and crashed into a low stone wall. Metal screeched and glass shattered as Nick watched in fascination. "That's stopped him. Let's get out of here!"

Leilani cut the wheel hard at the end of the alley and did a four wheel drift skid. They ended up in the middle of a road that paralleled Kamehameha Highway. She looked at him and smiled. "I don't think he'll be following us anymore tonight." She brought the Estate Wagon to a shuttering halt on the side of the road. They piled out. And examined the damaged car.

"Daddy is going to be so mad. Look at that huge dent in the bumper! The sides are scraped up something awful and all that broken glass. But at least I think it will get us home."

"Home?" Nick looked across the Woody. "No, we've got to make a run for the naval base!"

"Can't. It's twice as far and I'm not sure this car will make it." As if to reinforce the point, a blast of steam escaped from the side of the hood. Leilani shrugged. "Well, I've had worse. It's still drivable for a while. Hop in."

Nick looked back towards the alley but didn't see any movement "You're right. Let's get out of here before someone else tries to run us off the road."

It was pitch black now, and without street lights, it was difficult to see who else might have been lurking in the vicinity. Leilani moved the gear shift to first, popped the clutch, and spun the tires as she accelerated away. She turned a hard left and an immediate right putting them back on Kamehameha Highway. She bit her lower lip. "Daddy is going kill me! Nick, what are you mixed up in now?"

"Leilani, I told you. I was just suppose to deliver a package – nothing more."

"Don't you think it's a little odd that a Japanese cabbie tried to run us off the road?"

"Of course I do. And I aim to find out more. Maybe that's why FBI Agent Cook was against me taking the package."

"The FBI! Nick Grant, you'd better not be lying to me again!"

"Leilani, I'm not. If there was something else, something I couldn't talk about, I'd say so. No, something is fishy and it's not the ocean. "Where the heck was Boltz?"

"I don't know, Nick but it's got me worried too."

"I'd never deliberat,ely involve you in anything dangerous." *When I see Boltz, I'm going to give him a piece if my mind.*

Nick looked at Leilani's profile. She looked worried. *Who wouldn't be?* He wanted to hold her, to reassure her that everything would be alright, but before he could, he was bounced into the passenger door. Leilani had swung out and passed a slow-moving horse-drawn cart that had appeared suddenly in the bright headlights. She swerved back into her lane barely missing an oncoming truck. The truck laid on the horn as they left it behind. At the next intersection, she cut the wheel hard and slid into a turn, never slowing down.

Awed, Nick asked, "Where on earth did you learn to drive like this?"

"Oh, on the sugar plantation. Hanna and I raced the overseer's cars." She reached forward and pushed at the windshield with her purse until a small hole appeared in front of her face. "That's better. Now I can see again."

The warm island wind whistled through the opening.

Without warning, the damaged windshield began to crumple and fell onto the dashboard in a twisted mangled heap. The remaining fractured glass crashed on to their laps. The wind whipped at them, forcing tears to Nick's eyes. He pushed the mess onto the floor. Leilani did not need anything else to distract her. Nick leaned over and yelled. "Who usually won?"

"Hanna! She has no fear!" Leilani passed a car on the right, sending up clouds of red dust from the shoulder.

Nick gripped the dashboard and yelled back. "Remind me never to ride with her!"

Chapter Twenty Four: Home Sweet Home

6:42 p.m., Friday, December 20, 1935
Mauna Loa Heights, Honolulu, Oahu, Hawaii Territories

The Woody slid into a sharp turn as Leilani fought to keep it on the pavement. Nick recognized the long winding road that led up the mountain to the Porta's home. At the top, she took the gravel driveway and then shot past the palatial house. They came to a skidding stop in a cloud of white dust outside the garage.

Consuela ran out of the kitchen door smoothing her black housekeeper's dress and white apron. Mr. Porta followed. As the dust settled, Mr. Porta looked aghast at the Estate Wagon.

Leilani opened the Woody's door and flew into her father's arms. "Oh, Daddy, I was so scared!"

He hugged her back. "Leilani, what's this all about? Have you been racing again?" Porta gazed over to the Woody and noticed Nick. "Nick Grant? What on earth are you doing here?"

Nick retrieved his cap, amazingly still on the back seat. He got out of the car and walked over to Leilani's father. "Hello,

Mr. Porta." He extended his hand.

Porta disengaged from Leilani with some difficulty and shook Nick's hand. Then he sized up Nick. "Nice suit. So you came on the Clipper this morning?"

"Huh? Oh, the uniform. Yes sir, as junior flight engineer."

Porta turned back to Leilani. "So, young lady, what's this all about?"

"Daddy, Nick called earlier and Momma said that he was to stay with us, no argument. Then she left to go to her ladies' club. So I went down to pick him up from Pearl City. Then a cabbie rammed us and tried to run us off the road!"

"Oh my God! Are you two hurt?"

Nick answered, "No sir, but he did a lot of damage to your Woody."

"I can see that, Nick. Did either of you get his license plate number?"

Nick and Leilani looked at each other, aware that neither had thought of it.

Leilani said, "Daddy, I just wanted to get out of there. He was like a crazy man! I just wanted to get home."

"Well, all right. I'm glad that you two are safe. I want both of you to go inside and write down exactly what happened. Do it now, before you forget the details.

"I know you're pretty shaken up and I understand. Your mother will be home soon. She'll know what to say. I'd love to stay and comfort you but I have an important business meeting. Please do not disturb me until after my guest has left. Then we will call the police and file a report."

Nick grabbed the brown package and his overnight bag and followed them into the house. He'd have to report this incident to Boltz. But he'd have to wait. Boltz had left him to fend for himself, so now Boltz could wait. Besides, he needed to think it through. *It was so strange.*

* * *

They sat at the dining room table and wrote out the events

as best as they remembered. Even now, so soon after the incident, some of the details seemed to be fading from his memory. A bird called from outside and he looked up. Out the open windows, the estate looked the same. The side yard was full of flowering plants and their welcoming smells permeated the house.

Past the manicured lawns, and the low hills, he could see the Pacific. It was too far away to hear, but he remembered the sound of the crashing surf from his August nights on Waikiki. It amazed him that just twenty-four hours ago, he was 2,400 miles east, in Alameda, California. He had flown it twice now and still found it hard to believe how amazing that feat was.

Leilani looked up from her pencil and paper. "I can't figure out why Dad wasn't angry."

"He was pretty calm, considering the state of the Woody. I'd say he's a pretty cool customer."

"He's a real hot-head and gets upset fast. Mom says it's his hot Latin blood and that I got my Portuguese temper from him."

"Your Dad has a temper?"

"Oh, yeah! But he didn't blow his top today... and that's odd. In fact, he'd didn't even seem to care."

Nick looked at her. "Maybe he was worried about his business meeting. Any idea who he's meeting?"

She stood up and moved towards the open window. The trade winds blew the curtains open as she gazed at the ocean. "It's probably that creepy Mr. Moto."

"Who's he?"

"Oh, he's some local big shot. He wants to buy some of Dad's products."

Nick stood up and moved over to the window and behind Leilani. He placed his arm around her waist and held her. It felt so good to hold her again and he breathed deeply. She smelled so enticing. "What's so creepy about him? I mean, the economy is still pretty bad. It's great that your Dad has customers."

Leilani shrugged. "It's not that. Moto just gives me the creeps."

"Why?" Nick was only half listening. The feel of Leilani's body so close was intoxicating. His worries, concerns, and troubles seemed to melt away. He wished he could just hold her like this forever.

"Dad always discusses his business at dinner. I mean all the boring stuff in great detail. Said that we had to know the business, because someday we'd be running it."

"Sounds about right to me." Nick put his chin on her shoulder and closed his eyes to burn the feel of her skin into his brain. He never wanted to forget.

"Well, that's just it. He won't say a word about the deal with Mr. Moto. When I asked him specifically, he got mad and said that he didn't want to talk about it."

Nick noticed a large black limousine climbing the hill towards the house. "Looks like that might be him."

Leilani looked where Nick pointed. "It's him alright, riding in that enormous Packard convertible. It's so ostentatious!"

He turned back to Leilani. "Is that what you dislike about Moto?"

"No, it's his eyes. They are as black as coal and seem bottomless. It's like looking into something dead. He's so creepy–yuk!"

Nick remembered eyes like that... Miyazaki's. However, that was a secret for another day's telling. "I've seen eyes like that and I know the feeling. I wonder why the top is still up? It's such a beautiful evening."

The huge Packard stopped under the Portico, the Porta's covered driveway. The driver hopped out and ran around to open a door for the passenger. A well-dressed man stepped out and moved towards the front door. To Nick's utter horror, he recognized the passenger. He now understood why Leilani got the creeps when she was near this customer. The man she knew as Mr. Moto was in fact Lieutenant Commander Toshio Miyazaki!

Chapter Twenty Five: Who's Your Daddy?

7:32 p.m., Friday, December 20, 1935
Mauna Loa Heights, Honolulu, Oahu, Hawaii Territories

Nick blinked several times to clear his vision. It seemed that Miyazaki was the man called Mr. Moto. He turned Leilani around to face him. "Is *that* Moto?"

Leilani looked more annoyed than surprised. "Yes! What's wrong with you?"

Nick put his hands on Leilani's shoulders. He enjoyed the contact but regretted what he had to say next. "Leilani, remember when I told you about my old boss, Joe McMillan?"

"You mean that one that was murdered?"

"Yes! And that man you are calling Mr. Moto really is Miyazaki! Miyazaki is Mac's murderer!"

"What? Are you sure, Nick?"

"Absolutely! What is he doing here? And what does he want from your father?"

"I don't know, but I've got to warn Dad!" She tried to struggle free of Nick's grasp but he held firm.

"Leilani, wait!"

She pounded her fists on his chest. "Let me go! Moto or Miyazaki, I don't care! I've got to warn Dad!"

Nick simply hugged her to him. "Shush, your father is in no immediate danger."

She pushed back from him and looked him in the eyes. "How do you know that?"

"Leilani, you don't know who we're dealing with. Believe me, if Miyazaki wanted to harm your father, it would already be too late. No, he's after something, but what?"

Leilani thought for a few seconds. "What aren't you telling me, Nick?"

"Leilani, don't make this any harder than it is, please. I can't tell you much."

She looked up him. "No more lies, Nick. Remember?"

"I know, but some things I can't talk about. I told you that last time."

"But this is different! That's my father in there with a man you say is a murderer!"

Nick looked down at her. "You've got to trust me, that's all I can say...and you can't tell anyone about Miyazaki. There's no telling what he'll do if he finds out you know."

Leilani spun away from Nick and then turned to face him. Shaking with rage, she asked "What am I supposed to do Nick? Go out and curtsey to that monster?"

"Leilani, we've got to keep calm and use our heads. He's here for some purpose. He wants something that your dad has, or can provide. Think, what could it be?"

"How should I know?"

"Come on, has something unusual happened lately?"

She thought for a few moments. Then understanding lighted her face. "A convoy of Army trucks."

Nick was puzzled. "What would Army trucks be doing up here. Is there a training area behind your house?"

"No, the road dead ends at the next house up and it sits on a sheer cliff."

Nick racked his brain. "Have you noticed anything unusual

at the house?"

"There's the radio gear."

"What type of radio gear?"

"Oh, I don't know! I do know it had RCA RDF stenciled on the side of the boxes."

"Holy cow, that's sensitive stuff! It's only for U.S. military planes and the Pan American trans-oceanic airliners!"

Leilani bit her bottom lip. "Remember, when you first visited back in March?"

"Remember? How I could I forget? That's the first time we kissed!"

Leilani blushed. "No, not that! When we were in the garden, Dad took John Borger into the study and questioned him about the RDF."

"Oh, I remember all right! John was sore for days. He said I was making hay with you while he was getting the third degree from your Dad."

Leilani's eyes narrowed. "What did you tell him about us?"

"Nothing, but when Hanna and John found us the garden, well… I guess he put two and two together. But later he joked that your Dad would be a perfect spy."

Leilani giggled. "Daddy, a spy? You've got to be kidding! There's some weird stuff going on here...but I know there's a simple explanation. He's been storing the RDF gear in the pool house. Wanna take a look?"

"You bet!"

She grabbed his hand and pulled. "Come on!"

* * *

Nick replaced the top of the wooden packing crate. He turned the screws back in using the same quarter he'd used to remove them. "There's no doubt about it, that's Radio Corporation of America, lightweight Radio Direction Finding equipment. But how did your Dad get it and what's he going to do with it? It's very expensive."

Leilani was standing beside the window. She was keeping

an eye on the front of the house in case Porta and Miyazaki decided to come to the pool house. "He said something about outfitting our fishing fleet."

Nick shook his head. "That doesn't make any sense. For the cost of one these sets, he could outfit his entire fleet with maritime RDF equipment. There are four cases and the one we opened had three complete sets. How many fishing boats does your Dad own?"

Leilani looked back at Nick. "Last count we had 48."

Mr. Porta's wealth still amazed Nick. He shook his head. "No, I doubt they're for his fishing fleet."

Leilani stared at Nick. "Are you implying that my father is involved in something...unseemly?"

"No, but I can't figure it out. What do you think?"

Leilani looked back out the window. "I'm not sure what to think anymore. I can tell you this. An Army truck delivered these crates a couple of days ago."

"An Army truck?" Nick thought fast. *Does that mean that there's a traitor in the Army's ranks? Is Porta in cahoots with a traitor? Or is Porta a traitor too?* He moved up next to Leilani just as Mr. Porta and Miyazaki came into view. Nick and Leilani ducked out of sight below the window, and then slowly peered up over the sill. The men had stopped by the Packard and were discussing something. Nick couldn't hear the words, but it seemed friendly. Finally, Miyazaki bowed to Porta who bowed back. Then the driver opened the back door for Miyazaki who stepped inside. The driver closed the door, jumped in the front, and drove off. Porta stood under the Portico and watched until the Packard disappeared down driveway and was gone.

Leilani rushed to the pool house door and jerked it open. She quickly marched towards her father. Nick jogged to catch up with her.

She stopped in front of her father and glared at him. "What are doing with that man?"

Mr. Porta raised an eyebrow then lowered it to form a

straight line. "Conducting business, young lady, and I don't care for your tone of voice."

Undeterred, Leilani continued. "Daddy, I told you that man give me the creeps. Why do you have to have him here at our home?"

Porta spread his hands. "He is not the first businessman that I have entertained in our home."

"If you must deal with him, why don't you use your fancy office downtown?"

"He has asked for a less public place to conduct his business and I agreed." Porta put his hands on his hips and stared down at his daughter. "Besides, this deal is very important to me."

"Why Daddy? Did Mr. Miyazaki offer you lots of money? And how much do we really need, anyway?" Leilani gestured toward the lavish house, the pool and garage filled with fancy automobiles.

Mr. Porta paled at the mention of Miyazaki's name. "What name did you say? His name is Moto!"

"Moto...Miyazaki, who cares? Daddy, that man is trouble and I want you to end your dealings with him. I'm afraid for you, for all of us."

Porta looked at his daughter and sighed. "It's too late for that now, dear. I have to go through with the deal. If I don't, the whole family may be in danger." He looked at the ground unable to meet Leilani's eyes. "I can't tell you any more. I'm sorry."

Leilani looked at her father, then at Nick, who had silently witnessed the exchange. "Well then, I'll just leave you two secret keepers to yourselves. I'm sure that you will have nothing to talk about!" She walked into the house and slammed the front door with such force that the house seemed to shake on its very foundation.

Chapter Twenty Six: Protégée

8:42 p.m., Friday, December 20, 1935
Mauna Loa Heights, Honolulu, Oahu, Hawaii Territories

Mr. Porta and Nick stood in stunned silence, staring at the front door. Finally, Nick broke the silence. "Mr. Porta, could I use your phone to make a local call?"

Mr. Porta narrowed his eyes in suspicion. "Why? Who are you planning to call?"

"I have to call Captain Tilton and let him know that I have accepted Mrs. Porta's kind invitation, that I will not need the room at the Royal Hawaiian Hotel."

Porta seemed confused. "Captain? What kind of captain? Army, Navy, or Coast Guard?"

"None of those, sir, The *Philippine Clipper* Captain."

"Oh, yes of course. Sorry. But what invitation are you referring to?'

"Mrs. Porta's offer to stay here instead of the Royal Hawaiian. But if you'd rather I go –"

"No, no, stay by all means. I'm already in enough trouble with my daughter." Porta seemed to visibly age before Nick's eyes. "It's been a long day."

Nick picked up his bag. "Okay, so can I make the call?"

"What? Oh yes, I'm sorry." But Porta put a hand on Nick's shoulder and stopped him from entering the house. "But I have to ask you one more thing, Nick."

"Yes, sir?"

"Any idea why Leilani called Mr. Moto 'Miyazaki'?"

"Who's Miyazaki?"

They eyed each other for a long moment before Mr. Porta dropped his hand. "No, I didn't think so. Go ahead and make your call. Then see Consuela. She'll find you something to eat."

"Thanks." Nick entered the front hall and rubbed his shoulder. Porta had used a lot of strength. He looked back and watched Porta slowly walk towards the garden. *I don't think he believed me.*

Inside, Nick put down his bag and the package next to the hall telephone stand. He sat in the chair, opened his notebook, and dialed the hotel's number. The desk clerk connected him and a sleepy Tilton answered the phone. "Hello."

"Hello Captain Tilton. It's Nick Grant."

"Nick, where the devil are you?"

"I'm at the Porta House. They've asked me to stay here while I'm on Oahu."

"Porta House? Explain."

"It's Leilani's family home. Mrs. Porta insisted that I stay with them and I can't refuse. I hope that's okay."

Tilton sounded more awake. "Let me get this straight. Your girlfriend's mother asked you to stay with them...under the same roof?"

"Well, sort of. I will be staying in the pool house on the grounds."

Tilton laughed. "Well, I'll be! These island girls sure move fast. You watch your step, young man. If you're not careful, you'll be married before we return from the Philippines!"

"Oh, it's nothing like that, Captain."

"I guess it's okay. I mean it is certainly a modern concept, but, what the heck, these are modern times."

"Do you need me tomorrow?"

Tilton turned all business. "Yes, be at the Pearl City facility at 10:00 a.m. sharp. We're going to review the flight from Alameda, start to finish."

"Aye, aye, Captain. See you at ten sharp."

"Okay, good night, Nick. Try to stay out of trouble."

"I'll try. Good night, sir."

The line went dead.

Nick looked around. He didn't see anybody, so he risked another call. He dialed the next number in his notebook.

A male voice answered. "Coral 6-257."

Nick was a little taken back. "Hello, I'd like to speak with Commander Boltz or Chief Ellis, please."

The man paused then asked, "Who's calling?"

"Nick Grant."

The man shot back. "Are you in a safe location?"

"What? I don't know what you mean."

"Are you safe?"

What the heck? "Yes, I'm safe."

"Good. Hold the line, please."

About thirty seconds later Nick heard a familiar voice say, "This is Chief Ellis."

Nick exploded. "Where were you guys? I've still got the package. What do you want me to do with it?"

"Easy, Nick. One question at a time, okay. Something came up and we got delayed."

"Delayed! Some cabbie tried to kill me and my girl and all you can say is you got delayed?"

"Yes, we know. We have him in custody."

"How could you have him in custody? What's going on, Chief?"

"I can't say over the phone. Can you get to our office, say about 0800 tomorrow morning?"

"How do I find it?"

"Get to the Pearl Harbor main gate and go into the visitor shack. Wait for me there."

"What about your precious package?"

"Oh that. Uh, yeah bring it along. Sorry, gotta go. Bye, Nick." Ellis hung up.

Thanks a lot!

Nick slammed the phone on its cradle. He'd almost been killed for that darn package and now it seemed like an afterthought to Ellis! Disgusted, he rose from the chair, grabbed his luggage and the package. He almost threw it at the wall, but decided against it at the last moment. Instead, he shoved it into his bag and headed for the kitchen to find Consuela. It had been a long day and he felt like he could eat an entire roast pig by himself.

* * *

9:02 p.m., Friday, December 20, 1935
Fort Shafter, Oahu, Hawaii Territories

Major Forrest Davis, U.S. Army Counterintelligence Corps, replaced the receiver in its desktop cradle. He'd just finished speaking with his top agents and things were not good. *Who the hell was Nick Grant?* He sighed, opened his bottom desk drawer and removed a dusty bottle of Jack Daniels Whiskey and a shot glass. Davis didn't often drink, but when he did, it was never more than one, and always the finest Tennessee sipping whiskey. He poured a generous portion into the glass and sniffed deeply before holding up the glass to the single light bulb that illumined his small office. *Ahh, tonight I need this. Just when everything was going so well, now this. Who was that guy?* He tossed it back and then replaced the glass and the bottle.

Davis leaned forward and toggled the switch on his RCA desktop intercom. "Special Agent Clendenny."

Clendenny answered instantaneously, his voice tinny on the intercom speaker. "Yes, sir?"

"Top, call the team members. I want a meeting in the secure conference room at 0730 tomorrow."

"Yes, sir. But I'm not a First Sergeant."

"You're my top NCO and I'll call you anything I darn well please."

"Yes, sir, just don't call me late for dinner. Anything you to want me to tell them?"

"Tell them the mission is in danger and we're going to move up the timeline."

The door opened and Army Counter Intelligence Special Agent Ron Clendenny walked into the room. His intense green eyes never wavered from Davis's face. His stare looked for answers to unanswered questions. He was slender but muscular and stood about five feet ten. "Sir, is that wise?"

Davis smiled. "You trying to tell me my job, Ron?"

Clendenny shook his head. "You know better than that, Forest. How long we been working together now?"

Davis sat back and folded his hands behind his head. "Must be, what, seven years?"

"Eight. And you always said, 'If you got a problem, come see me'. So what, now that you're wearing major's rank, you're starting to act like all the other officers?"

Davis smiled. "I'm a mustang and I'll always be one. Officer Candidate School graduates seldom rise above major and you know it. You'd be wearing major oak leafs too, if you hadn't chickened out of OCS. So state your problem, Top."

Clendenny turned a desk chair around and sat facing Davis. Clendenny folded his arms across the back of the chair." The way I see it, Forrest, we start screwing with the timeline and we risk the entire op. There's too much riding on this and we've got a good chance to nail this guy. And stop calling me Top."

"You call me by my first name and you want me to stop calling you Top?"

"Need I remind you, Major, sir, you said I could use your first name when out of public earshot."

"Point taken, Ron. But you want to tell me why some seventeen-year old Pan American flyboy knows the real name of our target?"

"When did that happen?"

"About five minutes ago. Protégée just called me."

Clendenny clinched his fists and bit back a curse. Then he focused his green eyes on Davis. "Does our target know yet?"

"God, I hope not. If he does, Protégée is dead along with his entire family and Miyazaki slips away...again."

Chapter Twenty Seven: The Cord

6:02 a.m., Saturday, December 21, 1935
Mauna Loa Heights, Honolulu, Oahu, Hawaii Territories

Nick awoke with a start. He sat up and looked out the window onto a tropical scene. *What?* Disoriented, he heard a myna bird song and tired to think. *Where the heck am I?* He looked out the pool house window, into the dawn and remembered. The sunrise streamed through the tall cumulus clouds and reminded him of last summer on the Pacific atolls. The horizon was streaked with hues of pink and gold, offset by the azure blue of the Pacific. He rubbed the sleep from his eyes and wondered if he'd ever return to Midway and Wake. *Not enough sleep! Too many dreams.* Wearily, he grabbed his toilet bag and made his way to the bathroom.

After a long hot shower and quick shave, Nick dressed in a clean shirt and his Pan Am uniform. He checked his appearance in the floor length mirror. His reflection showed a young man who was a little too tall and could have used a few more pounds. He checked his tie and followed the scent of fresh coffee over to the main house.

He walked into the kitchen and Consuela smiled. "Good morning, Nick. Did you sleep well?" She handed him a mug of steaming coffee.

"Not really, Consuela. Thinking about stuff." Nick sat at the table and took a sip from his mug. "Mmm, this is good coffee." He noticed Leilani silently eating her breakfast. "Good morning, Leilani."

Leilani ignored him. "Consuela, do we have any mango jelly for the banana bread?"

"Yes, dear." Consuela put the jelly on the table. "Where are your manners? Aren't you going to say good morning to Nick?"

Leilani stopped eating and looked at Nick. "No."

Nick stared back, and then winked at her. *Was that a glimmer of a smile?* He turned to Consuela. "Any chance of getting some eggs?"

"Sure, Nick. How do you want them?"

"Scrambled...like my life."

Leilani giggled.

Encouraged, Nick asked. "Will you share the bread, Leilani?"

She wordlessly slid the loaf over.

"Thanks."

She continued to eat her breakfast.

He looked out the window into the glorious morning and changed tactics. "Ho hum, another day in paradise. If my girl would talk to me, it would be perfect."

That time Leilani did smile...but briefly.

Consuela placed a plate of scrambled eggs in front of him and refilled his coffee cup. The coffee smelled wonderful. He lifted the cup and took a sip. "Consuela this coffee is really great!"

Leilani's smile lit up Nick's world. "It's from Daddy's Kona coffee plantation on the big island."

Nick put the cup down and smiled back. "Your smile is better but isn't this the big island?"

Leilani picked up her plate and took it over to the sink. "You're still a silver-tongued *Haole*."

Leilani returned to the table and sat down. "No, silly, it's the island of Hawaii. Daddy closed a deal with a distributor a few weeks ago. He shipped two tons to the mainland last week and will ship two more each month. And it has nothing to do with Mr. Moto." She crossed her arms and looked at Nick.

At the sound of Moto's name, Consuela clucked her tongue. "I don't like that man. Best your father should not have dealings with him. But no one ever asks for my opinion."

Leilani and Nick smiled. Then Leilani reached across the table and took Nick's hands. "Oh Nick, I'm not mad at you. I'm worried sick about Daddy."

Nick gently squeezed her hands. "Will you give me a ride to town? I have a meeting at eight. If you drive, maybe we can talk."

"Would you rather borrow a car? We have so many."

Nick shook his head. "I'd rather that you drove."

Leilani stood. "Okay, but if I wreck another car, I'll be grounded for life."

"Then we'll have to be more careful." Nick carried his half-eaten breakfast to the sink. "I'm sorry, Consuela, I guess I lost my appetite."

"Oh, that's okay, Nick. It must be love."

"Excuse me, Consuela, what did you say?" Nick wasn't sure that he'd heard correctly.

"Oh nothing, Nick. I was just thinking out loud." Consuela turned back to the sink and began humming.

Nick was confused. *Were his mixed-up feelings a sign of love?*

Leilani looked at the wall clock. "Come on, Nick. It's time to go."

At the garage, Leilani choose a cream-colored 1935 Cord Roadster. Nick helped her remove the ragtop and stow it under a small snap-on cover. Nick ran his hands along the

Cord. *It's long, low and very fast.* "Wow! I can't believe that your Dad lets you drive the Cord."

Leilani started the engine and they shot out of the garage. She downshifted at the first sharp curve without slowing down. The car felt solid as a railroad car. It sat the road without a noticeable body lean. She tucked a lock of hair behind her ear. "Haven't you ridden in a Cord before?"

"Leilani, I've never seen this one close before. I thought only movie stars drove Cords." Nick ran his hand along the walnut dashboard. He loved the feel of the soft leather seats. *This car is absolutely sinful when so many are still hungry.* He pushed those thoughts aside. It wasn't his car...unfortunately.

Leilani accelerated out of the curve and shifted into third gear. "A client went broke and gave it to Dad for payments he couldn't make. Dad says he's going to sell it, but he can't seem to find a buyer."

Nick yelled over the noise of the howling wind. "I don't wonder! Back home this car costs as much as a house."

Leilani gave him a sly look. "Do you want to drive it?"

"You have to be kidding! Of course I do!"

She eased off the gas, pulled over and they switched positions. Nick dropped the gearshift lever into first gear, popped the clutch, and promptly stalled the engine. Sheepishly, he looked at Leilani. "It's nothing like the clutch on my old truck."

She leaned over and kissed him on the cheek. "Treat it gently, more like a woman. And remember, if you scratch it, it's not my neck."

"And what a pretty neck it is." Nick dropped a quick kiss on the back of Leilani's neck. "My lady."

She giggled. "Come on, let's go! And this time don't stall it." She moved to the back seat. "Now you're my chauffer. Drive on!"

A few minutes later Nick turned the Cord into the main gate of Pearl Harbor Naval Base. When they stopped in the line of cars awaiting admittance, everybody turned to gawk at the car.

Leilani was in a playful mood. From the back seat, she waved her hand as if she were a movie star in a parade. In his Pan American uniform, Nick looked a great deal like a chauffeur and he acted the part.

One of the Navy guards, a Shore Patrolman, or SP, took a look and started to move the other cars out of the way. Another SP quickly stopped the inbound traffic.

They waved Nick through and as the car passed, two SPs came to attention and saluted. Unsure what to do, Nick returned a cavalier salute and drove on. He stopped next to the visitor shack and an astonished Chief Ellis.

Nick killed the engine and handed the keys to Leilani. She looked back at the cars in line. The other drivers were gawking at them and Leilani smiled. "What was that all about?"

Ellis stood with his fists on his hips. "Grant, where on earth did you get a '35 Cord?" Without waiting for an answer, Ellis leaned over and ran his hands over the gleaming cream hood. "This is the fastest production car in the world. You got Carol Lombard stashed in the trunk?"

"There are no movie stars aboard, Chief. Sorry." Nick nodded toward the main gate. "What gives with those SPs? That was weird."

Ellis chuckled. "Oh, those knuckleheads thought you were the Admiral."

"The Admiral? I'm a bit too young, don't you think?"

"It's the car. The Admiral has a cream-colored Ducati and they're too dumb to know the difference. All they know is that it's the same color!" The Chief opened the car door and helped Leilani out.

"Whatever you say." Nick turned to Leilani. "Chief Ellis, this is my girl, Leilani Porter. Leilani, this is Chief Boson's Mate Ellis, U.S. Naval Intelligence."

They shook hands." Nice to meet you, miss. Nick kiss your girl goodbye, Commander Boltz is waiting."

Nick hugged Leilani and she threw her arms around his

neck. "So are you still sore at me, Leilani?"

Her green eyes sparkled. "Maybe a little." Then she kissed Nick lightly on the lips.

Nick smiled. "Then I guess I better take you out to dinner and beg for mercy."

"You'd better." She giggled again and looked over his shoulder. "Right now, the Chief looks impatient." She let go and waved. "Good bye, Chief Ellis."

Ellis touched his cap. "Goodbye, miss."

Leilani gracefully walked to the driver's seat, sat behind the wheel and started the engine. Then she pulled a U-turn in front of the four lanes of traffic entering the naval base. Horns blared and the SPs scrambled to stop the traffic. Leilani punched the accelerator and the Cord leapt out onto Kamehameha Highway. She drove away, oblivious to the chorus of angry car horns and shouts.

Nick watched the receding car. *God she's so beautiful. I sure hope she lives!*

Ellis watched her go, too. "Dames," he sighed. "Don't they make the world go around?"

"I'm beginning to think she is my world."

Ellis looked hard at Nick. "You know, Grant, we just might make a sailor out of you yet."

Nick cocked his head. "Not if I can help it."

Ellis chuckled. "We'll see."

Chapter Twenty Eight: Who's Fooling Who?

8:00 a.m., Thursday, December 21, 1935
Building 3801, Pearl Harbor Naval Base,
Oahu, Hawaii Territories

Commander Steven Boltz looked up from the pile of papers strewn across his desk as Nick followed Chief Ellis into the room. Boltz held up his hand. "Just a minute, Nick. Ellis, cover the wall map."

"Aye, aye, sir." Ellis deftly pulled a curtain over the wall map, but not before Nick saw red pins struck into a map of the Pacific Ocean. The cover was navy blue with white stenciled letters:

**TOP SECRET CODEWORD
SPECIAL INTELLIGENCE**

Boltz stood. "That's better. Come in, Nick. Have a seat!" He extended his hand. "It's good to see you again, shipmate. Would you like a Coca-Cola or maybe some coffee?"

Nick took the offered hand and felt the firm grip. "Is it Kona Coffee?"

Boltz looked at Ellis. "Chief?"

"No sir! It's Navy coffee – best in the world."

Nick shook his head. "No thanks, I'll have a Coca-Cola. I've tasted Navy coffee."

Boltz chuckled. "Nick, you're such a civilian. I hope to change that someday."

Nick sat down and then tossed his package at Boltz. "You forget about this, Commander?"

Boltz snatched it from the air then handed it to Ellis, who glared at Nick. A big man, Ellis resembled a prize fighter more than a sailor.

"At ease, Chief," Boltz said. Then he looked at Nick. "That was impolite, don't you think?"

"Impolite? Not showing up for a meeting with me after I traveled 2,400 miles is impolite." With every word, Nick's temper escalated. "Impolite would be failing to leave word, or even making a phone call. Pan Am has telephones operators who take messages for crewmembers! You could have gotten me or my girl killed!"

Boltz banged on his desk. "You were in no danger until you disobeyed your instructions. You didn't wait!"

Nick shot to his feet. "I hadn't slept in two days but I *waited* almost ten hours! And *you're* angry? Give me a break!"

Boltz leaned across the desk. He was at least a head shorter than Nick, but his fury made him seem taller. "I told you to wait. I thought I could trust you. I gave you a key part to play in this operation. Then you go and blow the whole thing!"

"How? I waited for hours. I called your office, but you weren't available. What was I supposed to think? I figured something else more important came up and you forgot to let me know."

Boltz looked confused. He sat down and looked up at Nick. "Is that what you thought?"

Nick lowered his voice. "It wouldn't be the first time that an adult blew off a kid."

Boltz gestured for him to sit back down. "I don't think of you as a kid. I thought you knew that." He looked at Ellis.

"Chief, please get coffee, Nick's Coca-Cola and then rejoin us."

Ellis nodded, placed the package on Boltz's desk, and left.

Boltz stared at Nick a few moments then blew out a breath. "Okay, let's start again. My message said we had a good chance at nailing Miyazaki – remember?"

"I remember, but my part was to deliver that package." Nick gestured towards the package.

"Well, no…actually, *you* were the bait."

Nick leapt to his feet. "What!"

Boltz waved Nick to sit. "I regret that I couldn't tell you for security reasons. However, let me ask you this…if I offered you a part in nabbing Miyazaki, would you take it?"

"Yes."

"Even if I told you it would require you being used as bait?"

"Absolutely! You know how I feel about Mac's murderer. I would have waited until hell froze over, had I known. Why didn't you just tell me?"

Boltz leaned back in his chair. "Do we still have our deal?"

"You mean about not spilling the beans to the press or anyone else?"

"That's the one."

"Yeah, I guess."

Boltz leaned forward. "I have to make sure, Nick. I'm taking an awful risk. If word gets out that I've shared classified information with a high school student, I could lose my commission… maybe even go to the brig for a few years."

"I gave you my word and I will honor it. Still *you* wouldn't trust me. Why didn't you tell me?"

"We call it Operational Security, or OPSEC. Good OPSEC means that very few people know all the details. The more who know, the greater the chance that we blow the op. I want Miyazaki as much as you do, Nick."

"Oh yeah? Why, Commander?"

"He killed José Padilla, a close childhood friend." For a moment Boltz seems lost in thought. Then he continued. "The Navy stationed my dad in the Philippines when I was kid. José was our housekeeper's son and we grew up together. He was the closest thing I had to a brother."

"So your Dad was Navy, too."

"The Boltz men have been Navy for five generations," Boltz explained with pride.

Nick nodded. "How did José get killed?"

"José loved the idea of democracy. The U.S. had planned to hand over the former Spanish colony to the Philippine people. But the Japanese had other ideas. José worked for Naval Intelligence as a local agent. Through hard work and taking risks, he found out about a Japanese directed fifth column movement."

"What's a fifth column movement?" Nick asked.

"It's a multifaceted attempt to overthrow a government. It consists of propaganda, lies, false accusations, sabotage, and murder of elected officials. The story line was that the U.S. never intended to give the Philippines back to the people. Riots had already broken out and many people were injured; some were killed.

"José uncovered a truly horrifying plot. He'd worked his way into the local Japanese-Philippine Friendship Club. That was the front for Japanese fifth column efforts in Manila. He discovered a plan for Philippine sympathizers to blow up the *USS Cleveland* while in dry dock. Jose said he knew who the mastermind was." Boltz paused a moment.

"Miyazaki?" Nick asked.

"Exactly."

The vision of the ensuing inferno stunned Nick. "My God! Hundreds of civilian workers could have been killed or wounded."

Boltz nodded solemnly. "I told José that he should never have come contacted me directly, especially at my duty station in broad daylight. He'd broken all our elaborate cut-outs, cover routines, and safeguards. Essentially, José had blown his cover. Luckily, he came in time to stop the plot and we arrested the Philippine perpetrators. Unfortunately, the

Japanese got wind of the raid and Miyazaki got away.

"José claimed that the police were corrupt and they had tipped off the Japanese. Since he was on Subic Bay Naval base he was safe, but he worried about his wife and child who lived in Manila. He said he had to get them and bring them on the base.

"I agreed and left to arrange for a car and a couple of big tough SPs to join us. By the time I returned, he was gone. I knew where José lived and we drove there as fast as we could. However, Miyazaki got there first.

"When I ran upstairs to his apartment, Miyazaki had backed José into a corner. José was standing in front of his family, holding a chair to ward off Miyazaki's sword." Boltz stopped, swallowed hard, and then continued. "José held his stomach in the other. Miyazaki had slashed José horribly and blood had soaked through his shirt.

"I drew my .45 automatic. But, before I could shoot, Miyazaki whirled and kicked my hand just as I fired. I missed Miyazaki. The SPs heard the shot and charged up the stairs behind me. They burst in and fired wildly and missed as well. With the Devil's own luck, Miyazaki dove out the window and took off across the rooftops.

"I told the SPs to check on José's wife and child, little José. Then I went to my old friend's side. He had collapsed onto the floor. Blood was everywhere. Miyazaki had sliced open José's belly. When José dropped to the floor I could see that Miyazaki had disemboweled him. I could not believe José had remained standing...let alone fighting. He knew he was dying but managed to ask me to find Miyazaki and kill him."

Nick looked at Boltz. "Commander, I had no idea. What happened to José's wife?"

"Maria, too, died by Miyazaki's sword. José never knew. His death preceded hers. But their son lives. I pay for his keep with the Sisters of Mercy Orphanage – Irish nuns that do God's work in the Philippines. Young José is much like his father, and I'll make sure that he gets a good education. I owe that to my old friend."

Ellis knocked, and then came in with the tray of drinks. Nick took a sip of Coca-Cola then asked, "Why were the Japanese stirring up trouble in the Philippines?"

Boltz sighed. "The U.S. Navy was considering stationing the Asiatic Fleet there. The Japanese are intent upon Pacific expansion, and our fleet could have threatened those ambitions. They hoped that their fifth column movement would foil any hope of that eventuality."

Nick sat back in his chair and let the details of the story sink in. Then a frightening thought hit him. "Commander! What about my family back on the mainland? Are they in any danger?"

"I don't think so, Nick. Special Agent Cook has men watching your house."

"That's a relief." Another thought hit him. "Did Agent Cook know the details of this mission? He was very much against me taking the flight out here."

"No. If I could have told him, I could have told you. Apart from the Chief and me, no one else had the details. I don't trust our long haul communications. I'm convinced that the Japanese are reading our out-bound messages. Miyazaki always seems to be one step ahead of us and that could be part of the reason."

Nick decided to share some information. "Do you know where Miyazaki is right now?"

"No. Your girl picked you up at the terminal and it threw a monkey wrench into our well-laid plans. When the cabbie followed you, we followed him. That meant we broke our cover. Miyazaki or one of his men was almost certainly there and watched us pull out to pursue you. He would have recognized the trap. We nabbed the cabbie, but he's not talking."

"I'd like to give him my compliments."

Boltz smiled. "I'll bet you would, but you're not going near him!"

"Too bad."

"Nick, we have no reason to hold him and we're turning him over to HPD today."

"HPD?"

"Honolulu Police Department. If the cabbie sees you, Miyazaki's going to find out that we're still in cahoots."

"Commander, Miyazaki is here in Hawaii, masquerading as Mr. Moto, a rich Japanese business man."

Boltz shot him a look of astonishment. "How can you know that?"

"He visited my girlfriend's father last night, and I saw him there."

"My God, did he see you? No, strike that. If he'd seen you, you'd be dead." Boltz got up and paced behind his desk. "What was he doing at the Porta house?"

"I don't know. I couldn't hear and Porta wouldn't talk about it. But I also found some very sensitive RDF equipment. I think Miyazaki's working some sort of a deal with Mr. Porta. I'll bet it's got something to do with the RDF equipment. It's the same stuff that we use on the Clippers, and the Navy uses for its carrier based aircraft."

Ellis sat forward. "Grant, are you sure it's RCA RDF equipment?"

Nick turned to face Ellis. "I saw the crates, Chief, and I opened one. It's RDF all right. I carried a lot of components ashore at Midway and Wake. I also became proficient in RDF operations for my flight engineering exam."

Ellis looked at Boltz. "You know anything about this, sir?"

Boltz shook his head. "No, it's news to me, Chief." He looked at Nick. "What else can you tell me?"

"Mr. Porta stores the RDF equipment on the first floor of the pool house. I'm staying on the second floor."

Boltz rubbed his chin. "Pretty big pool house?"

Nick nodded. "It's only a bit smaller than my parents Alameda home."

Ellis put his coffee cup down on the tray. "How on earth

did Porta get his hands on such sensitive equipment?"

Nick looked at Ellis. "Leilani said that an Army truck brought it up a few days ago. Does that mean that there's a traitor in the Army?"

"Maybe." Boltz started pacing again. "But it could be something else." Boltz looked at the wall clock. "It's 9:18. You'd better scoot. Ellis tells me you have a 10:00 appointment."

Nick stood. "Commander, what's in the package?" He gestured to the package on Boltz's desk.

"It's a red herring."

"A what?"

"It's false information designed to mislead the Japanese just in case it fell into Miyazaki's hands. They are lists of fictitious agents in the Philippines, Japan, and occupied China. We also included a fake collection plan. It's a pity that Miyazaki didn't get his hands on it."

Nick shook his head in disbelief. "You think of everything, Commander."

"No, Nick, I planned on nabbing Miyazaki or at least spreading disinformation. I didn't plan for Miyazaki getting his hands on our cutting edge RDF technology."

"Are you going to catch Miyazaki?"

"What do you think?"

"I think you might. Can I help?"

"We'll be in touch, but contact me immediately if he shows up again."

Boltz looked at Ellis. "Chief, please take our young agent. Get him to his appointment, and get back here pronto. We've got a spy to catch."

"Aye, aye, Skipper."

Chapter Twenty Nine: Dinner for Two?

4:00 p.m., Saturday, December 23, 1935
Pan American Hawaiian Operations Building,
Pearl City, Oahu, Hawaii Territories

Nick looked up from the desk to see Mr. Berst enter the workshop. Berst was wiping his greasy hands on an equally greasy rag. "Mr. Berst, can I ask you a question?"

Berst nodded.

"It's this sentence… it doesn't make sense." Nick handed a technical bulletin to Berst, who now stood over him.

Berst reached into the top pocket of his *PAA* overalls, withdrew a pair of reading glasses, and placed them at the end of his nose. "Let me see." He read the sentence, and then looked down at Nick. "You're right. It doesn't make a lick of sense. Why use twenty-eight foot pounds of torque on one cylinder, and only eighteen on the others? It must be a typo. The retaining studs could sheer off during maintenance or worse – they could fail in flight. Where did you get this?" Berst held up the bulletin.

"I pulled it from the clipboard by the engine repair stands.

185

Do you think anyone has used it yet?"

Berst pushed his cap back on his head and scratched. "No way to tell. I'll have a chat with the rest of the boys."

Nick nodded. "Should I send a telegram to the Wright Engine Company and ask about the glitch?"

"I'll do it, Nick. I've got a few other questions before the *Philippine Clipper* makes the hop back to the mainland."

A car horn sounded outside and they looked out the window. They saw a cream-colored Cord convertible driven by a cute island girl.

Berst looked back to Nick. "That your girl?"

Nick beamed with pleasure. "Yes, Mr. Berst."

"Well don't just stand there with your mouth open. Get your stuff and get going!"

"But I still owe you 30 minutes."

Berst smiled and waved the bulletin. "I'd say we're even. Now clear out before I change my mind."

Nick grabbed his beat-up messenger bag and his hat, and then headed for the screen door. "What time Monday, Mr. Berst?"

"Monday's Christmas. Are you planning on being here?"

"No, I guess not. I forgot. See you Tuesday, then."

"See you Tuesday. Merry Christmas!"

"Mele Kaliki Maka!"

Nick pushed the screen door open and stepped into the late afternoon sun. Leilani waved, pushed open the driver's door, and scooted toward the passenger seat. He glanced around to see the mechanics at the engine stands staring at them. He threw his bag into the back seat and sat down behind the wheel. Immediately, Leilani leaned over and kissed his cheek and the mechanics let out a series of loud, long whistles.

Nick waved, feeling a bit self-conscious, and then drove off. He made the right turn onto Kamehameha Highway and merged with the eastbound traffic headed for Honolulu. He looked over at Leilani, her dark hair billowing as they drove.

The sun was still high in the cloudless sky. "What a glorious day. Too bad I had to spend most of it inside."

Leilani grabbed her hair, twisted it, and pulled it back. "Yes, it was lovely and I spent most of it at the beach."

Nick could smell coconut. Do you have a trunk full of coconuts or something?"

"No silly, it's coco butter tanning lotion." She lifted her darkly tanned arm to his nose.

Leilani had pinned a red and white hibiscus flower behind her ear and was beaming at Nick. She wore a modest one piece bathing suit and had a towel wrapped around her middle.

Nick looked down at her tanned legs. *God, she was so pretty!* "It's hard to tell, you're already so tan. If I'd gone, I'd be red as a lobster. Where did you go?"

"I went to Hanauma Bay with some of my school friends. They're all dying to meet you."

Nick passed a slow moving horse-drawn cart. "They are? Why?"

"The radio interview today."

"What radio interview?"

"You mean you haven't heard? Captain Tilton spoke today on the local NBC affiliate. He mentioned you by name. Said that you're the youngest flight engineer in Pan American's history."

Nick wondered what Commander Boltz would think. "He did? Why would he mention that?"

"He was talking about Pan Am's efforts to reach out to the American youth."

"Great! Now the guys on the crew will never stop ribbing me!" Nick made the turn onto Manoa Road and started up the steep grade. At the Porta's property he started for the garage.

However, Leilani pointed to the cabana. "Park it there – by the front door. We'll need it later tonight."

"We will?"

Leilani opened the passenger door and stepped out. "Yes. You're taking me out to dinner, remember?"

Nick stepped out onto the crushed coral driveway. "But I haven't made any reservations yet."

"Don't worry, Daddy already made them at the Royal Hawaiian. They have a great floorshow, and Arty Shaw's band is playing tonight. It will be so much fun!"

Nick hurriedly dug into his pocket. He pulled out some crumbled bills and loose change. He counted it up and realized he had fourteen dollars and seventy-six cents. He shoved the money back into his pockets. Sheepishly he looked at Leilani as he put the money back in his pocket. "I'm sorry, Leilani, but there is no way I can afford the Royal Hawaiian."

Leilani walked around the car. She hugged Nick, and then looked up at him. "It's okay. Daddy will pay for everything."

Nick shook his head. "No way, Leilani. I may be poor but I pay for my dates."

The front door opened and Mr. and Mrs. Porta emerged from the house. Mrs. Porta wore a long formal dress while Mr. Porta wore a white dinner jacket and black pants. Nick heard a car approach and turned to see the huge black Cadillac pull up beside them. Maleko, the Porta's chauffer, opened his door. "Hello, Mr. Grant. It's good to see you again."

"Hello, Maleko." Maleko bowed, and then opened the car door for the Portas, who took a seat. Nick moved to the open door. "Aloha Mrs. Porta, you look lovely." It was obvious where Leilani got her beauty.

Mrs. Porta smiled. "Aloha. Why thank you, Nick. Are you excited about tonight?"

"I beg your pardon, ma'am, but I need to speak to Mr. Porta about that."

Mr. Porta smiled at Nick. "Yes, Nick what is it?"

"I don't want to seem ungrateful for your wonderful hospitality, but I simply can't let you pay for my date with Leilani tonight."

The Portas exchanged puzzled looks. Then Mr. Porta

asked. "Is that what Leilani told you?"

Confused, Nick nodded. "Yes..."

Mr. Porta chuckled. "That little *Menehune*! Leilani's always into mischief." He looked warmly at his wife. "She gets that from you, my love."

A sly smile crossed Mrs. Porta's face. "Guilherme, it helps the weaker sex keep the males on their toes."

Mr. Porta turned back to Nick. "Has Leilani told you that we're going to pick up her sister at the harbor?"

Nick smiled. "No. It'll be great to see Hanna again. Is she on the Matson Liner?"

Mr. Porta frowned. "No, we had to book her on the *Hiiyü Maru*."

Nick was puzzled. "Why a Japanese ship?"

"We couldn't get passage on the Matson Liner. You know, too many Christmas passengers."

Nick brightened. "This time next year, she can fly home with me on the Clipper."

Mr. Porta looked at Nick. "Will Pan Am have its passenger service by then?"

"We should. The mail runs have gone off like clockwork. Imagine, Hanna could be here overnight from San Francisco, instead of five days."

Mr. Porta looked thoughtful, and then closed the car door. He spoke to Nick through the open car window. "Right now, we need to pick Hanna up from the dock, or she'll think we've abandoned her. You drive the Cord down and we'll meet you for dinner at the Royal Hawaiian. It's my treat Nick, no arguments."

"Okay, Mr. Porta, no argument tonight. A family dinner isn't really a date. Thank you and we'll see you later – at the Royal Hawaiian."

Maleko put the Caddie in gear and drove off. Nick looked at Leilani. "You sure set me up with your parents. You want to tell me what that was all about?"

Leilani giggled and bolted for the front door. "Sorry, Nick, it will have to wait. I have to go upstairs to dress for dinner."

Leilani's lithe figure and swaying hips mesmerized Nick.

She looked back over her shoulder. "Caught you staring." Then she giggled again.

Nick grinned. "Guilty as charged. Say, I'll have to wear my Pan Am uniform. I didn't bring another coat and tie. Will that be okay?"

Leilani stopped at the door. "You'd better, fly boy. I want to show you off."

"Leilani! You're impossible!" Nick couldn't help a big grin. *I'm the luckiest guy in the world.*

Chapter Thirty: The Royal Hawaiian Hotel

7:30 p.m., Saturday, December 23, 1935
Royal Hawaiian Hotel, Honolulu, Oahu, Hawaii Territories

The main ballroom took Nick's breath away. He had seen ballrooms in San Francisco, but nothing this spectacular. He looked in awe at the room. It formed a semi-circle with high arches that reached up to a balcony that ringed the room. Under the arches, dining tables spread out towards the central dance floor and back to the open *lanai*. Pulmaria and orchid-scented breezes blew off Waikiki beach and rustled the palm fronds. Nick could hear the surf gently kissing the sands and thought that it was like being in a movie, only this was in living color.

Nick and Leilani swayed to the rhythm of Artie Shaw's *Any Old Time*. When the music ended, the dancers clapped enthusiastically. Then Artie Shaw stepped to the microphone, "Folks we're going to take a ten minute break. But stick around because we're coming back with more hot tunes we brought to the islands from the Imperial Theater in New York City!"

Nick looked at Leilani. "Have I told you that you look

ravishing tonight, *darhling*?" She wore a long, close-fitting red satin dress. It offset her figure and long hair, which she wore loose with a red hibiscus flower tucked behind her right ear.

"Not nearly enough, *darhling*."

They laughed. It was a famous line from *A Top Hat*, a Fred Astaire and Ginger Rogers movie. Nick led Leilani back to their table where they sat. He was perspiring freely and he picked up a napkin to mop his brow. "This wool uniform is too darn hot. You know, that would be a great title for a song." He glanced at Leilani. "You look quite comfortable." He picked up his lemonade and drink deeply.

She was gently fanning herself with a ruby red bamboo fan. There was no trace of perspiration on her face or bare arms. "It's amazing that Pan Am hasn't designed a cooler uniform. You guys are going to die in August when the trade winds stop blowing for weeks at a time."

They chatted for a few more minutes until the band reappeared. Artie Shaw opened with a foxtrot. Nick stood and took Leilani's hand. "Come on, I want to see how fast you can move in that dress."

Leilani smiled as she stood and hand-in-hand they headed for the dance floor. Then she dropped Nick's hand and put both hands to her face. "Oh, my God! Hanna!" She rushed and embraced her sister and then kissed her on both cheeks.

The Portas had entered from the *lanai* and Nick walked over to greet them. "Aloha, Hanna. It's good to see you again."

Hanna disengaged from her sister's embrace and, to Nick's surprise, hugged him. She kissed him on each cheek and looked up at him. "You get more handsome every time I see you, Nick. You'd better not break my sister's heart, or you'll have to deal with me."

Leilani chided her sister. "Hanna, don't you mean, I'd better not break his heart?"

Hanna looked at her sister and shook her head. "Still the same girl, I see."

Mr. Porta pointed to their table. "Come on, let's sit down.

I'm hungry enough to eat a humpback whale – raw."

Nick looked confused. "Do they serve whale here?"

Everybody laughed as the group moved to the dinner table.

After dinner, Mr. Porta and Nick took turns dancing with the women. Nick enjoyed Mrs. Porta's conversation as they danced. She told some very funny "little *Menehune*" stories about Leilani.

Hanna enthralled Nick with her experiences at Johns Hopkins medical school. "It's my first semester and it's been very challenging. Still, I've never felt so alive. I just love it."

"How many women are in your class?"

"Including me? One."

Nick smiled at Hanna's tenacity. He had considered medical school last summer when he worked for Dr. Kenler on the Pacific atolls. However, now he was certain that aeronautical engineering and flying were his future.

Best of all, Nick enjoyed dancing with Leilani despite his unbearably hot uniform. "Do you mind if we step outside for some air?"

She winked. "Got anything else in mind, flyboy?"

Nick tugged at his collar, trying to vent some heat. "Maybe later, but right now I just want to cool off."

They walked through the doors. Leilani turned to him. "Are you having a good time, Nick?"

He took her in his arms and kissed her. After a moment, they parted. "Does that answer your question?"

Another couple joined them. The young man said. "Aloha, Leilani!"

Leilani smoothed her hair, and then turned to face the new comers, "Aloha, Kenan. Is this your friend from the mainland?"

Kenan replied. "Sure is, Leilani. This is Clara Rothschild. Her family is visiting from New York City. Clara, this is Leilani Porta and Nick Grant."

They exchanged hellos and shook hands. Nick was relieved

that the Hawaiian men didn't feel the need to kiss. "Kenan, let me guess, you knew who I was because of the uniform?"

"That was my first clue. And the fact that Leilani has been talking about nothing else for the last few days." He smiled and his white teeth contrasted with his dark complexion. "It had to be you!"

Leilani blushed then turned to Clara. They were quickly engaged in conversation.

Kenan asked. "Nick, tell me what it's like to fly on the Clipper."

"Have you flown?"

"I took the stick of a Jenny a few times, but I've never had a lesson."

"Maybe we could go up sometime. I'd be glad to give you a few tips."

"Would you? That would be great!"

"Sure, next time I'm in Honolulu. I look forward to it."

Kenan continued, "I've been accepted to the Hawaiian National Guard flying program. I'll attend pilot school at Wright-Patterson Army Air Corp Base next summer. Have you considered joining up?"

Nick was tempted to tell Kenan about Commander Boltz and Naval Intelligence but thought better of it. "No, I hope to keep working for Pan Am next summer. After I graduate, I plan to attend the Boeing School of Aeronautical Engineering."

"Wow, what a great school. Which campus — Seattle or Oakland?"

"It will have to be Oakland. I live in Alameda and can still work part-time at Pan Am. Besides, I can't afford the dormitories in Seattle." Suddenly, Nick felt quite poor again despite his opulent surroundings.

Kenan clapped Nick on the shoulder. "I'd give my left eye to work for Pan Am, and attend the Boeing School. The Army flight school is only six weeks then I come back home to go to Kamehameha College."

Nick laughed. "Kenan, I don't think you can sell anybody

that your life is a hardship. I'd give almost anything to live here in Hawaii. It's paradise and the girls are so beautiful." He caught Leilani's eye and she smiled at him, obviously pleased.

The magic feeling Nick enjoyed on the *lanai* was broken as Hanna appeared. "There you are. Come on, it's time to go. I'm beat from all the travel and Daddy's getting tired."

Leilani protested. "But it's only eleven o'clock! Why can't we stay and drive ourselves home?"

Hanna shook her head. "Don't shoot me. I'm just the messenger. Take it up with the parents." She marshaled them off towards the hotel's main entrance and the valet parking stand.

The Portas stood outside waiting for the Cadillac and Leilani didn't waste a moment. The instant she saw her parents, she launched into her plea. "Daddy, I'm not tired and neither is Nick. Right, Nick?"

Nick was very tired but he played along. "Oh, not at all, Mr. Porta."

Porta looked from Nick to Leilani, and then to his wife. "Dear, it is early for these young people. What do you say we let them stay a while longer?"

Mrs. Porta thought a moment and then looked at Leilani. "Leilani, you may stay until twelve-thirty, but I want you home by one a.m. We've got church tomorrow and I won't have you falling asleep in service." She turned to Nick. "I will expect you to bring my daughter home on time. Don't listen to her if she protests. Do you agree?"

"Yes, Mrs. Porta and thank you."

Leilani threw her arms around her mother. "Thanks, Mom, but can't –"

"You certainly may not! If you argue, you will come home now."

Leilani slumped. "Yes, mother."

The Cadillac arrived and the valet opened the doors. Hanna and her parents boarded and Maleko eased the big car into traffic.

Nick was trying to stifle a yawn when he caught movement out of the corner of his eye. A yellow cab moved out from the cabstand. When it passed the hotel entrance, the bright lights momentarily illuminated the cab's dark interior. The cab had no fare in the back. *That was odd.* Then Nick recognized the driver and grabbed Leilani's arm. "Oh my God! It's him!"

Chapter Thirty One: The Road to Hell

11:06 p.m., Saturday, December 23, 1935
Royal Hawaiian Hotel, Honolulu, Oahu, Hawaii Territories

"Who?" Leilani shielded her eyes from the lobby lights and stared after the disappearing cab. "Was that the cabbie that ran us off the road?"

Nick nodded as the cab turned after the Cadillac.

Leilani tugged on Nick's sleeve. "We've got to help them. Let's go!"

"Wait! I've got to call Naval Intelligence first."

"No! You said that cabbie works for Miyazaki. We've got to help my parents!"

"We will." Nick put a hand on Leilani's shoulder. "But if Miyazaki is headed to your house, we're going need all the help we can get!" He dug into his pocket, fished out a nickel, and tossed it to her. "Call your house and warn Consuela. Tell her to lock all the doors and let no one in. I'll use the other phone to call Naval Intelligence."

Leilani dropped the coin into the slot and waited. "Manoa 3-125, hurry!"

Nick dialed. "Coral 6-257... Yes, I'll wait."

Leilani looked stunned. "What? Are you sure, operator? ... Oh, no." She hung up. "Nick, the line's dead!"

He nodded and held up his hand. "Yes, please get the message to Commander Boltz immediately. It's urgent!" Then he hung up.

"Oh Nick, I'm so scared. Maybe we should call the police."

Nick shook his head. "What are we going to tell them? That a cab followed your parents from a hotel? No, they will never believe us."

"What about the Navy? Will they help?"

"I don't know. The duty officer said that he'd try to get the message to Commander Boltz, but he didn't know where the Commander was. It looks like we're on our own."

They ran hand-in-hand to the car park. Nick saw the Cord keys hanging on the wall behind the valet stand. He ignored the valet's shouts, grabbed the keys and tossed them a buck. "Sorry guys, we're in a hurry!" They ran to the car and Nick jumped behind the wheel. He fired up the Cord's big engine as Leilani jumped in the passenger seat. He turned to Leilani. "Let's see what this baby can do. You'd better hold on to something." Then he floored the accelerator and popped the clutch. The two valets dove out of the way as Nick left a patch of rubber twenty-five feet long in the parking lot. The valets' curses followed them as they disappeared into the night.

* * *

11:12 p.m., Saturday, December 23, 1935
Mauna Loa Heights, Honolulu, Oahu, Hawaii Territories

Miyazaki waited inside the Porta house. Two Japanese men had gagged and bound Consuela to a dining room chair. They stood next to her, their faces impassive, waiting for their next orders. She had ceased struggling only a few minutes ago.

Miyazaki sat in front of her contemplating his next move. He took a long drag on his cigarette. She would probably have to die, but she did not need to know that yet. He moved to stand directly in front of the woman. "Consuela, I told you, cooperate and no one will be harmed. Are you willing to help me now?"

She nodded, eyes wide with fear. Miyazaki nodded to one of his men and he removed the gag.

Immediately, Consuela started to scream. "Help! Somebody, help!"

In a lightning move, Miyazaki rose and backhanded Consuela hard, splitting her lip. Her head jerked to the side. "Gag her!" he told his men.

"Foolish woman! With your help, we could easily capture the Portas. Now, who knows what will happen. If any harm comes to them it will be your fault."

Consuela continued to struggle with her bonds even as her blood soaked through the gag.

*   *   *

11:28 p.m., Saturday, December 23, 1935
Fort Shafter, Honolulu, Oahu, Hawaii Territories

The phone rang on Major Davis' desk. He reached for it but Clendenny snatched it up first. "Army CI... Yes, that's right... How long ago?... Good, stay with him but keep out of sight. The last thing I want to do is to spook Miyazaki." He replaced the phone in its cradle.

Davis glared at Clendenny. "What's the deal, Ron?"

"It's a go. All our agents are in place and we've got a squad of Military Police."

"A Squad! I asked for a platoon. How long have you known we were short thirty MPs?

Clendenny looked at his watch. "Oh, about twenty seconds. You want to call it off?"

Davis shook his head. "No, but I don't like it. Things could go to hell in a handbag and I'd like to have more firepower on that hill. If we get into trouble, no one's going to be able to reach us in time."

Clendenny leaded forward. "Forrest, I know it's a risk, but the odds are he'll never know what hit him."

"You'd better be right about this, Ron. There's too much at stake. Does Protégée know about the operation tonight?"

"No, there was no way to contact him without tipping our hand. Our counter surveillance team saw Miyazaki's man watching the Porta party at the Royal Hawaiian."

Davis looked out the window. "Is our squad in position?"

Clendenny nodded as her un-holstered his .45 caliber Colt automatic, removed the magazine, and jacked the slide to the rear. Noting the weapon was not loaded, he released the side, then replaced the magazine. "Yes, everything is set. Stop worrying. You ready?"

Davis stood and checked his pistol. "Ready as I'll ever be. Let's get this show on the road."

* * *

11:31 p.m., Saturday, December 23, 1935
Kamehameha Highway, Honolulu, Oahu, Hawaii Territories

Nick turned sharply from Kamehameha onto Manoa Drive, the Cord somehow holding the road. As the headlamps briefly illuminated the woods, Nick caught the image of an olive drab Army truck and two very white faces under metal helmets. He looked over at Leilani. "Did you see that?"

"Yes. What was an Army truck doing there?"

"I've no idea."

"Do you think they might help?"

Nick shook his head. "Maybe, but it would take too long to explain why. I think we'd keep going."

Leilani bit her lip, then said. "I hope my family is all right. The night just keeps getting weirder!"

Nick hid his worry from Leilani. Miyazaki had already killed three men and one woman – that he knew of. He'd probably killed countless others. Nick pulled over to the shoulder, stopped the car, and switched off the lights. "Let's walk from here."

"Do you think someone might be watching the road?"

"Yes, and let's hope they haven't seen us yet." Silently, he cursed himself for his impatience. *I should have thought of that earlier!*

Leilani opened the door and walked around to the trunk. She opened it and removed a baseball bat. She handed it to Nick. "You might need this." Then she withdrew a tire iron and quietly closed the trunk.

Nick looked at her tire iron. "Be careful with that thing."

"I'll be careful. But if they've hurt anyone in my family, I'm going to bury this metal bar into someone's head." She spoke with a determined fury.

"Okay, but remember, I'm on your side." Nick took Leilani's hand and they walked up the road towards the house. It lay just beyond the next bend.

They walked along in silence, both deep in worry and thought. Suddenly Nick froze. He pointed to a glowing cigarette end close to the road about twenty-five yards ahead. He placed a finger to his lips. As silently as possible, he moved Leilani off the road and into the brush. He pulled her down gently and he placed his lips next to her ear and whispered. "I need you to walk up the road and distract that man!"

"How?" she whispered.

"I know, you could say your car's broken down. Ask him for help."

Leilani looked concerned. "He'll never believe me!"

"He'll be startled. And that will give me time."

"For what?"

Nick hefted the baseball bat. "I'll circle around and attack from behind." He looked at his watch. The luminous dial showed 11:35. "Can you see your watch?"

Leilani looked at her watch in the faint moon light. "Yes."

"Set it to 11:35. Then wait five minutes before you start up the road. That should give me time to get into position."

Chapter Thirty Two: Strike One!

11:39 p.m., Saturday, December 23, 1935
Manoa Road, Manoa Heights, Oahu, Hawaii Territories

Nick kissed Leilani on the cheek and set off cross-country. It was tough going. The underbrush caught at his wool uniform and continually snagged on his wool uniform. He found himself unable to move quickly. The weak moonlight did not help either. Twice he fell and just managed to grab a bush before tumbling down the slope and back to the road.

He checked his watch. He'd been gone four minutes and was nowhere near where he needed to be. He moved closer to the road to try and catch a glimpse of the man. *Where was he?* Suddenly, the cigarette glowed again. *Omigod!* The man was less than twenty feet away but Nick was still downhill from him. Worse, Leilani was walking right up to him!

Nick moved with less caution pushing through the shrub, oblivious to snags, scratches, and his crashing noises that had to be waking the dead. He had to get into position before anything happened to Leilani! Too late! He heard Leilani. She was sobbing!

202

"That darn car! It always breaks down!" She stopped and acted as if she had seen the man on the road for the first time. "Is that you, Maleko? Come here, I need your help!"

She continued to walk up to the man, seemingly unafraid. The man reached out and grabbed her left arm. Enraged, Nick charged from the bushes. The man kept his hold on Leilani but turned to face Nick. Nick hoisted his bat just as Leilani cold-cocked the man with the tire iron. He crumpled to the road without a sound.

"Leilani, are you okay?" She stood over the body. Nick was unsure if she intended to hit the man again.

"Do you know who this is?"

Nick looked down at the crumpled figure. "No."

"It's the cabbie. I think he recognized me just as I hit him."

Nick removed his belt and knelt at the unconscious man's side. He spoke softly. "That must have felt good."

"Oh, it did. Will he live?"

Nick examined the cabbie's head wound. "Probably." The moonlight showed that he was bleeding from the forehead. His eyes were closed and his breathing shallow.

He removed a handkerchief from his pocket and tied it around the man's head. "Give me a hand. I want to tie him up before he comes around."

Leilani helped Nick roll the cabbie over. She held the man's hands behind his back, while Nick looped his belt around his wrists. When he finished, Nick tied the loose end to the cabbie's belt. Next he untied the cabbie's shoes and retied the laces together.

Nick stood. "That should hold him for a while. Let's drag him off the road."

Together they moved the inert form behind some low bushes.

Leilani looked up towards her house. The lights were just visible through the trees. "Do you think anybody heard?"

Nick looked up the hill. "It's hard to tell. Come on, let's get up there." He grabbed Leilani's hand and moved along the shoulder of the road.

When they reached the driveway they saw the Yellow Cab. It was parked alongside the Cadillac. Someone lay between the two cars.

Leilani gasped. "Oh my God, it's Maleko!"

"Shush!" Nick whispered. "They'll hear us!"

They crouched low and covered the distance to the cars, wary of anyone seeing them from a window. Maleko lay crumpled on the ground beside the open driver's door. Nick reached down and felt for a pulse. "He's alive. Looks like someone whacked him about as hard as you hit the cabbie."

"My poor Maleko. Will he be alright?" Leilani looked around, tire iron at the ready.

Nick examined Maleko's head wound. "It looks like a nasty bump but there's no sign of a cranial fracture. Of course, we won't know until we get him to a hospital. I don't think he's in any immediate danger."

Leilani looked down Maleko. "He's more like family than a servant."

"Let's look for the rest of your family."

She nodded and they crept toward the dining room bay window. They moved slowly, as the coral of the driveway crunched under foot. When they reached the side of the window, Nick risked a quick look. He saw Mrs. Porta, Hanna, and Consuela gagged and tied to the dining room chairs, their backs towards him.

Nick also saw Mr. Porta. He stood, his right side toward the window. Miyazaki stood in front of Porta while two men flanked him. Porta's hands were tied behind his back. His head hung and his face was red and swollen. Nick moved his ear closer to the window and heard Miyazaki speak.

"I grow tired of asking, Guilherme. Where are Leilani and that meddling Grant boy?"

Porta raised his head. "Told you," he rasped. "Leilani is spending the night at a friend's house. Grant's with the Clipper crew at the Royal Hawaiian."

CRACK! Miyazaki backhanded Porta. Porta's head jerked as the blow connected. Blood flew from Porta's mouth and splattered Hanna's hair.

Miyazaki seemed enraged. "Liar! I have men at the hotel watching the crew. Grant is not registered and he has not been seen!" He looked at the man closest to the window and said something in Japanese. Nick was still trying to translate when the man slapped Hanna. The gag muffled her scream.

Porta shouldered the man holding him, hard. He lost his grip on Porta's arm and staggered backwards. Then Porta shouldered Miyazaki aside and charged the other man. He head butted the man, square in the chest. Stunned, the man toppled over backward. Miyazaki recovered, leapt into the air and landed on Porta's back. Porta crumpled to the floor. Miyazaki snapped to his feet and kicked Porta in the ribs. The other two men regained their feet and hauled Porta upright.

Rage filled Nick as he watched, but he felt helpless. What could he do? There were three of them. Besides, Miyazaki alone could kill him. Then in the distance, he heard a truck grinding up the hill in low gear. It was faint and he doubted anyone in the house could hear it…yet.

Leilani tugged on Nick's sleeve. "Tell me, what did you see? What's happening in there?"

Nick chose his words carefully. He didn't want Leilani to charge in, tire iron flailing. "Miyazaki has your family tied up and he's questioning them."

She looked suspicious. "About what?"

"Where we are. I think he wants me."

"Oh, God. We've got to get help!"

"I know. Do you hear the truck climbing the hill?"

She cocked her head. "…Yes, now I do."

"I think it might be that Army truck we saw earlier. Since they're on their way up here, I'm going to try to get their help."

"How you going to do that?"

"Throw myself in front of the truck and tell them what's

going on."

"Think they'll believe you?"

"They *have* to!"

"What should I do?"

"Let's get back behind the car and I'll tell you."

Back at the Cadillac, Nick peaked over the hood and then ducked down again. "Stay here with Maleko and keep watch. Miyazaki is after the RDF equipment and he still thinks he's got the road covered. I doubt he'll come out."

"Okay. What should I do if Miyazaki sees me?"

"Run like hell."

Chapter Thirty Three: The Cavalry's Here!

12:01a.m., Sunday, December 24, 1935
Manoa Road, Oahu, Hawaii Territories

Major Davis and Special Agent Clendenny occupied the front seat of an olive drab Plymouth sedan, the lead vehicle. Davis sat in the passenger seat looking intently out the windshield. "Ron, are you sure you can see the road?"

"Quit your bellyaching, Forrest, I'm only doing five miles an hour. Besides, I've always had better night vision than you."

"Maybe, but it wasn't good enough for flight school."

"I asked you not to bring up that subject ever again."

"Sorry, guess I'm a little nervous."

Behind them, far too close for Davis's comfort, the MP truck followed. Neither vehicle burned their headlights. The only time Davis saw the truck was when Clendenny braked. The red glow of the brake lights made the truck look huge in the outside mirror.

Suddenly a dark shape of a man loomed out of the darkness. "Look out, Ron!" Davis yelled.

The man's dark suit made him almost invisible in the night. Clendenny hit the brakes but not before the figure glanced off the hood and rolled off the passenger side.

The car stopped abruptly but too quickly for the truck. When it hit, it bumped the car forward a foot.

"Damn it, Ron!" Davis pulled himself off the dashboard. Concerned that they had fallen into a trap, he drew his automatic and opened his door.

Clendenny followed Davis's lead, drew his weapon, and exited through the driver's door. "Find the lookout, Major Davis..." Behind him MPs piled out of the back of the truck, rifles at the ready.

* * *

Nick had run hard for about three-quarters of a mile when he rounded a corner and saw the car. It had no lights, but he could see a huge white star painted on the hood. The car brakes squealed and he hit the star. The next thing he knew, he was flat on his back, looking up into the largest gun barrel he'd ever seen.

As his eyes focused a man spoke. "Freeze! Easy now, this .45 will make a big hole in you."

Nick slowly held up his empty hands. "What's with the guns and who are you?" he demanded.

Another man joined the first, his pistol leveled at Nick's chest. "More to the point, who the hell are *you*?"

"I'm Nick Grant from the Pan Am Clipper. I need help!"

The first man holstered his weapon. "What are you doing here?"

"I'm a guest of the Portas. A Japanese gang is holding them hostage in their house. I slipped away to get help."

The second man lowered his pistol. "Major Davis, what do you want me to do with him?"

Nick was thrilled. "A Major! That's great! Can you contact Commander Boltz of Naval Intelligence?"

Both men stared at Nick. Then Davis spoke. "Why should

we contact the Navy? This is an Army operation."

Nick considered carefully what to say next. These two were clearly Americans but were they really in the Army? As he thought about what to say next he was surrounded by Army MPs.

One of them asked. "Special Agent Clendenny, are you okay, sir?"

Nick was elated. "Special Agent? Are you with the FBI?"

Clendenny shot back. "You shut up! I'll ask the questions here!"

He sure sounded like the FBI! Nick decided to gamble. What choice did he have? "I'm here on a Naval Intelligence operation."

Everybody's head jerked around to stare at him. Major Davis extended a hand and pulled Nick to his feet. "What operation?"

Nick swallowed. "Does the name Miyazaki mean anything?"

Clendenny leaned in close and spoke close to Nick's face in a threatening tone. "What do you know about Miyazaki?"

"I know that he's the one up in the house holding the Portas."

Clendenny thought about that for a moment. "So you know Commander Boltz. Tell me, what's the name of his right hand man and what does he look like?"

"That's easy. Master Chief Ellis, late of the China Gunboats."

"Okay, so what does he look like?"

"Like a prize fighter that went one round too many?"

Clendenny chuckled. "Major Davis, I've know the Chief for years. I'd say Grant knows him."

Davis turned to the MP Sergeant. "Get your men back on board. And tell your driver to keep his distance or he'll be charged for damaging government property!"

"Yes, sir." He turned to his men. "All right, you knuckleheads. You heard the Major. Get back on the truck!"

Davis opened the passenger door. "Grant, get in. Ron, let's go. And for God's sake, keep your eyes open this time!"

They piled in and Clendenny started the car up the road. Nick quickly explained the situation. "They've got the family tied and gagged in the dining room. My girl, Leilani, is outside with the driver. He's out cold."

Davis interrupted. "How come they're not tied up?"

"Leilani and I arrived after the Portas. When I looked inside, Miyazaki was slapping Mr. Porta around pretty bad. He wanted to know where we were."

"Why?"

"I've met Miyazaki before on two occasions and we have some unfinished business."

"Like what?"

"Like the death of my old boss, Mac McMillan, and FBI Agent Franks."

Davis looked at Clendenny but said nothing. He turned back to Nick. "Does Commander Boltz know that Miyazaki is holding the Portas?"

"No, I didn't speak with him. I left a message to come to the Porta's house about forty-five minutes ago. I said Miyazaki's driver was at the Royal Hawaiian. That he'd followed the Portas when they left to go home."

"Ron, stop before that last turn. We'll have to hoof it from there."

"Yes, sir."

* * *

Nick, Davis, and Clendenny quietly moved up the road. Rivulets of sweat poured down Nick's face and back. He was swimming in sweat but did not slow for a moment. The Portas were in danger and nothing could deter his desire to catch Miyazaki.

The MP squad followed behind, half on one side of the road and half on the other. Most were carrying Springfield rifles, but the NCOs had Thompson sub-machine guns. Their combat gear clanked and rattled. They made so much noise that Davis ordered them to slow down, lest they give up the element of surprise.

Nick reached the house first with Davis and Clendenny right behind. He was relieved to see Leilani cradling Maleko's head in her lap, the tire iron at her side. "Thank God you're okay!" he whispered. Maleko moaned softly.

Leilani stroked his head, "Shush, everything will be alright."

Davis and Clendenny moved beside them. Nick asked Leilani, "What's happening?"

Leilani looked at Nick, eyes filled with tears. "Miyazaki and one of his thugs dragged Daddy to the pool house. I didn't see anyone else. Nick, you've got to help them!"

He put his arm around her shoulder. "This is Major Davis and Special Agent Clendenny. They have a bunch of MPs headed this way. I'd say the cavalry has arrived."

Davis looked at Clendenny. "Ron, this complicates things. We don't have enough men to cover both buildings. I knew we needed a full platoon."

Nick was worried. "What do you propose, Major Davis?"

"We concentrate on the pool house first. If we can nab Miyazaki, the others will either run or surrender."

"No way! Those men are Black Dragons. They'll kill everyone first, then commit *seppuku*. They will never be taken alive," said Nick.

Davis looked angry. "What are you talking about? *Seppuku*, what's that?"

"It's ritual suicide. Death before the dishonor of being captured. You don't know what these men are capable of."

Davis was defiant. "We'll do it my way!"

Just then the MP Sergeant ran over, bent double. "Sir, the men are spread out in the trees. What are your orders?"

"Sergeant, deploy your men to cover the doors and the window of the pool house." Davis pointed out the building. "Keep your men hidden and apprehend anyone who tries to flee. Instruct your men that there is a hostage in the pool house and more hostages in the main house. Then both

Special Agent Clendenny and I will enter the pool house to arrest the suspects."

The Sergeant nodded.

"Further instruct them that they are to fire only in self-defense or to prevent a suspect from escaping. Remember, we want these men alive, if possible. You got it?"

"Yes, sir."

"Deploy your men, but quietly – very quietly."

Nick was incensed. He couldn't believe that they were going to put the Portas at such risk. He had to do something.

He turned to Leilani. "Help me get Maleko into the Caddie. I'm going to go into the house and free your mother, Hanna, and Consuela. When they come out the front door, get them into the car and drive your family to the hospital. I'll join you there later. Once you get going, don't stop for anything."

Leilani reached up and hugged Nick. "I love you, Nick. Be careful."

"I love you too, Leilani." He picked up the bat and ran crouched to the side of the main house, toward the garage.

Chapter Thirty Four: Strike Two!

12:16 a.m., Sunday, December 24, 1935
Porta House, Manoa Heights, Oahu, Hawaii Territories

Holding a death grip on the bat, Nick dashed into the garage and ducked behind a Packard. The big black car was parked on the side of the garage next to the adjoining kitchen. Carefully, Nick inched forward, his heart pounding, toward the kitchen door. He tried the door knob and was in luck. It was unlocked. He slipped off his shoes and socks, took a deep breath and slowly opened the door. He stepped inside.

The house was quiet. Too quiet. *Where was that other goon?* He moved as quickly as he dared, his focus on the kitchen door that led to the hallway. It looked clear. He moved through the door, the bat at his side, and flattened against the hallway wall. Inadvertently, he gently bumped the telephone stand. It started to tip over!

Nick reached down and grabbed the phone with one hand and used the bat to stop the table from crashing into the floor. *Whew, that was close.* He tipped the table upright with the bat and replaced the phone. He could hear his father's voice in his head admonishing him *"Be more careful Nick, you're like a bull in a china shop!"* He shook those thoughts away and continued down the hall towards the dining room. He heard sounds and froze.

Someone was weeping, perhaps Consuela. It was hard to tell as the sound was so muffled. He tiptoed until he reached the dining room doorway. He steeled himself and took a quick look. The man guarding the Portas stood, his back towards the hallway door. The three women were still tied to the chairs that faced the doorway. Hanna saw him and her eyes widened. Her face was red and swollen from the thug's slap but she betrayed no other emotion.

Nick raised the bat and quietly stepped into the room. The thug still had his back to the door. *Good! Now if I can just get closer before he notices.*

When Hanna saw Nick, she started to struggle with her bonds. She tried to yell, but the gag muffled her voice. Then she pushed herself backwards and rocked her chair. Nick was amazed. Hanna was distracting the Japanese thug while he made his approach. *Good girl!*

The thug kicked her chair. "Quiet!" Then he reached for a knife and flicked it open. He held it high in his right hand. "Stop it now or I'll cut that pretty face of yours!"

The knife was a wicked-looking switch blade, the kind Nick had seen in countless gangster movies. Filled with fury, Nick was raised his bat. The thug must have sensed Nick's presence because he whirled around, knife ready. Too late. Nick swung with all his might.

WHAP! Nick's bat connected.

The sound was not unlike the day Nick had walloped a cantaloupe with Timmy's bat. Both his Mom and Timmy had been furious with him – his mom for wasting food, Timmy for leaving a stain on his bat.

The blade flew from the thug's hand and Nick heard bones break. Nick continued with the upward follow-through and the bat impacted with the man's head.

The man crumpled without a sound. Nick turned, bat in hand, ready for another assailant, but none came. Slowly, he lowered the bat and started to get control of his emotions and his racing heart. He looked down at his victim. The man was motionless and blood poured from his caved-in head. *Oh my God! Did I kill him?* Then another, darker thought crossed his mind. *Do I care?*

The three women's muffled yells brought Nick back to the present situation. Mrs. Porta was closest and he untied her first. He removed her gag and she gasped.

"Oh, thank God, Nick. Moto, or Miyazaki, took Guilherme to the pool house."

"I know. Help is here," Nick said calmly as he moved to untie Consuela. "The Army brought a squad of MPs and they're going to deal with Miyazaki. This time he's as good as captured or dead."

Consuela stood and helped Mrs. Porta to her feet. They were both unsteady. Nick moved over to Hanna and started to untie her. "Hanna, you were great! You distracted that goon long enough for me to get a great swing."

She nodded and stood, rubbed her face, and walked over to the prostrate thug. She kicked him hard between the legs. He groaned.

Well, at least I know he's alive! Nick moved to Hanna.

Hanna drew back to kick him again. "You low-down snake! You're a son-of-a —"

"Hanna!" Mrs. Porta stood straight and proud. "You will not swear in this house!"

Hanna bent down and picked up the thug's knife. "After what he did to our family, I'm tempted to castrate him!"

The sound of a car climbing the hill made them all turn. Fear crossed Hanna's face. "I hope that's not more of Miyazaki's men."

This was getting out of hand! Nick snatched the knife from Hanna's hand. "Leilani is outside in the Cadillac. She has Maleko, too. We need to get him to the hospital and all of you to safety."

They moved out the front door just as Nick caught a glimpse of a grey Navy Chevy on the road below. "Oh no! It's got to be Boltz! He'll spoil everything! I've got to stop him."

He turned to Hanna. "Please get into the car, we've got to get you out of here!"

Mrs. Porta crossed her arms. "I'm not leaving without Guilherme!"

Nick turned to Hanna. "Please, get in. We don't have much time. Your father would want you safely away."

Hanna put her arm around her mother's shoulders. "Mother, Nick's right. We need to get out of here so the men can deal with Moto, or Miyazaki, or whoever the hell he is!"

Mrs. Porta started to cry. "But your father, I said I'd never leave him. He's hurt. I must go to him." She sobbed into her daughter's chest.

Hanna patted her mother's head. "Come on, let get Maleko to the hospital. Nick will bring Dad to us as soon as he can."

Nick picked up his bat. "I will, Mrs. Porta. I promise! But first I need to stop Boltz"

Nick opened the front door and ushered the Porta family to the Cadillac, then stood on the running board. "Once we reach the car coming up the hill stop in the road so he can't get around you."

"Will do, Nick."

"Once you start the engine, all hell is going to break loose around here." The pool house was on the west side of the main house and out of view. "Don't stop for anyone or anything until you reach Boltz."

Nick gently closed the driver's door. "Hanna, Leilani says that you can drive fast."

Hanna looked up at Nick. "She tell you about the plantation races?"

"Yep." He leaned in close. "God knows who else is out there tonight. Floor it and keep going. You ready?"

She nodded.

"Okay. Fire up the beast and don't spare the horses." Nick looked to the west. *Where was everybody?*

Hanna hit the floor starter switch and the Cadillac's huge eight cylinder engine growled to life.

Hanna gunned the Cadillac and it fishtailed out of the driveway. As the headlights crossed the yard, Nick saw some of the MPs in their hiding places. Eyes wide with astonishment, their forms were quickly engulfed in darkness as the lights passed.

Hanna gained the road and the first switchback. As they dropped below the ridgeline Nick saw the navy's Chevy and started waving madly.

Ellis drove and Boltz sat next to him. At first they were blinded by the Caddie's lights then saw Nick and waved back. Both cars stopped and Nick hopped off the running board.

Boltz rolled down the window. "Nick, are the Portas safe?"

"Everyone's here except Mr. Porta. Miyazaki's got him in the pool house."

"With the RDF?"

"Yes. I'll show you."

"No, I need you to escort the Portas to the Pearl Harbor Hospital."

"I can't leave until Mr. Porta's safe. Besides, the Army will probably shoot first and ask questions later. They know me. I'd better take you up."

Boltz thought a few seconds and decided. "Chief, give me your Tommy Gun and drive the Portas to base. We'll meet you later with Mr. Porta."

"I'd better go with you, sir. You can't hit the broad side of a barn with a Tommy Gun."

"Gimme the Tommy and get going, Chief. That's an order!"

"An order?" He opened his door and handed the sub machine gun to Boltz. "Grant, you better drive."

"Right, Chief." He trotted around the car and hopped behind the wheel. Ellis took Nick's position on the running board.

"Better hold on tight, Chief. Hanna drives faster than her sister!" Nick warned Ellis.

"Don't you worry about me. You just bring back my skipper in one piece!"

Nick grinned. "Aye, aye, Chief!" Then Nick turned his thoughts to the pool house and Miyazaki.

Nick flipped off the Chevy's headlights and inched the car up the road. He stopped below the ridge line. "We'd better walk from here."

Boltz, nodded, grabbed the Tommy Gun, and they stepped out.

Chapter Thirty Five: Strike Three!

12:31 a.m., Sunday, December 24, 1935
Porta Grounds, Manoa Heights, Oahu, Hawaii Territories

Miyazaki was startled by a car suddenly starting up and accelerating out of the driveway. "Who was that?'

His assistant looked out the window and then back at Miyazaki. "The Cadillac is gone!"

Miyazaki looked out the window. He didn't see anyone or any movement. Surely, that had been a signal for an attack. But everything seemed to be okay. He wondered if one of his new men lost his nerve. "We'll have to use the cab! When I find out who has run away, he will pay with his life. Now, we've got to move."

Porta was seated on the couch, hands still bound behind him. He sat at an awkward angle. "It won't fit! You'll have to make at least two trips."

"We will use another one of your cars."

Porta nodded towards the wooden crates stacked against the wall. "You'll never fit those crates in the cars. Look at the size of them."

Miyazaki smiled. "Then we will take the equipment out of the crates."

"No! You can't!"

"Why not, Guilherme?" Miyazaki looked suspicious.

"Ah, the equipment is specially packed. If you remove it from the crates, you'll damage it."

Miyazaki nodded to another assistant. "Open that top box."

Porta looked desperate. "No, not that one. Start with the one we've already opened."

The assistant stopped and looked at Miyazaki.

Miyazaki nodded to the top box. "Do as I tell you."

The assistant grabbed the heavy looking crate marked U.S. ARMY PROPERTY, and easily lifted it to the floor. He took out a coin and used it to remove the screws. Once done, he lifted the wooden top off and stood back.

Miyazaki walked over and looked at the packing straw. He reached down and fished around in the straw. He grabbed something from the crate. It was a heavy metal bar. He said, "No! You will pay for this insult with the lives of your family!" Miyazaki stepped toward Porta. "Each will die a slow death while you watch. You will tell me your codename and the names of everyone in your network."

Miyazaki tossed the metal bar at an expensive lamp on the couch end table. The lamp seemed to explode on contact. The matching lamp at the other end of the couch remained the sole light source.

Porta was sweating freely. "You were the one who wanted to meet here, not me! Let my family go! They had nothing to do with this."

Miyazaki opened a gold case and selected a cigarette. He inhaled deeply and blew a cloud of blue smoke at the ceiling. "Guilherme, Guilherme, you are such a fool, as are most U.S. Intelligence officers. The point of coming here was your family. They give me great leverage over you."

Enraged, Porta attacked. Miyazaki easily side-stepped the

bull-like charge and punched Porta in the kidneys. Miyazaki then swept his leg under Porta's, crashing him to the floor. "That will be enough head butting for one evening."

Porta rolled over. "Wait! I know where the real RDF equipment is hidden. I'll lead you to it…just let my family go!"

"Oh, so you can help me after all." Miyazaki turned to his assistant and in rapid Japanese said, "Shintarou, go tell Atsushi to get the women into the Packard and wait for me. Then take the cab and pick up Mutsumi. Do you remember where we left him?"

"Yes, master. At the first bend."

"Good. Take Mutsumi to the warehouse and get the truck. Then meet me at the dead drop. I will need you two to transfer the RDF equipment to the submarine. And speak English from now on. Once we're back in the city, I don't want any unnecessary attention."

Shintarou bowed and replied in English. "Yes, Master."

* * *

Nick walked up the road cradling his bat. At the entrance to Porta's land, an MP NCO stepped out of the bushes and leveled a Tommy Gun at them. Nick whispered. "It's me, and this is Commander Boltz, US Navy."

The NCO looked surprised but then brought his weapon to a salute. He whispered back. "I sort of figured. The Commander stands out like a light bulb in that white uniform with all those medals. No offense, sir."

"None taken. I was at a ball and didn't have time to change, Give me an update, sergeant."

After the MP updated Boltz, he turned to Nick. "I'll wait here with the sergeant. You circle around and find Major Davis. Let him know I'm here."

Nick nodded and walked around the parking lot perimeter keeping to the shadows. About halfway there he saw someone moving toward the house. He raced to intercept. He tackled the man at the knees and they both skidded across the gravel in a heap. Nick's arms wound up pinned under the man. He could feel the sharp coral cutting through his trousers and into his knees. The man pushed away as they stopped, did a back flip and landed on his feet.

Nick jumped up just as the man attacked. Without conscious thought he blocked the man's kicks and punches with the bat. *This guy is good!* Nick found himself giving ground in an effort to avoid the fury of the man's attack. Soon he would be up against the house and have no place left to go. Still his attacker pressed the fight.

Nick's left heel touched the wall. He'd run out of room. He deflected a kick to his head and heard the bat strike bone. The attacker jumped back and Nick saw an opportunity. He threw the bat as hard as he could. The man easily sidestepped the bat but winced when he landed. He was favoring his left leg.

Nick leapt up and landed close to the man's left side. He ducked as a round house punch barely missed his head and chopped at the injured leg. *Bingo!* The man screamed and jumped back, his left leg collapsed and he fell to one knee. Nick risked a quick look at the pool house just in time to see Davis and Clendenny enter. It was a mistake to take his eyes off his opponent. A fighting star hit him in the chest and stuck fast.

* * *

Davis broke right while Clendenny went to the left. They rolled and came up kneeling with their pistols extended and scanned the room for targets. Davis saw Porta sitting on the floor and Miyazaki standing behind the couch. Then the light beside the couch exploded into a thousand fireflies, plunging the room into darkness. Something whistled past Davis's ear and impacted in the wall behind him. Davis rolled to his left He had to link up with Clendenny or they might shoot each other, or Porta, by mistake.

CRASH!

"Oomph."

"Ron, where are you?"

Nothing. He heard labored breathing close by. His eyes were starting to adjust to the darkness and he saw something lying on the floor. He kept his pistol ready and edged over to the figure. A man was on his back, but Davis could not determine if it was Porta or Clendenny. He ran his empty hand over the man and found a handle of a knife sticking out of his stomach. He felt Ron's badge and knew it had to be Clendenny.

Davis heard a noise behind him. He dug his lighter out of his pocket and tossed it across the room. It hit, but nothing moved. Then he sensed movement just before something hard smashed into his face. An explosion of light erupted behind his eyes and he drifted away into nothingness.

* * *

Nick looked down at the fighting star protruding from his chest. *When I feel that thing, I'm going to pass out.* Determined to finish the fight, he hefted his bat, stepped forward, and brought it down squarely on the man's head. The man's eyes fluttered and closed, and then he dropped another fighting star from his hand and pitched forward.

Nick sat down heavily on the gravel. Strangely, he still did not feel any pain. Gingerly, he touched the steel and felt something move inside his jacket. Then a wave of relief washed over him. He grabbed the star in the center and yanked it out. Smiling, he reached inside his jacket and removed his flight log. Nick looked at the thick leather bound volume and saw that the star had cut through the cover and many pages. If the star had hit a few inches either side, he'd be dead or dying.

Ruefully, he wondered if that was what Mac had meant when he had told Nick, "Always carry it with you. You never know when you'll need it."

Still a little shook up from his close escape, Nick heard the crash of breaking glass. He looked up to see the side window to the pool house shatter outward followed by a pool chair. Immediately a dark figure dove out the window and ran into the trees.

Someone yelled, "Stop or I'll shoot!"

Then Nick heard a Tommy Gun open up followed by a scream.

Another voice called, "Allenbeck, you okay?"

The question was greeted by silence.

A few seconds later a different voice from somewhere else call out. "He's over here, Sarge!" Another scream followed the call and ended in a gurgling sound. Then someone opened up with a machine gun.

The staccato of the machine gun seemed to go on forever. When it stopped, Nick heard intermittent rifle fire. The sounds were retreating as if the MPs were chasing someone down the hill. An even longer burst of machine gunfire sounded and then silence followed.

Chapter Thirty Six: Pool House Blues

12:49 a.m., Sunday, December 24, 1935
Porta Grounds, Manoa Heights, Oahu, Hawaii Territories

Nick got to his feet and wearily walked towards the pool house. He kept the bat ready and approached the door warily. Boltz stepped into the dim light from the open garage door. He cradled the Tommy Gun muzzle down. A white smoke wisped from the barrel and the open bolt.

"Did you get him, Commander?"

Boltz's white uniform had gunpowder stains across the chest and both arms. He shook his head. "Missed him, but Miyazaki got the Sergeant."

Nick grimaced. "Is he dead?"

"Yes, Miyazaki sliced him to ribbons."

Nick nodded, saddened that Miyazaki had claimed another life. "Let's find Mr. Porta."

They moved to the pool house door. Nick stopped at the door jam and called. "Hello, anybody in there?"

Mr. Porta spoke. "Nick, is that you? Come quickly. Major Davis and Special Agent Clendenny are wounded!"

Nick felt his way into the dark pool house carefully. The floor was strewn with debris and he did not want to step on anybody. "Where are you, Mr. Porta?

"Over here near the window. Stop where you are. There's a light switch behind you. Turn it on."

Nick patted the wall until he found the switch and turned it on. In the harsh light he saw Davis and Clendenny flat on their backs. Clendenny had a knife sticking out of his belly. Porta was also on the floor, close to the window.

"Oh My God, Mr. Porta!"

Porta struggled to stand and looked at Boltz. "Who are you?"

Nick did the introductions.

Porta asked Nick. "Where's my family! Untie my hands."

"They're okay. Commander Boltz's side kick, Chief Ellis, drove them to Pearl Harbor in the Caddie. Maleko is hurt pretty bad, he's unconscious." Nick untied Mr. Porta.

"Thank you. How did they get away?"

Nick shrugged. "Their captor had a little run in with this." Nick lifted the bat.

Porta was visibly relieved. "Thank you, Nick. I'm sorry that you had to get mixed up in this. Miyazaki took out these two, then left through that window," Porta nodded to where Clendenny and Davis lay. "Let's see to their wounds."

Porta walked over to the cabinet and reached for a white bag. As Porta put it down next to Clendenny, Nick recognized the big Red Cross on the side.

Porta bent down and examined Clendenny's wound "This doesn't look good. The only good news is that the blade seems to have missed the major arteries. Now the question is do I remove it or leave it until we can get him to hospital."

Nick was busy tending to Davis. Davis had a broken nose and a deep cut to his right cheek. He was also bleeding profusely. "Mr. Porta, toss me a compress and two bandages. Major Davis is bleeding pretty badly."

Porta tossed them to Nick. "How's his breathing?"

"Ragged, but it's too early to start artificial respiration."

Porta wrapped a large white compress around the knife hilt. "I'm going to leave the knife as it is. Right now, Ron's hardly bleeding. If I remove the knife I might make matters worse."

Nick finished bandaging Davis's head as the MP Sergeant walked in.

"Holy Mother of God! Are they alive?"

Nick looked up from Davis. "Yes, but we've got to get them to a hospital, STAT!"

Boltz asked, "Did you get Miyazaki?"

The sergeant removed his helmet. "No, sir, but he got three of my men. I've got two wounded and one dead. The driver is bringing the truck up now. We'll load the wounded and head for the Naval Station. Do you want to ride with us, sir?"

Boltz nodded. "Nick, don't hang around. Miyazaki's still out there somewhere. It's unlikely that he'll return tonight, but you never know."

"Don't worry, Mr. Porta wants to rejoin his family. We'll gather up a few things and follow shortly."

Nick walked over to the sink by the cabinets, turned on the water and started to wash his hands. *Ouch!* The soap stung cuts that he had been unaware of. Gingerly, he rinsed his hands under the warm water. Then he opened a bottle of iodine and poured some over one palm, then the other, wondering where he'd picked up the cuts. It stung, but was nothing compared to the fury he felt that Miyazaki had once again slipped through the noose and escaped.

A few minutes later the truck pulled up to the pool house. The sergeant ordered his remaining men to retrieve Davis and Clendenny from the pool house and the two wounded Japanese men. He had them loaded with the dead MP. He turned back to Porta and Nick. "We will need to get your statements. Can you both come down to Fort Shafter tomorrow, say about thirteen hundred? I'll have an NCO waiting at the gate to greet you and escort you to the Provost

Marshal's office."

Mr. Porta looked at wreckage of his pool house. "That depends on how my family is doing."

The sergeant smiled. "Do you need a ride?"

Suddenly, Nick had a thought. "Sergeant, did you pick up any Japanese on the road below the house?"

"No, sir." He turned to Boltz. "Sir, do you want to ride shotgun?"

"No, I'll ride with the wounded and see if I can help."

The sergeant hopped up front and motioned the driver to go. The truck gathered speed and disappeared behind the first turn.

Nick turned to Porta. "Sir, we'd better take a look at the first bend on the way down the hill. Leilani clobbered one of the Japanese agents. He might still be there."

Porta looked amazed. "My Leilani took out a *Black Dragon*? Isn't that amazing?"

"You should have seen her! Bam! He never knew what hit him!"

"Good, because it's not going to get any easier for any of us."

Porta jumped into the Packard's passenger seat. "You drive."

Nick started the car and backed it out of the garage.

They stopped at the bushes where Leilani and Nick had hidden the cabbie, but the Black Dragon was gone. Nick found his belt but nothing else. Back in the car, under the dome light, he looked at the tattered remains of his Pan Am uniform. "Captain Tilton is going to kill me! I've destroyed this uniform."

Porta looked at Nick's torn sleeve. "Let me take care of that. When does the Clipper leave for the mainland?"

"The day after Christmas. How can you help?"

Porta stroked his swollen chin. "You let me worry about that. Now let's get to Pearl Harbor and see how everybody is doing."

Chapter Thirty Seven: The Army–Navy Games

0150 hours, Sunday, December 24, 1935
Main Gate, Pearl Harbor Naval Station,
Oahu, Hawaiian Territories

Nick approached the gate and remembered to dim his headlights. The SPs had lowered the steel pole that blocked approaching traffic. Three SPs stood on the other side of the barrier, cradling twelve-gage pump action shotguns. The SP petty officer stooped under the bar and approached the driver's side. The other two kept a wary eye on the big black Packard.

Nick rolled down the window and handed over his Pan American ID. "What's up, Petty Officer?"

The Petty Officer looked at the ID and turned it over in his hand. Satisfied, he handed it back to Nick. "Your passenger got some ID?"

Porta dug out his driver's license and handed it over to the Petty Officer.

The Petty Officer examined it, looked hard at Porta, and then handed it back. He turned to the two behind the barrier.

"Seaman Jones, hand your shotgun to Walsh and come over here!"

"Aye, aye, Chief!" Jones handed his shotgun to Walsh and trotted over.

The Petty Officer turned back to Nick. "Commander Boltz's compliments, Mr. Grant. Jones will direct you to the hospital where Mr. Porta's family and servants are being treated."

Porta leaned over. "Can you tell me anything about their condition?"

"No, sir. They came through here about an hour ago. Then we got word to go to high alert. No one in - no one out."

"Thank you. Let's go, Nick."

Jones got into the back seat and leaned toward Nick and Porta. His directions were unerring and they quickly arrived at Hospital Point.

Chief Ellis met them in the foyer. "Nick, you took care of my skipper. Thanks. I heard it was a nasty toss up after we left."

"We didn't see each other until the fight was over. But you're right."

"Right? 'Bout what?"

The Commander can't hit the broad side of a barn."

"Officers! They think they know it all!"

Nick smiled, "This is Mr. Porta." They shook hands.

Porta asked, "Can you take me to my family?"

Ellis nodded. "Sure, right this way."

They followed Ellis up a flight of stairs and down a corridor. At two large doors, a couple of armed SPs stood guard. The SPs opened the doors for them and stood aside. They entered a ward room with six beds, three to each side. Mrs. Porta, Hanna, and Consuela sat up in hospital beds on one side. One the other side, two nurses looked at charts and conferred with a doctor.

Nick scanned the room. The three other beds were empty. "Where are Leilani and Maleko?"

The doctor answered. "Maleko is in X-Ray, but it's just a

precaution. Miss Porta is, well…"

Mrs. Porta interrupted. "Leilani is in the ladies' room. She will be here shortly."

"Thanks Mrs. Porta." Nick followed Mr. Porta towards her.

Porta swept her up in his arms and kissed her. "Thank goodness you are safe! Are you hurt?"

She shook her head. "No, dear, but Doctor Miles is being unreasonable."

The doctor turned at the sound of his name. "Don't blame me. Commander Boltz is the one who ordered you admitted."

Ellis interjected, "The Commander thought they would be safer here."

Nick had a thought. "It would have been safer if you and the Commander had come to the Porta house a whole lot earlier."

Ellis looked a little sheepish. "Yea, well, how were we to know that the Army was running an op on the same guy?"

Nick was incredulous. "You didn't know? How is that possible? The Army and the Navy *are* on the same side… aren't they?"

Ellis looked at the floor. "That's officer business and I don't know nothing about being on no sides."

"Special Agent Clendenny said that you two know each other. He's hurt pretty bad. Miyazaki killed at least one MP and wounded a couple more. Do you at least know how the wounded are doing?"

"The two wounded MPs will live. Major Davis is up and around with only a mild concussion. But Clendenny is another story."

Nick was suddenly fearful. He wondered if Miyazaki had killed another. "How's he doing, Chief. Will he live?"

"Live! That Scotsman is the luckiest man on earth! The knife missed every major artery and only nicked his stomach. He'll be sore as hell for a few weeks, but it's not too serious."

Nick let out a long sigh. "I'm relieved to hear that."

"You're relieved? That doughboy still owes me fifty bucks!"

The doors opened and Leilani entered. As soon as she saw Nick, she ran to his arms. "Oh, Nick! I was so worried that you had been hurt!"

Porta walked over and tapped Leilani on the shoulder. "I'm okay too, Leilani."

Leilani broke from Nick's embrace. "Oh, Daddy, of course you are. I was just so worried about both of you, and then when I saw Nick…"

Porta looked a little hurt but managed to smile. "Yes, I know it's love. Still, young lady, I am your father."

Leilani hugged her father. "I know, Daddy."

The ward doors opened again and Commander Boltz walked in. "Nick, Mr. Porta, I need to see you in my office." Boltz looked at Porta's swollen, red face. "Do you need medical attention, Mr. Porta?"

Porta shook his head. "No, let's get this over with."

"Okay, then let's go." Boltz headed for the doors.

Porta stopped at the threshold. "But I warn you, Commander, I can't say much without Major Davis present."

"As I suspected. I've asked Lieutenant Colonel Peterson to join us. He's waiting in my office. Major Davis will be out of pocket for a few days while he recovers."

Porta seemed satisfied. "The Major's boss will do just fine."

Hanna called after them. "When does the rest of the family get to know what tonight was all about, Daddy?"

Porta walked over to his daughter, and kissed her on the forehead. She had white bandages crisscrossing her face. She had needed several stitches to repair her face. "I swear to you Hanna, I will make that man pay for leaving a scar."

"Daddy, I just want our family to be safe again."

Porta looked back unsmiling. "As long as Miyazaki is free, that can never be. I must help bring him to justice."

* * *

0215 hours, Monday, December 25, 1935
Naval Intelligence Building, Pearl Harbor Naval Base,
Oahu, Hawaiian Territories

Boltz closed the door of his office. Peterson, Ellis, Porta, and Nick sat at the table. Boltz took a seat and began. "Tonight could have turned out even more tragic than it was.

"Let me give you a rundown. We've taken two of Miyazaki's associates into custody but they're not talking. Miyazaki and his main henchman both got away. The MP Sergeant swears he winged Miyazaki, but I'll let Lieutenant Colonel Peterson tell that story."

Nick was puzzled. "I don't understand why Mr. Porta is here."

Peterson turned to Nick. "What I'm about to tell you does not leave this room. Commander Boltz says I can trust you. Can I?"

Nick looked from Boltz to Peterson. "Yeah, I guess so."

Peterson retorted, " 'I guess so' doesn't cut it, Grant. Can I trust you?"

Nick nodded, a little tired of playing games. "You can trust me. Now please explain why Mr. Porta is privy to this conversation?"

Peterson continued. "Mr. Porta is a counter-intelligence agent for the United States Army, code name Protégée."

"Holy smoke, Mr. Porta! And I wondered if you were in cahoots with Miyazaki." Then it dawned on Nick. "So the RCA RDF equipment was a trick?"

Porta smiled. "Yes, Nick. I got the idea to try and trap foreign agents after I spoke to your friend, John Borger."

Nick looked astonished. "John gave me hell after we left Oahu. Claimed that I was making time with Leilani while you were pumping him for information."

Porta glared at Nick. "Were you making time with Leilani?"

Caught off guard, Nick swallowed hard. "Well no, not then. I mean we held hands, but nothing more. You can ask her."

Porta still did not smile. "I did. And what does 'not then' mean?"

Boltz interrupted. "Gentlemen, Nick is honorable." He kicked Nick under the table. "Aren't you, Nick?"

Nick jumped. "Absolutely! I have deep feelings for Leilani."

That got a laugh from everyone but Porta. Peterson continued. "Major Davis overheard Miyazaki discuss a submarine pickup. Trouble is we don't know where."

Boltz added, "I asked the Admiral to move the destroyer squadron out to sea for an 'exercise', and he agreed. But we only have six DDs and two sub chasers in port. It's a pretty thin screen for the island. Even if we don't intercept the sub, maybe we can scare it off before the rendezvous."

Nick looked at Boltz. "So why are you telling me all this?"

Boltz looked at the floor. "Miyazaki's still at large and likely to pay you a visit, sooner or later."

Peterson stood and paced. "If not him, then his agents on the mainland. How well do you know Roger Tanaka?"

Nick hadn't thought about Roger for a long time. "He was one of my Karate instructors and the brother of a girl I know."

Peterson looked at Boltz. Boltz nodded and began, "Nick, Tanaka is telling the FBI and Military Intelligence some things. However, we believe that he knows a great deal more than he's sharing. We want you to visit him when you return to the mainland."

Nick sat thinking for a long time. "I thought he was cooperating fully. What isn't he telling you?"

"The names of local agents. We believe that he's not willing to name other Japanese-Americans. The FBI now considers him a flight risk and has had his bail revoked."

Nick thought about that for a few more minutes. "If he's back in jail that will only strengthen his resolve. I'm not sure that I can influence him. Besides, what's in it for him?"

Peterson stopped pacing. "The government can go easy on him during the sentencing. The trial outcome is a foregone conclusion. He's admitted his complicity in the plot to sabotage the Clipper. He could still get twenty years for interfering with the mail."

Nick jumped to his feet. "Twenty years for interfering with the mail! Bit harsh, don't you think?"

Peterson pointed at Nick. "Tanaka was charged under US Code 2109-Sec. 2109. Public vessels. Since the government can make a good case that he endangered the crew, the maximum penalty is 20 years' hard labor. The government is willing to consider reducing the sentence for his full cooperation."

Nick knew that the *China Clipper's* crew had barely escaped death. "I'll let him know. But loyalty is pretty important in the Japanese community. He's afraid that, if he names names, his family will be shunned, and the business will suffer."

Peterson did not look sympathetic. "Either Tanaka comes clean, or he'll be behind bars until 1956."

Boltz turned to Peterson. "Have you given any thought to a cover story for the Portas?"

Chapter Thirty Eight: Christmas and Aloha Hawaii

11:47 a.m., Monday, December 25, 1935
Our Lady of Peace, Catholic Church
Honolulu, Oahu, Hawaiian Territories

Nick looked in the mirror of the church men's room. He had to admit it – the suit that Mr. Porta had miraculously made appear was very nice. It fit much better than the "off the-rack" uniform he had drawn from the Pan American supply room before the flight. He straightened his new silk tie and walked out into the vestibule.

Leilani was there. She stood with her back towards him looking intently at a large painting of a priest. Leilani wore a red *Mu'u Mu'u*. Her hair hung loose down her back to her waist. She had a red hibiscus flower tucked behind her right ear and she smelled wonderful - like a tropical morning.

Nick walked over to her. "Where are your parents?"

Leilani continued to stare at the painting. "They went to our family pew. There's so much to explain to the congregation. Everyone was understandably worried when they heard about our 'robbery'."

"Yeah, I can only imagine. Are they buying it?"

"Hook, line, and sinker." She turned to face Nick. "Do you know who this is?"

Nick looked at the portrait of a bearded priest wearing small wire rim glasses. "No, sorry."

"It's the Blessed Father Damien of Molokai. Have you ever heard of him?"

Nick shook his head. "I can't say that I have."

"Few people on the mainland have. He was a Belgian priest who came to Hawaii in 1864 during a leprosy epidemic. Very few westerners would treat the victims, afraid that they might contract leprosy themselves. In those days, if you had it, you were sent to the Molokai Leper Colony.

"Father Damien asked to treat the lepers and the Archdiocese granted his wish. He served at the colony until his death from leprosy in 1889."

"The poor guy. He should have known it would happen." Nick frowned.

"He did. He even prayed for it so he could be more like his flock. But his writings and letters raised awareness of the dreaded disease in Europe and America. Aid flowed in from all over the globe. Doctors started to work on cures and medicine to ease the suffering. Clothes and food came by the boat load."

Nick looked back at the painting with a new respect. "Seems like a pretty amazing human being. But why did you tell me the story?"

"Simple. He cared for my great grandmother when she fell ill. He nursed her until she was free of the disease. She was able to see her children and grandchildren again."

Nick stared at the face of the man who had done so much for Hawaii and humankind. He wondered if he could ever be so selfless.

Leilani took his arm. "Come on. The nave is beautiful and I want to show it to you."

Inside the high vaulted nave, Leilani stopped by a bowl of holy water attached to the wall by the door. She dipped her fingers in and made the sign of the cross. Nick followed her example.

Leilani smiled. "I didn't know you were Catholic."

"I'm not. I'm Episcopalian. We do this too."

"What's that?"

"You know, it's like Church of England. In the States, it's called Episcopalian."

She frowned. "That means you can't take communion. What a shame."

"Do you think God will really mind after what I've been through?"

Leilani shook her lovely head. "No, I don't think He will and in many ways, it's easier."

Nick looked up in awe at the grandeur of the nave. Then they were at the Porta's pew. Members of the congregation listened as Mr. Porta told the cover story Lieutenant Colonel Peterson and Commander Boltz had concocted with Mr. Porta. "Then the robbers tied us up and started hitting me. They demanded to know where I hide the family jewels."

A parishioner interrupted. "But Guilherme, everyone knows that you keep your jewels in a safe deposit box at the bank."

"Well those boys didn't. They must have been fresh off the boat. They looked like they might have been sugarcane workers."

A murmur of fear spread through those listening.

Then Mr. Porta noticed the Procession forming at the entrance to the nave. "Let's talk later at the coffee. It looks like Mass is about to begin."

As the congregation took their seats, Nick could not help but notice there were Polynesians, Chinese, Japanese, Portuguese, American, and German families as parishioners. They joked, smiled, and waved to each other, seeming oblivious to what was happening in the world. He wondered if someday mankind could get along as well when they weren't in church.

* * *

After the service, the Portas joined the congregation for coffee on the grounds. The palm trees seemed to reach for a sky that was an impossible blue. Big puffy cumulus clouds hovered near the Pali pass, although no one thought it would rain.

Nick took Leilani's hand and walked through the garden. "I love it here. I don't ever want to leave."

The trade winds rustled the palm fronds high above them and the mina birds chattered away happily. Nick loved the deep hues of the Bird of Paradise flowers that lined the pathway with fragrant pulmaria blossoms. Oahu was like Heaven on earth – a paradise. Its people were so friendly. He could imagine how wonderful it would be to have year round summer, where he could swim in the ocean every day.

Leilani interrupted Nick's reverie. "Speaking of which, when do you have to go back?"

Nick squeezed Leilani's hand. "Tomorrow."

Leilani pulled him along the path. They found a secluded gazebo and sat in silence for a while, still holding hands.

It would especially nice not to have to say Aloha to Leilani. Finally, the silence stretched on until Nick could stand it no longer. "It's not like I want to leave you. But I've got–"

She put her finger to his lips to silence him. The she leaned over and kissed him. When they parted, she whispered in Nick's ear. "Come back to me, Nick."

"I will, Leilani. I promise!"

* * *

CHINA CLIPPER

1357 hours, Tuesday, December 26, 1935
Aboard the *Philippine Clipper*
The point of no return, the Pacific Ocean

Nick sat in the back compartment of the Martin M-130 on an uncomfortable airmail sack. He was cold and smelled musty, but he needed a place to be alone. He unfolded the letter Commander Boltz had delivered just before their Pearl Harbor take off.

> *Nick, old friend!*
>
> *Some news. The Destroyer Squadron's exercises went well but they were unable to turn up the targets we had hoped they would find. Our friend from the Rising Sun seems to have taken his watery leave without saying goodbye. We don't know when we'll be able to play more games with our friend. He is, for the moment, incommunicado.*
>
> *We all enjoyed your visit and the recipes that we shared. I told our mutual friend, the Cook, that you would swap recipes when you arrived. He was so excited, he said he would meet you dockside.*
>
> *Keep in touch and keep a sharp look out for more Black Dragon spices and fine recipes to share.*
> *Steve.*

Nick left the back compartment and entered the adjacent lavatory. He closed the door and tore the note into smaller and smaller pieces until he could tear them no further. He threw them into the toilet bowl and flushed. The paper bits swirled around once then the flap opened and the contents jettisoned at 6,000 feet. For a brief instant, Nick saw the deep blue of the Pacific below before the flap closed and the bowl refilled. He checked to insure that none of the note remained. Satisfied, he left that lavatory and moved forward.

He wrapped his silk scarf around his neck more tightly

and rubbed his hands together. As they flew away from the tropics, the temperature dropped. He peered out one of the portholes and saw only a few clouds. The weather was cooperating at least. Maybe this time he could get this unwieldy beast's wings level and at altitude. Captain Musick had said it best. "The M-130 is unstable on every axis. She may have great endurance but is exhausting to fly." Be that as it may, it was his turn to sit the co-pilot position for some multi-engine time. He couldn't wait!

Chapter Thirty Nine: The Deposition

7:48 a.m., Tuesday, January 7, 1936
Federal Court Building, San Francisco, California

The tall buildings that lined Golden Gate Street funneled the cold winter wind. It cut through Nick's overcoat and chilled him to the bone. Somewhere out over the Pacific a storm was brewing, and it made him miss the Islands a little more with each step.

When he reached the Federal courthouse, Nick was surprised to see Nancy and Mr. Nieshe standing under the neo-classic façade, between two immense Corinthian columns.

Nick sprinted up the steps and bowed. "Hello, Mr. Nieshe, Nancy. It's good to see you again." They returned his bow. Nick noticed that Nieshe also wore a suit and tie under his overcoat. "Roger's sentencing isn't until ten. Why are you here so early?"

Nieshe rubbed his hands together for warmth. "I got a call last night from a bailiff. He said there was a mix-up in my transcripts, and I had to review them before court. Nancy

242

agreed to keep me company. Why are you here?"

"The same. I got the call after dinner."

Nancy Tanaka looked particularly attractive this morning. So much so that Nick was struck by her beauty, and that surprised him. The sun reflected in her almond colored eyes and she wore her hair swept up under a cute hat. Dressed to the nines, she looked like a young woman in her twenties, especially in her long dark coat and high heels. But she also looked troubled. "Did you get a chance to speak with my brother again?"

Nick smiled and gently took Nancy's arm. "Yes, but let's move inside out of this wind." He caught her scent as they moved toward the entrance–*sandalwood*.

Working from scaffolding inside, twenty artists labored on the foyer's murals. The court house was a Work Projects Administration venture. Like everything WPA, the building and the art were larger than life. One mural depicted San Francisco stevedores loading a cargo ship. All the men were young and strong with heroic expressions.

Nick recalled something one of his teachers had said. "Art is as important to the recovery as the building and infrastructure projects. The art's meant to inspire, to bring hope to the people, hope that someday the economy will improve." The Great Depression had lasted for seven of Nick's seventeen years. He wondered if it would ever end.

Nick took their coats to the cloakroom and returned. "I spoke with Roger in the lockup, yesterday, after the verdict."

Nancy smoothed her elegant calf length dress. "Was he receptive?"

Nick nodded. "Yes, he's finally agreed to name names. I'm afraid there is going to be more arrests in the Japanese community."

Nieshe frowned. "That is regrettable but perhaps it will help Roger. His lawyer said he's likely to get fifteen years at hard labor."

Nick winced. "Ouch! Let's hope his recent change of heart

combined with my testimony helps." He looked at Nancy. "Are your parents here too?"

"Not yet. Dad has a few things to do at the office, but they will be here by ten."

Nieshe looked to his watch. "It's almost eight. We'd better meet that bailiff."

They moved beyond the foyer and waited at the elevators. When the doors opened, a uniformed Japanese man bowed his head. "Going up."

The elevator operator did not smile but looked intently from Nieshe, to Nancy, and then to Nick.

Nick bowed slightly and said, "*Konichiwa.*"

Strangely impolite, the operator did not return Nick's greeting as the trio entered the car. Nick continued in Japanese, "Where are your manners? Third floor, please."

If the operator was surprised that Nick spoke in Japanese, he did not show it. When the car reached the third floor, the operator pulled the doors open and they stepped onto a deserted floor. The doors quickly closed behind them.

Nick looked around a little confused. "Yesterday, this hallway was crowded. Where is everyone?"

Nieshe looked puzzled as well. "The bailiff said to wait outside the courtroom and someone would come."

Nancy had been uncharacteristically quiet and now looked around with apprehension. "I feel like something's wrong, like something's out of place. I can't explain." She shivered. "Maybe I'm just dreading Roger's sentence. Poor Roger, how did this happen to him?"

Nancy's heels clicked on the highly waxed floor as they walked down the deserted hallway. When they reached the courtroom door, Nick pulled the handle. It was locked.

Nieshe tried the opposite courtroom door but it was also locked. There were only two courtrooms on this floor so they would have to wait in the hall until the bailiffs arrived. At the far end of the hallway, an elevator bell dinged. Nick turned and read the sign over the single set of doors:

PRISONER ELEVATOR
U.S. GOVERNMENT PERSONNEL ONLY

The arrow indicating the floors touched three and the doors opened. Hands manacled in front of him, Roger exited the elevator, escorted by two U.S. Marshals. Roger smiled when he saw them. "Hello Uncle Yoshe, Nancy! Nick! I'm glad you could come today."

Nick was amazed at Roger's cheerful greeting. "You still plan to tell the court everything?"

Roger's face darkened. "Absolutely! You were right. Miyazaki played me for a fool. Now I'll have to pay for being so gullible."

This elevator operator was also Japanese and he stared intently at the group. Just as the doors closed, Nick noticed the operator pick up the intercom. *That's odd.* Nick turned his attention back to Roger. "Maybe our combined testimony will sway the judge."

The Marshals stopped Roger in front of the courtroom door. One of them tried the door and looked at the other. "Hey, it's locked. What gives, Joe?"

Joe looked at his partner. "I don't know, Pete. When the bailiff called, he clearly said to bring Tanaka up early and through the hallway."

"Who was the bailiff?"

Joe looked puzzled. "A new guy, one I never heard of. Said his name was Kirk. You ever heard of him?"

"Nope. Looks like there's been another foul-up with sentencing. Let get the prisoner back to the cellblock."

Nick heard a faint click from the courtroom as someone unlocked the door.

Crash! The courtroom doors burst open. One door knocked Nick and Nancy to the floor. The other knocked Nieshe backward toward the elevator. Two *ninjas* dressed in black leapt out brandishing *hanbōs* – hard wooden staffs. They also wore *Samurai* swords sheathed across their backs.

The Marshals recovered and reached for their pistols, but

too late. The *ninjas' hanbōs* struck them down. The Marshals lay motionless, sprawled across the floor. The *ninjas* turned their attention to Roger.

Roger flipped sideways repeatedly, narrowly escaping a *ninja's hanbō*.

Nick scrambled to his feet. *It was a trap! Somehow, Miyazaki found out Roger was going to talk. They must be Black Dragons sent to kill us all!*

Nick hauled Nancy back to her feet. Normally, she would not need any help, but her dress hindered her. She quickly dropped her purse, slipped out of her shoes and tossed them aside. She hiked the hem of her dress exposing her thighs and dropped into a horse stance. It was just like she had so many months ago at the sock hop. But this was no demonstration – they would be fighting for their lives.

One *Dragon* pressed the attack against Roger while the other swiveled to look at Nancy, Nick, and Nieshe. Nick heard a shout from behind. He glanced over his shoulder and saw that their elevator operator had returned, brandishing a *Samurai* sword. Nieshe snapped his belt from his trousers and wrapped it around his right hand. Nick turned back to the fight in front.

Roger backed up as the *ninja* lifted the *hanbō* high over his head and struck downward. Roger raised his manacled hands to block. The *hanbō* hit the chain between the handcuffs and stopped cold.

Roger grabbed the *hanbō* with both hands, rotated on one foot, and kicked the *Black Dragon* hard in the chest. The assassin lost his grip and slammed into the wall. Stunned, he drew a short blade and lunged. Roger ducked and swept the *hanbō* at his opponent's feet. The *ninja* fell spread-eagled on the floor. Roger dropped the *hanbō*, jumped onto his opponent's back, and drew the *samurai* sword. Hands still shackled, Roger stabbed down as the *ninja* swung his knife around at Roger's knees. The razor sharp sword sliced through the *Black Dragon's* body and embedded in the floor.

He flapped like a speared fish for a few seconds then lay still in a pool of spreading blood.

The surviving *Black Dragon* threw his *hanbō* at Roger. It clattered against the wall inches from Roger's head. Then the assassin drew his *Samurai* sword. Roger tugged on his sword's hilt to no avail. It wouldn't budge. As the *ninja* charged, he scooped up the *hanbō* and called out, "Nick! Get the handcuff keys from the Marshals!"

The *ninja* slashed and Roger parried. Wood chips flew.

Nick reached the Marshals. "Where are they?"

Roger swung hard at the *ninja's* head. More wood chips flew as the ninja blocked. "On their belts, by the holsters"

"Okay!" Nick dove to the floor and started to search.

The *ninja* stabbed at Roger but he deflected the sword. Then he rotated the staff, struck the *ninja's* head and kicked him in the chest. The *ninja* tumbled backward past Nancy, recovered quickly, and then lunged at her.

She nimbly dodged his sword and called out. "Roger!"

At the opposite end of the hallway Nieshe continued to battle for his life against the elevator operator.

Nick looked up and saw Nancy slip on the polished floor. She recovered, barely escaping a sword slash. *Oh God, she wouldn't last long!*

Roger replied, "I'm coming, Nancy!" As he passed Nick he shouted. "Find the keys. I've got to get these handcuffs off!" Then he lunged at the *Black Dragon*. As the *ninja* turned to face Roger, Nancy landed a well aimed round-house kick on his lower back.

Roger jabbed at the assassin's ribs. "Where's that key, Nick?"

"I'm looking!" Nick fumbled with a Marshal's belt. Then he heard Nieshe cry out. Nick glanced up. Nieshe leapt back cradling his right arm. *How had Nieshe stayed alive so long?*

Desperate, Nick opened the Marshal's holster and yanked at the revolver. It would not budge! *The pistol lanyard!* It was wrapped around the holster making it impossible to dislodge.

A flash of movement caught Nick's eye. Nieshe had maneuvered the operator's back towards Nick!

Nick drew the Marshal's night stick, stood and charged. He promptly tripped over the tangled Marshal's bodies, landing face down on the slippery floor. He slid a few feet and stopped at the operator's feet. Nick swung the stick at the man's ankles. CRACK! The man screamed in pain and swung his sword down. Nick thrust the stick upward between the man's legs and connected.

The man doubled over. Nick followed through ramming the end of the night stick into the man's solar plexus and then into his face. The operator dropped the sword and crumpled next to Nick. Nick stood and whacked the man's head until he stopped moving. Then he noticed Nieshe's blood gushing to the floor. "We've got to stop that bleeding!"

Nancy's yell interrupted. "Nick, get back here! Roger's hurt!"

Nieshe grabbed Nick's shoulder with his uninjured hand. "Never mind me! Go help Roger!"

Nick spun around. Roger was on his knees attempting to fend off the remaining *Black Dragon*, the *hanbō* whittled to almost nothing. Blood poured from Roger's injured leg. Nick picked up the sword and moved cautiously toward the assassin.

The *Black Dragon* looked back, pulled a fighting star and threw it. Nick ducked and the four sided cutting blade flew past his head, narrowly missing Nieshe.

Roger grabbed his sister and pulled her behind him as the well-trained *ninja* turned and threw another star. This time the weapon found its target and imbedded in Roger's hand. It cut deep into the tendons and the remnants of Roger's *hanbō* dropped to the floor. The *ninja* stabbed forward and his sword pierced Roger's chest to the hilt.

Nancy screamed. "No!"

Wide-eyed, Roger reached up with both hands, grabbed the sword handle. He looked up at the *Black Dragon* and smiled. The assassin kicked and pulled, but somehow Roger held on. Nick was close....one more step. *Now!* He swung at the *ninja's* back.

The assassin leapt aside and drew a short sword. Its thick blade glinted in the overhead lamps as he turned to face Nick. The bloody floor was slick and the *ninja* almost lost his footing. Nick didn't swing his sword, afraid he'd hit Roger.

The *Black Dragon* seized the opportunity. He spun and slashed the double-edged weapon across Roger's side and then back toward Nancy. Roger pushed himself sideways to shield his sister and the blade sunk deep into his side. The *ninja* withdrew the weapon and turned to face Nick.

Behind the *ninja's* back, Nick saw Nancy working the *Samurai* sword back and forth in the dead *Black Dragon*. She was breaking it free! Then the *ninja* moved, blocking Nick's view.

Nick tried to calm his fears. He had very little sword instruction. *What was it Mr. Nieshe had said? Oh yeah, keep the tip moving and watch the eyes!* He moved his sword tip in small circles, his eyes fixed on his opponent's eyes. It wasn't difficult. The black mask hid the face except for the coal black eyes. The *ninja* attempted to circle but Nick's sword tip stopped him. *At least the Samurai sword had a longer reach!*

Nancy appeared out of nowhere with the sword! She sliced at the *ninja's* back. The man arched forward but Nancy's tip caught him. He did not cry out but lifted his blade to strike Nick.

Nick parried and his blade easily sliced through the *ninja's* wrist. The detached hand, still clutching the knife, hit the floor. Blood erupted from the severed wrist and the *Black Dragon* dropped to his knees. He looked up, eyes calm as Nick pulled back for the *coup-de-grace*. But Nick had second thoughts and checked his swing. *Maybe he's worth more alive. He might talk.*

Nancy had no such qualms. She put her full force into a swung that caught the *ninja* at the base of his neck. His severed head thunked against the wall, as a fountain of blood spurted towards the ceiling. Then the headless torso fell sideways.

Nick turned to see Nieshe struggling to reach them, his belt wrapped around his bloody arm. "How's Roger?"

Roger had collapsed sideways, the sword protruding from his body. Nancy sat at her brother's side and cradled his head in her lap. Roger's eyes were open and he blinked. She looked up. "He's hurt bad. We need a doctor."

Nieshe kneeled by his nephew's side, unable to hide his horror at the extent of Roger's wounds. Then he composed himself. "Roger, you fought well today. You have honored your family."

Nick was searching his mind for some way to stop Roger's bleeding but came up empty. Nancy wept.

Roger coughed blood then spoke. "Couldn't let anything happen to Nancy." He smiled weakly at her. "Better this way ... I cannot bear the shame any longer. Ask father for his forgiveness."

Nancy stroked her brother's hair. "Shush, Roger. Don't talk now."

Roger gagged and spat blood. "Nick, you fought well." Roger looked into Nick's eyes. "Promise me?" He coughed more blood.

Nick bent down closer. "Anything."

Roger nodded slowly and grimaced with pain. "Protect Nancy..." Roger's voice was faint.

Nick took Roger's hand. It was stone cold. "I will. You have my word."

Roger started to smile but convulsed instead. He jerked once, then again, and he was still. His unseeing eyes gazed at the ceiling.

Chapter Forty: A Walk with a Friend

9:39 a.m., Tuesday, January 7, 1936
Federal Court Building, San Francisco, California

Mr. Tanaka replaced the sheet over his son's face. Roger's body lay on an ambulance gurney. Mr. and Mrs. Tanaka had arrived expecting to listen to their son's sentence. Instead, as the medics worked to bandage the wounded, Nieshe spoke in hushed Japanese tones.

"Hirohito, all three fought well, and Roger sacrificed himself to save Nancy." Nieshe bowed, his face a frozen mask of pain and despair. "Roger asked for your forgiveness."

Hirohito Tanaka nodded, "Go on, Yoshe and none of that 'unworthy *sensei*' business either. We both know that is not the case."

"After Roger fell, Nick attacked and, together with Nancy, they slew the remaining *Black Dragon*."

Mrs. Tanaka asked. "You are sure they were *Black Dragons*, Yoshe?"

"Sadly yes, Akina." Nieshe pointed to the dead *ninja's* wrist tattoos. "There can be no doubt."

Mr. Tanana turned his gaze to his son's lifeless body. "So they have finally come to repay me. I had thought to leave that all behind when I abandoned my culture. But that was not to be. You realize that this changes everything, Akina?"

Mrs. Tanaka nodded, the pain evident on her face. Somehow the Tanakas retained their composure as the medic wheeled Nieshe out to the waiting ambulance.

When Agent Cook had finished debriefing Nick, Mr. Tanaka said, "Nick, if you have a moment, I wish to speak with you."

Nick looked at Agent Cook, who nodded. Nick stood. "Sure, Mr. Tanaka." He ushered Tanaka over to an empty corner of the courtroom. Nick gestured to a bench but Tanaka shook his head.

"My brother-in-law told me about your honorable actions. Had you not fought so well, doubtless I would have lost both of my children."

Nick started to protest. "Roger's the hero—"

Tanaka raised a hand, cutting him off. "Your modesty is most appropriate. As a former *Samurai*, I appreciate what you did and I wish to thank you." Tanaka bowed deeply and slowly rose. "I am humbly in your debt."

Embarrassed, Nick bowed back, "*Supashi-bo!*"

Nick was in shock. *Roger was dead!* Maybe if he'd fought better, Roger would still be alive. Both *Black Dragons* were dead, but the elevator operator was alive and in custody. Perhaps he would shed some light on how Miyazaki was able to pull off the ambush. The two U.S. Marshals had also lived and were headed for the hospital.

Nick looked at Tanaka's sad eyes. "Do you know when you will hold Roger's funeral?"

Tanaka stiffened. "We are *Ko-Shinto*. The *Shinto* rites require that Roger be buried within two days. Tomorrow the family will hold a private wake. The funeral will be Thursday and the priests will cremate Roger's body."

Nick could hear the despair in Tanaka's voice and wondered if it would be disrespectful to ask. After a second of indecision, he decided to ask regardless. "May I attend the service?"

Tanaka stared intently at Nick and blinked a few times. Then, once again, he bowed deeply from the waist. "It would be a great honor. I will contact you when I have worked out the details." He handed Nick his business card, bowed again but not as deeply, and left. Then he, Mrs. Tanaka, and Nancy, escorted Roger's body to the elevator

* * *

12:10 p.m., Sunday, January 12, 1936
Grant Home, Alameda, California

Nick was trying to read Shakespeare's *As You Like It* and failing miserably. He needed to read Act One before English class tomorrow but his mind keep wondering.

He thought about Roger's *Shint_* funeral. The flames from the open air funeral pyre still leapt through his head. And that ghastly business of shifting through the ashes for Roger's bones!

Nancy had explained. "It's an essential part of the ceremony. Without the correct funeral and post-funeral rites, Roger's spirit would become a ghost who wanders about endlessly."

Then Leilani's smiling face filled his mind and he could hear her soft voice. *"Why did I fall in love with a boy on the other side of the Pacific?"* He smiled at the image and knew he'd figure a way back to Hawaii to see her again. *It was so frustrating!*

Leilani's voice still echoed in his mind when the phone rang. "Hello, Grant Residence."

"Nick, it's Nancy Tanaka. Can you meet me at Crab Cove?"

"Sure, Nancy. How are you doing?"

There was silence on the line for a few seconds before she answered. "That's one of the things that I need to talk to you about."

Nick checked his watch. "Okay, then see you in about twenty minutes."

She hung up.

Nick threw on a coat and walked the few blocks south to the Bay Shore. The storm that threatened on Tuesday had blown out and the day was partly sunny and warm. Nick removed his jacket, tossed it across his shoulder, and walked to the railing. Ferries, cargo ships and passenger liners worked the harbor. The smell of the brackish water filled his nostrils as it lapped against the shore. Seagulls wheeled in the air and squawked intermittently.

He looked back towards the parking lot in time to see Nancy pull up in her father's Chevy. He thought about waving, but decided against it. He didn't feel too chipper and he was sure Nancy didn't either.

She closed the car door and slowly walked toward him. When she got there, she collapsed into Nick's arms and started to weep. Sobs wracked Nancy's body as Nick held her. It wasn't like holding Leilani. It was like holding Jude when she cried as a little girl. After a while Nancy slowed and her sobs became intermittent and she composed herself. "I'm sorry. I didn't mean to cry."

"It's okay, Nancy. I understand. I miss him too. I can't imagine how you must feel."

"I didn't ask you here to weep in your arms. But seeing you again brought back those awful last minutes with Roger. I keep asking myself why did I wear high heels? Why the long dress?"

Nick offered her a handkerchief, suddenly glad that his mother always made him carry one. He pushed a strand of long dark hair out of her face. "I know why."

She blew her nose. "You do?"

Nick smiled. "To look your best for the judge. You'd do anything to help your brother."

She nodded and looked out over the bay. "Tell me about Leilani."

Leilani's name sounded strange coming from Nancy. Still, he felt a deep rush of pleasure thinking about her. Nick told Nancy how he'd met Leilani and their Hawaiian experiences. He didn't mention Miyazaki but told Nancy the cover story instead.

However, Nancy wasn't buying it. "You went to Hawaii to trap Miyazaki, didn't you?"

Nick was about to protest but decided he just didn't have the heart. "If I did, I couldn't talk about it."

She gently pushed back from his sheltering arms. "I didn't think you could. Anyway, I want to help."

"Help! Are you crazy?"

"No, I want revenge against Miyazaki and Imperial Japan!"

"Nancy, think what you're saying. Could you really turn against your people, your culture?"

"My culture?" Nancy gestured around her and across the bay to San Francisco. "This is *my* culture! I'm an American, Nick! Sure, I don't look like one, but I am! Roger was the conflicted one, not me. I want to work for the FBI. I can help in so many ways. I can translate documents and help with interrogations. Will you tell your friends at the FBI?"

Nick thought about Nancy's request. "And break my word to Roger? I promised that I'd protect you. Had you forgotten?"

"I don't need your protection! Oh, you men are so frustrating. I can take care of myself!"

Nick had to admit that she had a point. "Yeah, I guess you can."

"But I want to help and there's something else."

"What?"

She turned and looked at a passenger liner headed toward the Golden Gate. The ship's paint scheme announced that she was Japanese. Nancy turned back. "Miyazaki must die."

Nick looked into Nancy's brown eyes. They were still swollen and red but they also showed determination and a hardness Nick had not seen before. He held her gaze for several moments then slowly nodded. "I have been thinking of nothing else since Roger died."

Nancy nodded, and turned back to the bay. "Nick, I need some time alone."

"Sure, I've got homework to do anyway." Nick gently placed his hand on Nancy's arm. "It will be difficult and dangerous."

She turned and looked at Nick. "I know but it must be done. Miyazaki must die."

They briefly embraced and parted. Nick considered, "I'll think about it. Give my regards to your parents." She nodded and then he headed home.

When he reached his house, another surprise awaited him. Special Agent Cook sat on the front porch steps. His tie was loose at his neck, his shirt was rumpled, and his Fedora was pushed back on his head. He looked up wearily as Nick arrived. "Got a minute?"

"Sure, Agent Cook. By the way, have you spoken to Mrs. Franks lately?"

Cook nodded.

"How's she doing?"

"She's taking it day to day. Raising the kids alone is going to be tough, even with the FBI pension. Still, she tells my wife that the kids are the only reason she can keep going."

"Please give her my sympathy when you speak to her."

Cook got to his feet. "Will do, Nick. Now about my visit. Can we take a walk?

Another walk? Why not?

They walked west in silence until they reached Park Street, then turned north. The shops were empty and business was slow. Few people were about. When they reached Tidal Canal Park, Cook motioned for Nick to sit on a bench.

"Nick, do your parents still believe your cover story?"

"So far. They have no idea that I was there when Roger was murdered. They think I was giving the deposition."

"Good. And how did you explain the abrasions and bruises?"

"Rough day at the *Dojo*."

256

Cook nodded thoughtfully. "Nick, I'm sorry for the mystery but we've finished interrogating the suspects and I wanted to share some information."

Nick braced himself. He knew the news would not be good. "Miyazaki was behind the attack."

"Tell me something I don't know, Agent Cook."

"Both elevator operators were involved."

Nick turned to Cook. "I figured that too. And?" he coaxed.

"We believe that Miyazaki meticulously planned the assassination. The elevator operators are not the regular employees. Miyazaki found out where they lived. He went to their homes, then bound and gagged the men. He stole the uniforms and his men presented themselves as new employees. They were, in fact, crew members from the Japanese national shipping line."

"I guess that figures. What do you know about the *ninjas*?"

"Nothing." Cook shrugged. "We can't find any record. Commander Boltz thinks they most probably slipped ashore from one of several Japanese ships in port a few days before the attack."

"Where's Miyazaki?"

"Military Intelligence said the trail's gone cold. He could be in California, Hawaii, or back in Japan. But it gets worse."

"Worse? How is that possible?"

"We found your parents' names, your address and a family picture on one of the dead *ninjas*. There's a very good possibility that, after they dispatched you, they were headed to Alameda to kill your family."

"Oh, my God! Why?"

"As a warning to others not to interfere."

Rage boiled in Nick but he spoke softly. "There's only one way to end this. Next time I see Miyazaki, I'm going to kill him!"

Cook grabbed Nick's arm. "Don't be a fool! We've got a team watching your house 'round the clock. You kill him and you could be charged with murder!"

Nick wrenched his arm free. "I'm willing to take that chance. As for watching my family – that's mighty nice of you. But Miyazaki will only bide his time and your guys can't stop him, anyway."

"You may be right, but we've got a plan. We've asked Pan Am to find a place for your family down south."

Nick was confused. "Down south? Where? Key West, Florida?"

"No, further. Rio De Janeiro."

"What? That's south in Brazil! How can you protect them in South America?"

Cook put a hand on Nick's shoulder. "Your family is a side-show to Miyazaki. What he wants is the RDF technology, the Clipper technology, to destroy the Skyway to Asia. The Clippers represent the pinnacle of aviation science. He won't abandon his mission to chase your family."

"That's a relief. Do they know yet? When do we leave?"

"Not yet. Juan Trippe will call your father tomorrow. But there's a catch."

"Of course! What's the catch?"

"Naval Intelligence and the FBI agree that you're needed here. You will finish high school and continue your work with U.S. Intelligence."

Nick felt his anger rise and got to his feet. He pointed a finger at Cook. "What about me? Do I get a vote? Maybe I'm tired of all this cloak-and-dagger stuff. Did you think of that?"

Cook looked up at Nick. "Are you?"

Nick sat down and put his head in his hands. "Yes. I hate it. People I know are dead. People I love are in danger. I just want it to stop!"

Cook put a hand on Nick's shoulder. "It's okay, Nick. We've asked you to do a great deal. Perhaps more than we should have. I'll tell the director that you prefer not to continue. You can go with your family to Rio. How's that?"

Nick was silent for several minutes.

Cook removed his hand from Nick's shoulder and waited.

Nick thought it through. He hated keeping secrets from his friends and family. He hated the skullduggery and was in way over his head. Still, if he wanted to make Miyazaki pay, he'd have to continue living in the distasteful world of counterintelligence.

Nick raised his head. "Agent Cook, I never said I wanted to quit. I want to catch Miyazaki and make him pay. But, it's all so sudden. Every time I think I've got my life figured out, something changes again. How do you do it?"

Cook looked confused. "How do I do what, Nick?"

"You know, figure out your life?"

Cook leaned back and roared with laughter. "Me? How do I figure out my life? Oh my, that's funny!"

Annoyed, Nick wondered if Cook was mocking him. "What's so funny?"

"Nick, I'm nowhere near figuring out my life!" He paused trying to regain his composure. "Hell, I'm making it up as I go!"

Nick started to laugh too. "But, adults act like they've got it all figured out. You mean that it's just an act?"

Cook stood, still smiling. "Nick, someone sure has handed you a line, and you swallowed it." Then he grabbed Nick's arm and hauled him to his feet. "Now remember, not a word to your family until Trippe calls your dad."

"Okay, Agent Cook, whatever you say." Then a thought struck Nick. "Wait a minute. Where will I stay?"

Cook smiled again. "In your home. Pan Am will lease it to cover your parents' mortgage."

Nick frowned. "That's a big house for one guy."

"Oh you won't be alone. Pan Am plans to put the bachelor pilots with you."

"Wow, now there's a change. Let me ask you something."

"Sure."

"Ever think of approaching Mr. Nieshe?"

Cook put his arm around Nick's shoulder as they walked. "Nick, I've been meaning to speak to you about that."

"Wait a minute, Agent Cook. Are you suggesting that I recruit Mr. Nieshe?"

Cook smiled. "We'll talk about that another time." He raised his hand and signaled. A black Buick slid to the curb and the front door opened. "I've got to get back to the office. Can I drop you?"

Nick looked at the driver and nodded. The young man nodded back. *He must be Agent Franks' replacement. Funny, he doesn't look much older than me.* "No thanks, I'll walk. I need some time to think."

Cook nodded. "I don't doubt it. We'll be in touch." He got into the car and the driver eased into the light Sunday traffic.

Nick shoved his hands into his pockets. He decided to walk to the Alameda Airport Café to get a cup of coffee. Maybe he'd strike up a conversation with a pilot. Besides, watching the planes come and go always calmed him. The sun peeked out from behind a cloud and warmed him. He headed west wondering how he'd cope with his ever changing world.

* * *

3:10 p.m., Sunday, January 12, 1936
Alameda Airport, Alameda, California

Nick watched a sleek Lockheed Orion, in Varney Speed Lines livery, splash through a few puddles and then climb into the clouds. At the Varney hanger, several mechanics applied a new paint scheme to the remaining Orions.

Nick recognized one of them. "Hello, Mr. Peterson."

Peterson, half covered in red paint, turned to greet him. "Hello, Nick. You here as a Pan Am spy?"

Nick was taken aback at first, but Peterson's broad smile reassured him. "Wouldn't do much good, would it?" Nick smiled back at Peterson. "Pan Am's an international carrier. Our planes are too big for your line of work."

"That may be true, but I'm just glad that Fresno doesn't have a lake big enough for your Clippers to land!"

Nick walked into over to the half red – half silver Orion 9E. "What's with you guys? Sell your soul to Transcontinental & Western Airline?"

"Nope, TWA bought these Orions, and good riddance, too!"

Nick nodded remembering the shocking news last August. Will Rogers and Wiley Post died in an Alaskan plane crash. "Wiley Post was a friend of yours, wasn't he?"

"That he was. He was bound and determined to have that Orion. Single engine aircraft got no business hauling passengers. Too dangerous."

Even here, death talk seemed to stalk him. Nick changed the subject "So are you guys giving up the business?"

Peterson dipped his brush into the paint can. "Not on your life! We're getting two Boeing B-247s next week."

Nick was impressed. "That's a big step up, two engines, lots of power. But I thought 'ol Varney was strapped for cash?"

"He was. Then he sold his southwest division to a new company called Continental Airlines. Ever heard of them?"

Nick thought a moment. "Can't say that I have."

The mechanic continued to paint. "They're a new group of Texas investors. Oil money, I hear."

After a few minutes Nick decided to leave. "Well, I'm going home to finish my school work. See you boys!"

"See ya, Nick. Give our regards to that 'ol pirate Juan Trippe."

"Sure, boys. I'm having tea with him this afternoon!"

Everybody chuckled. They waved goodbye and Nick wandered over to the airport café. A CLOSED sign hung on the door. He looked up at the grey sky. The ceiling was closing in. *Guess there won't be anymore flying today.* He turned up his collar at a chilly on-shore wind, shoved his hands in his pockets and started for home.

* * *

When he arrived, his mother sat in the living room knitting and his dad sat opposite reading the Sunday paper. His mom looked up. "Nick, you've been gone for hours. You said you were meeting Nancy for a few minutes?"

Nick hung his coat by the door, walked over to the space heater, and rubbed his hands together. Despite his brisk walk home, he was chilled. "I was, Mom, but she was pretty upset. I walked a while with her and we talked about Roger."

Nick's dad put his paper down. "Sit down, son." He gestured to the couch.

Nick sat and looked across the room to his parents. He felt tired and a little ashamed. He was bursting to tell them the news. They were leaving to go live in a foreign land. *How would they take it? How would his sister take it?* "Where's Jude?"

His mom smiled. "She's at the movies with a boy."

"Mom, I thought you said she was too young to date?"

"She's out with a group of boys and girls." She smiled. "But I think she's sweet on one in particular."

"It better not be Tommy!"

"Certainly not!" His mother frowned. "Tommy's a fine boy, but too old for her."

Nick relaxed. Tommy had always had an eye for Jude, but well... he decided not to think about it. He looked at his father. "Yes, Dad, was there something?"

His dad took a deep breath. "Your mother and I are worried about you, son. After all you've been through recently." He paused, seemingly searching for words. "Is there anything you want to talk about?"

Oh God! Was there ever! He bit back his emotions. There was just so much, and if he started, he knew he'd spill everything. He wanted so badly to tell them, but he'd given his word to Boltz and Cook. Did they really think he wouldn't tell his parents? He looked at his father. He was such a good man, but if he told his parents, they'd try to stop him from dealing with Miyazaki. "No, Dad, I'm still pretty broken up about Rogers's death, that's all."

Dad moved over to the couch and sat next to Nick. "Son,

we're so proud of you." He put his arm around Nick's broad shoulders. "We're relieved that you weren't hurt. You know I saw a few things in the Great War."

"You never wanted to tell me much about it, Dad." Nick was unsure where this conversation was going.

"That's true enough. Sometimes when a man has a shock like you've experienced, it takes a while to work through it. Your mother and I want you to know that we're here for you, that you can come to us with anything and we will still always love you."

Emotion roiled through him and he turned to hug his father. "Thanks, Dad. I'll remember that." He sat back feeling better but even more guilty. *If only it were true! But you'll be gone in a week! Then what will I do?* He stood up. "I've got to finish *As You Like It* by tomorrow."

Helen Grant put her knitting down on the side table and picked up an envelope. "Nick, I found this letter yesterday. It was tucked behind a bill." She smiled at him. "It's from Leilani."

"Really? Wow, that's great!" He took the letter and inhaled as her fragrant perfume wafted through his nostrils. A broad smile crossed his face. "I miss her."

"We know." His dad stood and moved back to his chair. "Your mother and I would love to meet her someday."

Nick beamed. "Oh, you will, Dad. I'm going to fly you to Hawaii one day! And I'll bet you'll love her, too."

His parents looked at each other and smiled. They seemed to be sharing some secret. Nick picked up the Shakespearean play and tucked Leilani's letter into the sleeve. "I've really got to get after this." He held up the book.

His mother looked at her son with obvious pride. "Well then, off you go, young man."

Nick bounded up the stairs with renewed energy. He knew that somehow, everything would work out.

God, it was good to be alive!

CHINA CLIPPER

And the adventure continues....

Mission: Shanghai

A Nick Gant Adventure

Chapter One:
Bushido and the code of the Samurai Warrior

2:32 a.m., January 17, 1936
4 Cherry Blossom Road, Yokohama, Japan

"Will there be anything else, Master?"

Lieutenant Commander Toshio Miyazaki looked up from his seated position on the mat. "No, Mitsu. You have been a faithful servant to the Miyazaki family for decades. Go to my mother's house now. However, do not deliver my death poem until after the cock crows."

Mitsu dropped to the floor, prostrate. "Master, I implore you! Let me get a second. I will be swift."

Miyazaki exploded upward in a flurry of white robes and anger. He crossed to where Mitsu lay, quivering on the floor.

267

His *tanto* knife flashed to the servant's neck, but at the last instant he stayed the death cut. The blade depressed Mitsu's throat but had yet to draw blood. In a cold voice that barely hid his anger, Miyazaki whispered into Mitsu's ear. "I do not need a *kaishakunin*! If you say another word, I will slice your throat from ear to ear. Do you understand me?" Miyazaki withdrew his blade.

Mitsu nodded.

"Fool! I have chosen *jumonji giri*. If I had wanted a second, I would have arranged it." Miyazaki's voice rose. "Do you think that I will cry out? Do you think that the pain will overcome my will to end this shame?" Miyazaki walked away.

Mitsu shook his head. His whole body trembled.

"Get up and do as I ordered!" Miyazaki trembled with rage. "Were your mission not so important, you would join me in death this evening for your insult! Now get out!"

Mitsu hastily stood, bowed deeply, and backed out of the room. At the sliding paper panel that served as the room door, he bowed once again before fleeing into the darkness, the death poem clutched to his chest.

Through the open door, Miyazaki looked out over his snow-covered garden. Like all traditional Japanese homes, the walls were made of wax-impregnated rice paper. The walls allowed softly filtered light to provide gentle illumination. The cherry trees would not bloom until April and he was sorry that he would miss them. Even more, he regretted that he could not settle the score with Grant.

How could a mere teenage boy have bested me? I am a Black Dragon, a Ninja! A proud member of Section Nine, Naval Intelligence! And yet, Grant has brought me to this.

The shame was unbearable. He frowned and slumped his shoulders, grateful that he was alone and did not need to mask his emotions. He slid the door panel closed and returned to his mat. He knelt and began the ritual to bring his body and mind back under control. He must be calm for what lay ahead.

268

Miyazaki replaced his ceremonial*tantō* on the ornate stand that also held his samurai sword. Like the sword, the *tantō* had been in the Miyazaki family for centuries. Miyazaki's father has used it for his own *seppuku* almost twenty years ago. Now it it was his turn to commit ritual suicide by disembowelment and release his spirit. *Seppuku* was a key part of bushido, the code of the samurai warriors. It was used by warriors to avoid falling into enemy hands, and to attenuate shame.

Shame. That is what I feel. I failed my class, my country, my admiral and, most importantly, my Emperor.

His mission had been to stop the American's China Clipper route, or the Skyway to Asia as the Americans called it. But because of that meddling Grant boy, American money and key airplane parts were reaching Shanghai in days instead of weeks. The Chinese air force was back in the skies. Their re-emergence had tipped the balance to the Chinese who had recently thrown back Imperial Marines outside Nanking. Admiral Shiozawa was most displeased.

Shiozawa had hand-picked Miyazaki for the mission over other senior Black Dragons; he expected success. However, Miyazaki's failure was total. He had also failed to capture the secret American Radio Direction Finding equipment. The American RDF was ten years ahead of the Japanese or German equipment. The Empire needed a lightweight and highly accurate RDF if the carrier planes were ever to find their way back from Pearl Harbor. It would take three or four raids to completely destroy the American Fleet based there. Japanese planes need to re-fuel and rearm to accomplish that much destruction. Without the RDF, many planes would be needlessly lost at sea.

He let his hatred for Nick Grant wash over him. Grant had also been responsible for the death of four Black Dragon operatives and his apprentice, Roger Tanaka. Worse, Tanaka had turned against him. All of his work developing the West Coast agent network was useless! The California network lay in shambles. The Neishi community would never trust him again. Even the most radical pro-Japanese Empire members were afraid after the FBI raids. Damn that Grant boy!

Miyazaki tried to calm his mind; this was not an appropriate way to face death. He had to clear his mind of all thoughts of this world and prepare himself for the next. He took several, deep cleansing breaths and began the calming routine he had learned as a child. He thought of the white robes he wore. Mitsu had bathed him, dressed in him, and fed him his favorite meal. When Miyazaki had finished, Mitsu placed the *tantō* on his empty plate. Now his sword was in the ornate stand in front of him, and seated on special cloths, Miyazaki prepared to die.

The white symbolized purification. He had last worn the novice white twenty years ago. After his father's *seppuku*, Admiral Shiozawa had taken him in, and trained him in the ways of the Ninja. He was an eager student and had won the kudan, a ninth dan black belt. His thoughts strayed again. *How had that boy bested me?* Feeling his anger rise again, he re-started the calming routine, determined to gain control over his mind and his emotions.

Normally, a *kaishakunin* would stand behind Miyazaki, sword drawn. Miyazaki would open his kimono, take up his *tantō* and plunge it into his abdomen, making a left-to-right cut. The *kaishakunin* would then perform *dakikubi*, the cut that usually decapitated the participant. Because of the precision necessary for such a maneuver, the second must be a skilled swordsman. Had Miyazaki chosen a public *seppuku*, the *kaishakunin* would make the cut as soon as he plunged the dagger into his abdomen.

Such was the depth of Miyazaki's shame that he could not bear a public ceremony and he would forgo the second. He had the honor to serve as *kaishakunin* and had seen the agony *seppuku* inflicted. He knew it would take an iron will to complete the cross cut and the final upward thrust into his heart. However, he felt confident he would bring honor to this ceremony. He also yearned for death's release. He feared death less than living with his crushing shame of failure.

Finally ready, Miyazaki opened his kimono, picked his *tantō* and slowly wrapped the wide white cotton belt around it and his right hand. This act would insure a firm grip when his intestines spilled out and covered his hands and the ritual mat. When he had finished wrapping, he took one last breath and placed the razor sharp blade against the left side of his naked abdomen. He was finally in the proper frame of mind for death.

CRASH!

The paper screen burst open and four uniformed men entered the room. In his trance-like state Miyazaki was only vaguely aware of the commotion. "Stop, in the name of Admiral Shiozawa!" a man yelled and tried to grab the sword.

Enraged, Miyazaki opened his eyes. He recognized Lieutenant Commander Nagasaki, Admiral Shiozawa's aide-de-camp.

"Nagasaki, I will kill you if you are not here by order of the Admiral." Interrupting a samurai's *seppuku* was punishable by death.

Nagasaki bowed deeply. "I apologize Commander, but here are the Admiral's orders." Nagasaki bowed again and held the letter in his out-stretched hand.

Miyazaki blinked and felt light-headed. He had reached the spiritual place where he longed for the deep peace his death would provide. Annoyed, he untied his *tantō*, and placed it on the stand. Then he retied his kimono and stood. He focused his mind, took the letter and opened it.

He read it with growing disbelief. "Is this a cruel joke? If it is, Nagasaki, you're a dead man!" He glanced at the escort. The three Imperial Marines did not wear the mark of Black Dragon, nor the karate rank. They would have no more than basic skills. He would kill them first then take his time with Nagasaki.

Nagasaki was from adjutant general corps, more of a clerk

than a naval officer. He swallowed hard. "Commander, I heard the Admiral say that you were needed for a mission, one that only you could perform."

Casually, Miyazaki reached down and picked up his *tanto*. "Is that so, Lieutenant Commander Nagasaki? And what mission would that be?"

"The same, sir. Destroy the Skyway to Asia. Steal the American RDF technology, and the American flying boat plans."

Miyazaki stepped closer to Nagasaki, his *tanto* aimed at Nagasaki's chest. "I have already stolen the Sikorsky S-42 plans. Our engineers have produced a better version, the H6K1 Flying Boat. It's faster, lighter and has greater range than the original."

"While that is true, Commander, the M-130 is yet another American technological leap. Our Bureau of Aeronautics insists that we must have those American plans. General Tojo has personally ordered it so."

Miyazaki shook his head. "Tojo will ruin this country and bring an end to the Empire. He's mad."

Nervously, Nagasaki glanced at the sword and then back to the three implacable Imperial Marines. In a hushed tone, he cautioned, "Commander, I must ask you to keep your thoughts to yourself! The Army is in charge of the government. They would love to hang more naval officers for treason."

Miyazaki shrugged. "At least I get another chance at Grant?"

Nagasaki frowned. "That is not your mission. Should Grant get in your way, well...that will be your decision. But you are not to target him deliberately."

"I can't see how he could keep away. Do you?"

Nagasaki smiled, his relief evident that Miyazaki no longer pointed the *tanto* at him. "No, Commander, I don't. You may get to have your revenge."

"We will see, Nagasaki. Now leave me! I must dress to meet the Admiral."

Nagasaki waited only long enough to see Miyazaki place his *tantō* on the side table and hurry to the bedroom before he left with the three Marines.

**For the rest of this story, read
*Misison: Shanghai, A Nick Grant Adventure.***

**For updates, please check out Nick's website:
www.nickgrantadventures.com**